AF436151

To my family.
For supporting my dreams.

Prologue

"And you're sure this will work?"

The scientist nodded.

"Yes, of course, Gorgon. I tested it *myself*, multiple times. All the results have been positive."

"Who did you test it on?" Gorgon asked. "Expendables I would hope. We can't waste the superior workers for something we can't control. Something we don't know about."

The scientist paused. "That doesn't matter. *Some* have been expendables... yes... others are a bit more *sophisticated*."

He waved his hands around in the air, shooing away the idea. "It doesn't matter anyway. Have you let William know?"

"I have. He is ready."

The scientist turned on his heel and headed for the door. He opened it just a crack before turning back around.

"Are you coming?" he asked Gorgon. "We need to finalize some details before mass producing the vaccine."

Gorgon nodded. "I'm only thinking," he said. "So... we give them the vaccine... and their emotions will come out in the form of... what was it again?"

The scientist closed the door, trying not to express his impatience, and walked back to Gorgon. He typed in a code on his watch and motioned to the wall behind him.

A projection appeared of a man. He was tied up in a white chair with gold restraints. No matter how violently the man yanked and writhed he simply could not free himself. Gorgon took a couple of steps toward the projector but stopped abruptly when the man began to scream. It was a violent, bloodcurdling scream. Gorgon couldn't help but grin, absorbing the delicious sound of the terrified shriek.

"He's afraid," said the scientist. "He's petrified."

Waves of purple fog began to emerge from the man. They clouded up the room, causing the projection to obtain a soft purple tint. Gorgon turned around and nodded at the professor, still smiling proudly.

"And the core..." Gorgon said.

"There." the scientist responded, pointing to the screen.

Amidst the billows of fear that continuously poured from the man, a blazing orb flew. It drifted around the room, glowing brighter than the rest of the fog around it.
Some cloudy tendrils circled the core, denser and darker than the rest of the fog. They orbited the thing, weaving and intertwining.

"That's the part that can be captured," Gorgon stated, eyes fixated on the screen. He took another step closer.

"The only part." the scientist mentioned. "The rest of the fog, it's useless. Just a measurement. Of how much emotion the person is feeling. And it's uncomfortable too. Thick and muggy and hot."

Gorgon smiled.

"This guy... he's *terrified.*"

"Paralyzed with fear in that ravishing way." the scientist agreed.

They watched as a different scientist entered the screen and faced the camera. He waved some of the fog away and showed that he had a jar.

"Here's a demonstration of what happens when the emotion is captured. The core of it, at least."

The scientist unscrewed the jar and scooped up the core, screwing on the lid tightly. The denser tendrils still circled the core, but the rest of the fog began to clear up.

The man continued to scream in horror, thrashing in his chair, testing the restraints, but the purple hue vanished and the fog wisped away into nothing.

The scientist in the video bowed and exited the frame.

Gorgon nodded.

"That's all I have to see. Thank you."

"Any other questions?"

"So he still felt fear once it was captured?"

The scientist sighed. "The four main emotions... they interlink. Anger and fear form sadness in the end. All the same, there would be no happiness without sadness. A single core *could* support all four of the emotions... they would just be harder to control."

"But once all of them are lost... there's nothing left to support them, yes?"

"Nothing can support the emotions, yes. They fade away. As does the person. We assume it's painful, but no one has lived to tell us how it felt. In the test trials, they sort of shuddered and then fell limp but they looked like they were-"

Gorgon began to head for the door.

"I think I've seen enough." he interrupted. "Thank you. Please begin the mass production of the vaccines, and then the vaccination process. Once it's up and running, they should begin to notice the whole ordeal in a couple of hours or so, and they'll be confused. Tell William to broadcast that their emotions are now their currency. We'll see how they react to that."

"Yes, of course." the scientist said. He furiously tapped at his watch, holding the door open for Gorgon with his foot.

Once the message to William was sent, the scientist couldn't help but smile, pleased to be working with such power. It felt fulfilling, to control the lives of others. It was a new high that he had never felt before. He was in charge. He was important. He wasn't an expendable, but instead... *sophisticated.*

A wisp of happiness poured from the scientist's fingers and danced around the room, pleased to be in the presence of such powerful figures all the same.

Chapter 1

I placed the bottles of swirling fog down on the counter. The core of each bounced off the glass in a rapid fury of terror. We had given our chickens fresh seed, the happiness that *should* have come out of them wasn't supposed to be terrified.

Atlas examined them closely. I could see his eyes following the tendrils, staring deep into their abyss, searching for the raw emotion.

He glanced back up at me.

I gave him a weak smile, confused about why he hadn't handed over the food already. Mom also told me to get cloth, if we could afford it but that was only if Mortia was working the stands because she was blind as a bat and as gullible as one too.

"Two bottles of what? Fear? I'll give you four meals kid."

I snatched one of the bottles back from him, scoffing at the fog inside the glass.

"Fear? No, we gave the chickens seed that would make them happy. These are happiness bottles, four meals *each*, if not more."

I watched the fog closely. I knew it was happiness inside the bottles, I just knew it. We had saved up for weeks to buy the chicken seed instead of the slim pickings of grass growing in the fence. I had watched the fog emerge from their beaks as they devoured the bag.

But I also knew Atlas was right.

The terror in the fog was obvious. It almost screamed every time Atlas or I would pick it up and examine it. A slight purple tint accompanied the tendrils.

"The chickens." I groaned, slamming the bottle back on the counter. I was glad it didn't break because that would only make me more angry.

A wisp of rage emerged from my shoulder blade. I could sense the men behind me, bumping each other and whispering. It was as if I could read their minds. Even though their happiness was probably traded long ago they were both keen on eradicating my emotions for the price of a couple of rations.

I knew they wanted my rage. Anger was pretty expensive because it wasn't very easily extracted from animals. Most animals only gave terror before they were slaughtered for meat.

Fear was the most common, followed by sorrow because the two were interlinked. Anger came next, most animals rarely got angry but fearful instead. Then happiness, the most sought after. The hardest to get and the most rewarding.

After the vaccine, people had trouble controlling their emotions of terror and anger. Many got snatched up and sold for food or clothing, leaving everyone even more terrified. It was an endless cycle.

Many people quickly became emotionless and faded away, reducing themselves to nothing.

It took everything in me to force a smile and deter the men from stealing my life away. They continued to watch after me though, just in case my core emerged. If my core came out and they caught it, it was over.

The walk home was grueling. The chickens weren't breeding as often as we needed them to and Mom and I were each one emotion away from fading. Mom's last emotion was happiness and mine was anger. Happiness was a very common last emotion since smiling and laughter were both things that existed during different times. It was pretty hard to get captured out of the blue unless it was given up willingly to feed children, or forced out by others for the same reason.

It was also the rarest because it seldom came from animals putting Mom in grave danger of raiders.

There was a time when children begged their parents for toys instead of emotions. When teenagers would plead their way out of grounding instead of plead their way out of giving up their happiness for the baby to eat.

Before the outbreak. Before the supposed cure which was hidden behind closed doors. What a cure it turned out to be. Extracting our emotions, turning them into capturable fog. It wasn't too long ago, but it felt like an eternity ago. Surviving just one day felt like an eternity, let alone a month or a year.

Mom was waiting for me outside. I could see the pain in her eyes as she saw the small bounty. Extraction processes aren't easy, especially if you have a soft spot in your heart for animals.

She grabbed two of the meals and examined them, looking them up and down as if more food would appear.

"How are there only-"

"Four meals?" I finished. "The chickens gave us fear instead of happiness. Fear! For seed!"

I picked an unlucky chicken from outside and carried it to the kitchen, not even minding the sharp beak on my knuckles. It wasn't one of the ones whose fear we captured because the fog began to fill the room faster than I could kill the thing.

It squirmed in my hands and scraped at my forearms with its talons. Clouds of mist made my eyes water. I could smell the fear- taste the horror. The thing choked on its terror and gagged at its demise. The core, the only part of the fog that mattered if it was captured, protruded from the chicken's beak and danced around the room. The core was bright and thick, an orb of raw emotion. Just wisps of fog would sell for nothing, they would disappear after the emotion wasn't felt anymore anyway. It was a shame they were even there, they only made the extraction process harder.

The chicken would die one way or another, one of them got us a meal and the other would be getting snatched by a hawk or shot by a rain of gunfire.

The core darted away before I could capture it. It slid through a crack in the door and floated into the street, for another lucky family to trap.

Sure, a bottle of fear could get us two meals but a dead chicken could get us more than so.

The fowl writhed in my grasp. I did the humane thing and extricated the creature from its misery. My blade only helped.

It cooked nicely, the thing. Juicy, white meat.

Just as I was taking a bite of the chicken and letting the juices dribble down my chin there was a pound on our door.

An Empath walked in. They work for the Empathorium, the palace in which our 'King' lives, but they aren't empathetic.

They're the opposite. Coldhearted. Cruel. Sometimes I hear rebellious teens call them the Apaths instead. One got shot over it just last month. It was right outside my street.

The man gestured toward the chair against the wall.

I heaved a sigh and my eyes widened when I noticed the fog that came out. Fog that seemed ready to pounce. Fog that was, undeniably, angry.

Shit. Not now. Not now.

If I were to lose my last emotion the Empathorium would certainly take it for personal gain. Another gold throne for our leader, William Rowen, to sit his shiny ass on as he watches his people fade away to nothing.

Luckily the core didn't come out.

The Empath stuck a disgusting-looking needle into my arm. I knew for a fact it hadn't been washed between uses.

"Name?" he asked.

"Seraphai."

"Seraphai...?"

"Vane."

The small screen in his hand glowed green. I still had the vaccine inside my bloodstream. Only the Lord knows what would have happened if I didn't.

"Last emotion?" he asked.

"Happiness," I said.

Mom taught me young to always say happiness if someone asked for my last emotion. In case someone tried to pry my emotions out of me.

She told me I'd much rather be primped and preened than abused and denounced as a last resort for a ration. And she's right, as always.

The Empath pulled the needle out and gave it a quick wipe with his bloodstained sleeve. I looked him dead in the eye as I reached for the bandages on the counter. He stared back, inspecting every move I made.

He didn't keep his eye off me as he moved to examine my mother in our bedroom. I couldn't care less about the chicken at this point. If Mom had somehow gotten rid of the vaccine in her bloodstream, she would indubitably die a horrible death, and I would end up getting my anger captured by her grave.

The Empath returned to the main room. I hadn't heard any gunshots or screams.

Yet.

He wavered for a bit by the food, taking in the horrid sights of our dusty cabinets and expired fruit. Cans of corn littered the top shelf while a sad-looking apple with a boot mark on it sat alone on the bottom. Dried sauces and crusts of meat littered the countertops.

"There's the door," I said, pointing toward the exit.

You could hardly call it a door, the thing couldn't keep out butterflies. It was fashioned from old planks using nails. Some parts were birch wood while some were oak. Then there's the holes.

Meanwhile, William's doors are marvelously fashioned. The highest quality. Superior.

The Empath glared at me for a while before finally taking a step toward me, making sure his boot landed directly on the chicken.

He smiled as he saw the tiny plume of anger drifting from my fingertips. The fingertips that would strangle his smug face if he wasn't white-knuckling a gun with his clammy hands.

"There will be much more where that came from," he growled as he walked towards the door. "If you lie about your last emotion again."

I watched him leave, just to make sure he really would.

I couldn't run after him or curse him out. Say one wrong thing about the government and they would find out. And they wouldn't only extract your last emotion and watch you fade away but they would do the same to every harmless soul in your bloodline. Your friends would be shamed, your coworkers would be embarrassed to have known you, and your house would catch ablaze, it's never-ending.

And it would all be because of you.

I tried to make do with the squashed chicken for dinner but it was obvious that even the pieces I picked out were dirty and flattened.

Mom knew but she ate them anyway. I did the same. Wasting food would be a bigger mistake than lying about my last emotion. I don't know how the Empath knew but he did. They always knew. Lying only worked on regular people, regular people didn't have access to all the fancy gadgets and whatnot.

When I finished dinner, I went to Mom and I's room and untied my boots, setting them on the floor next to our dresser.

I took a quick shower, but you could hardly call it that. There was only cold water, of course, but it didn't even come out in streams. Just a trickle that quickly turned brown as it ran over my hair and my body.

We didn't have soap or anything, way too expensive, so mom made soap out of old candle wax and roses. I hated using it, the wax made me feel like butter had been rubbed all over my skin but the roses smelled nice enough. I dried myself off with Dad's old shirt that had been sewn into a towel. It still smelled like him, just a little bit.

Mom was brushing her hair when I came out of the bathroom. She looked at me and gave me a sad smile, placing the brush on the nightstand and turning off the light.

I didn't sleep very well, there was too much to think about. Too much to be angry about.

I had to stop being angry, though, when I saw a wisp of fog protrude from my shoulder and dance around the room.

My stomach grumbled.

My waxy, rose-scented body was too big for the bed and for my nightgown.

The stupid chickens weren't mating.

The stupid Empath appeared in my nightmares.

And I, stupidly, resorted to stealing.

In every world, there are the rich and the poor.

In our world the rich are the poor and the poor are the half-dead.

I like to think Mom and I are somewhere in the middle but I know I just tell myself that to distract myself from the realization that we are undeniably poor. And not the rich-poor.

We have neighbors on the upper end of the spectrum. Their houses are made out of clay instead of wood. They breed pigs and cows instead of chickens or squirrels. They store up their emotions for later dates instead of rushing to get them traded for a portion of meat.

I knew that without the chickens reproducing we needed to steal from those a bit more well off.

And I knew that to steal we needed to act gracious.

I grabbed the last couple of eggs and the last sack of flour. What I needed was to make some nice homemade pasta and invite the new couple next door over for dinner. While Mom distracted them with a hot meal and some of her poems I could snoop through their neat emotions on their neat little clay shelves.

Mom went to the cabinets and picked out two brown and sad-looking tomatoes. She started to turn the tomatoes into sauce by smashing and boiling them. Even though it was rare to get, she used some of our salt and pepper which made me tense up because I didn't want to put this much effort into our victims.

"How many emotions are you going to steal?" She asked.

I squeezed and punched the dough, needing to take my anxiety out on something.

"Hopefully they haven't unpacked yet," I responded. "If the emotions are organized in boxes it'll be easy to snag a couple. But if they already unpacked everything they'll notice an empty spot on their shelf for sure."

Mom's gaze softened as she saw my hands tense up. The spaghetti dough almost split in two.

"Stir the sauce every five minutes." She said, placing her hand on my shoulder.

Then she went to the bedroom and closed the door behind her, not hard or angry, but soft and mysterious.

Through the crack down the middle, I could see her take out our two emergency emotion bottles. Both were just filled with fear, not much but they could get us some meals or maybe some rope if we needed it.

Mom returned shortly with two empty jars.

My eyes widened.

"The extra emotions!" I screamed. "What the hell? Did you set them free?"

"I put them in a separate jar," Mom said sharply. "You can use these as decoys. The insides of the bottles are fogged up from the emotions being in there for so long. They won't notice for a while."

I quietly slipped the jars in my pockets and started plating the spaghetti. Mom went over to the neighbor's house to invite them for dinner.

They walked through the door just as I had set the last chipped plate on the chipped table and filled up the chipped bowls. The table was crooked, from one of the legs being kicked by an Empath. The chairs had no more paint, only small pieces that could blow away in the wind if they wanted to. We didn't have a tablecloth or anything but I used one of my dresses as a stand-in and even included some wildflowers from outside, carefully positioned in an old emotion jar.

All three adults, including Mom, smiled at me when they came in.

Mom's teeth matched the vibe of our house. Chipped and a sad tan color. The neighbors' shiny smiles stuck out.

"Hi! You must be Seraph! I'm Hennie and this is my husband Drew!" The glistening lady said. She seemed so happy to visit our crooked house. It's too bad they would soon be two bottles too short of their richest emotions.

"Seraph, or Seraphai," I said. "Either or."

Ser was reserved for people I was closer with. I didn't dare tell them about that nickname. I hoped I would never be close with them, it would be too hard to be fake all the time.

I also hoped they couldn't tell that the bright smile I was giving them was fake.

Drew gave me his hand. I shook it but I didn't say anything.

Mom made conversation with Hennie and Drew but I just sat there taking in their aura.

They radiated this uncomfortable energy that felt plastic and stuffy. Hennie babbled about her strawberry farm and how she could use the deformed ones to make herself beauty supplies. Mom tried to smile and listen but I knew she was thinking the same thing I was.

How could you waste precious food just to make yourself look more presentable? For who? Your husband? The government responsible for your starving neighbors hosting you with their last rations?

"You know, we have the largest collection of anger on the block." Drew bragged. "Perhaps horror too but I haven't counted. It's simply too much!"

The table was suddenly filled with laughter, two sets of voices being bright and rich, the other two forcing out giggles.

Mom wiped her mouth with her sleeve and elbowed me under the table. I glanced at her.

"How did you get so much?" She asked.

Drew and Hennie's cheeks were both suddenly stuffed with spaghetti, making it 'unable' for them to answer the question.

I finished eating before anyone. I needed to.

"Excuse me," I said, getting up from the table. "I need to go see if the chickens laid any eggs."

"Drew, Hennie," Mom said. "You must come to our room and see Seraphai's old drawings!"

Hennie sighed gaily and pulled Drew towards the door.

I could smell their disgusting clothes from outside. Their shiny hair and shiny teeth. Shiny white slacks and dresses. It irked me.

Keeping my eye on the door I managed to hop the fence first try and slip through their door. Luckily it was unlocked.

Their house was as fake as them.

Boxes and boxes of fine glass silverware and pretty pink dresses. Crates of their famous strawberries and jars of cherries from their garden which I had accidentally trampled on outside.

They had eleven jars of rage. Seven jars of joy.

A whole box of sorrow and two boxes of fear.

I'm surprised they didn't have more anger and happiness based on how rich they were and how much Drew bragged, but it didn't bother me much because they had a whole box of sorrow.

Sadness gets you a good couple of meals or some fabric. If Atlas is in a good mood you can usually get some rope or a new pan for just one jar. If Mortia is there you can usually convince her it's happiness and she will give you something good like a fresh cake or a box of secondhand clothes. Not that the clothes are any good, it's mostly socks but sometimes you'll get lucky and end up with a shirt or some pants. One time Amin found a jacket *and* a wool hat. He talked about it for weeks, making everyone green with envy.

Even if Mortia isn't there, all it takes to get Atlas in a good mood is to compliment his unflattering outfits.

I slipped some bottles of terror inside my sack. Three bottles of sadness joined the lot. I placed one of Mom's fake emotion bottles in the rage box in exchange for a jar of the good stuff.

I also snuck a jar of cherries inside of my now lumpy bag.

I decided to explore the luscious rooms in search of anything else that could be useful.

The kitchen was a palace. It had smooth clay counters with shimmering stone countertops. And a giant fridge too, a real one, made out of metal and such.

I ran my finger along the fridge. Not a speck of dirt.

Bottles of juice were sprawled on the counter. I slipped one in my bag because they were too tempting to pass up. It was a red one, so that was intriguing because there could be many options.

Strawberry, cherry, watermelon, and raspberry.

My mouth started to water like a fool.

I placed my hand on the door of a room which caught my attention. There was a single drop of blood that stained the smooth clay door. Something so raw and mysterious seemed out of place in a pristine palace like this.

I had to push the door open since it was so heavy. It was filled with clay instead of hollowed out so it would be harder to open.

A very common child-proof lock system since children couldn't push open the heavy clay doors. These rooms usually contained weapons or big dangerous objects. Maybe even a kid-free bedroom or bathroom.

The room inside looked like a normal bedroom.

No secret emotions, or hell, even drugs that parents wouldn't want children to see.

But what peaked my interest the most is that of all the things the neighbors bragged about they didn't once bring up any children. Certainly in a picture-perfect family people who are so happy about their perfect strawberries this season would be just as happy about their children.

So who else would they be keeping out of the room that presumably had the same strength as a child?

"Hello?" I called. "Is anyone there?"

"Hello?" A little voice responded. "Mrs. Hobbs? Mr. Hobbs? Are you home early from dinner?"

Chapter 2

I walked into the room and my eyes widened.

I almost dropped the bag full of precious emotions right on top of the little girl chained to the wall.

She had wispy blonde hair that hadn't been combed in weeks. Her cheeks were hollow instead of the plump rosy type. Her dress was ripped and there were scratch marks on her arm.

She didn't even seem frightened by me. Just curious.

"Why the hell are you chained up?" I screamed. "Are you locked in here? Are they hurting you?"

I opened the jar of cherries from my bag and gave them to her. She examined each one before putting them in her mouth, a cautious little girl.

After eating and slowly enjoying three cherries she handed me back the jar, putting the pits inside before she did. Playful plumes of steam danced from her mouth and her hands as she wiped the juice from her chin onto her dress. The dress was stained with another red liquid that I presumed wasn't cherry juice.

The core of her happiness floated around her head, making her giggle as she swatted at it.

"My name is Grayce," she said, playing with the fog in midair. It swirled around her fingers as she tried to grab it.

I put my hands on her shoulders and made her look me in the eye. She didn't seem that bothered to be chained up as if it was all she had ever known.

"Answer me," I demanded.

If I needed to use a stern voice on a young child to get her to spill the horrid truth about this place I was prepared to. I knew I scared her a bit because the fog started to fade away. The once capturable core slowly faded into Grayce's arm. She watched it and laughed.

"Mr. and Mrs. Hobbs adopted me!" Grayce said. She put her small hands on my face and pulled my face closer.

"They take one new emotion every few days," she whispered. "I think happy is all I have left."

"But they surely won't take your last emotion right?" I said, my voice quivering. No. They couldn't. They wouldn't! No human being would be that heartless or resort to such things.

"I'm not the only one." Grayce continued, still whispering. "They adopt lots of little boys and little girls. For their emotions."

She pointed towards the closet.

"See?"

The closet was overflowing with adoption papers and signed documents. Grayce's was among the bunch at the very top. There was a small picture of her, smiling wide. Her hair was pulled into a braid, she wore a little dress and little shoes.

I turned towards the girl slowly.

"Grayce," I said cautiously. "Do you know what happens when you run out of emotions?"

"Hmm. Do you become outta emotions?'" she asked.

"No, no!" I cried.

I dropped to my knees and tried to get the horrible, rusty chain off of Grayce's arm. She started to cry as she sensed my panic, grabbing at her dress in utter confusion.

But no fog came out. They had already taken her sadness. Just so Hennie could buy another God-awful dress and just so Drew could plant another strawberry they weren't going to eat but instead brag about.

I struggled for what felt like an eternity before I gave up and slumped to the floor. Grayce was still crying.

"Tell me what happens! Tell me what happens!" she screamed, her hands clenched into fists.

"No Grayce, I can't." I cried.

"Tell me what happens!" she demanded. "Please! Tell me what happens! I wanna know what-"

"You die!"

Grayce fell silent. She looked at the numerous adoption papers in the closet. She inspected the scratches and bloodstains on the walls.

For a moment I thought that she'd finally stop crying. Crying was too loud and would surely catch the attention of Hennie and Drew, no matter how much conversation my mom tried to cover it up with.

Grayce's eyes filled with tears. She began to not cry but wail, screaming and thrashing. I pushed open the door and ran to the kitchen.

Some boxes were unpacked while some lay scattered on the floor. One of the boxes was filled with knives.

Mom and I have one knife. A giant one.

We use it for all things whether we use it for cutting a hunk of meat or cutting down a tree branch. Hennie and Drew had a suspicious amount of knives and they were all different sizes.

I didn't know which one to choose.

I found a rather large knife with a big handle. It would have to do, hopefully it would do.

Grayce continued to scream. It was piercing. She needed to stop or the neighbors would hear.

Not just the neighbors but her so-called parents.

"Shh. Grayce, it's alright. Please! Stop crying!" I pleaded, trying to cut the shackle from the wall.

The knife didn't even make a mark, not even a dent, and it was really hard to cut steady since Grayce was squirming and trying to rip her little hand away from the chains.

The knife wasn't getting anywhere and I was certain everyone had heard Grayce's screams.

"Okay well that's real nice to meet you then I hope you get home safe and *get out* more!" I heard my mom yell. Her words were rushed and loud so that I would hear them.

I knew she was telling me to get out but was I supposed to just leave Grayce? Cut her arm off?

I slid the knife under Grayce's dress. Hopefully, she was smart enough to use it later on.

I heard a door slam and feet scrambling across the floor.

The window was open.

I dove.

I flew.

I had a rough landing on top of some plants. I could hear Grayce's door being pushed open.

I heard her choked sobs.

I heard a slap.

I heard a kick.

I heard a punch.

I heard a whimper.

And finally, I heard a gunshot.

I didn't leave and go back to my house.

I sat, slumped against the wall, my satchel holding emotions that were probably harvested from Grayce. The emotions that would buy me a lump of wheat or a sack of potatoes could have also brought back a young girl's life.

I could still hear everything. I heard as they picked up the knife. I couldn't move in fear that they would hear me and simply kill me before giving me a chance.

"Honey, did you give her a knife?" Hennie asked.

"No," said Drew. "I wonder, did she snag it all by herself? She couldn't have. Are you sure you didn't put the knife in here to kill her later?"

"Not that I recall..." Hennie said. "Perhaps you did it while intoxicated."

"No." Said Drew. "I use my bare hands not a knife, I wouldn't want to kill her without all of her emotions."

"Well, you just did!" Hennie screamed. "We could have harvested her happiness, you know that? One more to the collection Drew, it's all about killing for you!"

"She was screaming!" yelled Drew.

His voice quieted down to a mere whisper. I had to stand up to hear what he was saying. My weight shifted and a leaf cracked which doubled my heart rate in a matter of seconds when they didn't begin talking again. The silence was deafening.

The silence meant that they could hear me. The silence would be broken one way or another and one way ending in my skull getting shot.

"Hen, the neighbors. They would've heard. It was way too risky. It's not all about the emotions and the money and the markets. At least to some people."

Hennie began to argue about gunshots every other day and how she wasn't that attracted to money at all so I took the piercing sound of her wails as my cue to leave.

Their house was circled in pricker bushes besides a small slot at the front door. I thought, perhaps, if I could make it to the front door that I could slip out without being noticed.

As I made my way around I heard their voices get quieter and then eventually fade away to nothing. I hoped it was just my bad hearing from the bombs last month and not that they had stopped talking and would make their way someplace so that they would see me. Their house didn't have many windows but just enough.

I had to freeze and duck when I heard them come into the kitchen, their footsteps loud.

Drew insulted our house and then Hennie insulted our food. They both laughed that same loud, fake laugh.

They seemed to stand in the kitchen for a while, drinking their wine or some other fancy drink. I could hear glasses clink and their maniacal laughter. A bunch of insults and cursing were thrown into the mix.

I knew I had to get home eventually or else Mom would get worried and end up searching for me which would ruin the whole operation. She was probably smarter than to come poking around in their backyard to get me but I didn't know what else she would even do.

I had to do a sort of duck walk to get around the house without them seeing me through the window. Crawling would be too risky because my bare hands would certainly get pricked by the hundreds of thistles and sharp branches that made up the edges of their yard.

Only the extremely rich folks had bushes and plants. Mom and I got lucky and have a couple of patches of grass but most of the town is covered with unforgiving dust and sand. Dust and sand don't feed the chickens.

Dust and sand can't grow crops.

I waited when I got to the front door, to make sure they wouldn't go anywhere besides upstairs. After about ten minutes I couldn't hear anything so I stood up and sprinted towards our yard, if you could call it that.

I cleared the fence that separated the houses with one leap and nearly squashed a helpless chicken who was trying to peer through the cracks in the wood.

Mom found me, panting and shaking, crying out to a little girl that couldn't hear me anymore.

She tried to get me inside but my legs couldn't move. I ended up having to tell her the story sitting in the grass, while the stupid poultry wandered around and squawked loudly.

I wanted to kill someone.

Or perhaps some*ones.*

"They're probably out right now. Searching for their next victim. A homeless baby on the sidewalk or a little boy without his parents. It's sick!"

I drove a twig into the fragile dirt.

"I know Ser." Mom said, trying to reassure me. "There's nothing anyone would or could do."

We sat in silence for a bit longer. Mom fiddled with her dress, picking out the grass and dirt specks. She was always conscious about how scrappy her clothes looked, especially next to such extravagant neighbors like Hennie and Drew.

Usually, I would tell her that she shouldn't worry about them, especially people who harvest emotions from children, but I couldn't move, let alone speak.

She stood up with much difficulty and began to make her way towards the door, silently begging me to come with her and get out of the unloving night.

She brought me a plate of spaghetti after a while.

The next morning it was still there, speckled with the beak-marks of those useless chickens.

"I'm going to work!" I told Mom. She was stirring a pot of mush and couldn't even look at me.

"Good luck Seraphai," she said, turning her head for a split second to smile at me. Her eyes looked tired. Her smile looked faded.

I smiled back but she had turned back around to tend to the bubbling slop spitting all over her clothes and our floors.

The jobs are very slim pickings here.

If you want to lose your self-worth you can get hired as an animal tender by the rich families. Or you could get hired to bring William another slice of ham if you looked respectable.

Some lucky people like Atlas get hired as traders by the city guards. They also have the responsibility of giving all the traded emotions back to the Empathorium. It's a mystery I've heard many rumors about, where the bottled emotions go after being traded away for a sack of flour or maybe a dress if you're really lucky.

Some people with select skills, like baking or sewing, run shops from their houses. They usually charge more money than the Empathorium though.

Other people, like me and Mom, have to get lucky.

I pushed open the door of the blacksmith with much difficulty. It too had a child-proof lock but the inside of the clay door was filled with melted steel so that not even a strong child could break in and steal any of our weapons.

"Ser, can you get started on the newest order?" Titus asked. "It's from that family right down there. Harry and Dean? Henry and Drew? Hennie and Drew!"

My heart dropped down to my dusty boots.

I snatched the order slip from Titus' hands. He eyed me curiously.

"Chains and a shackle?" I read aloud. "Why would they need chains and a shackle?"

I looked around the room, silently begging the rest of the workers to agree with me and wonder why they would possibly need something that would end up killing a small child if left unsaid.

"We don't ask questions," Emilie whispered. "Questions get us less meal slips. Less meal slips end in the death of your mother. Or you, so make the shackles."

She stuffed the welding helmet into my hands, looked into my eyes with much fear, and smiled at our supervisor for the day, Noura. The smile was fake, of course.

Noura didn't smile back but instead loosened the grip on her gun. She's a real crowd-pleaser, that one.

I got to work on the shackles, trying to make them as flimsy and breakable as possible without getting caught by Noura, who walked around white-knuckling the gun and peering over our shoulders.

I managed to slip away to the cutting room and cut numerous small divots in the chains, enough so that if a small child were to pull away frantically they would hopefully be able to break away from the wall.

I couldn't add anything else without being caught but I hoped it was enough.

Reluctantly, I tapped Noura on the shoulder and showed her my finished product. I kept the cuts hidden with my hands but she has an eagle eye.

"What material? They asked for our strongest metal." Noura said.

"We only have one type of metal." I groaned. "The only other material we have is iron but that's reserved for the king."

Noura inspected the chains once more. "Well. Make sure to tell them that then Sarah."

"Sera*phai,*" I said, wringing my hands around the chains. "Or Seraph or Ser but those are what my *friends* call me."

Noura picked up her gun but not to shoot me, to jab me in the back out of the door which she was freakishly able to hold open with just one arm and her left foot.

It slammed shut behind me.

I saw Amin heading to the neighborhoods so I picked up my pace to follow him before he got too far ahead.

He turned around when he heard my footsteps.

"Oh, hey Ser. You headed to your house?"

"Yeah, I have to deliver these chains to my neighbors," I mumbled, holding them loosely in defeat.

Amin pulled a jar of fear out of his pocket. He put it in mine. It didn't feel heavy but strong. Powerful.

"Here, my mother asked for me to give this to you. For the eggs last season. Maybe you can give it to your mother on the way. We are doing much better now."

"Thank you, Amin," I said, gently touching the bottle with my fingertips. "I thought you had forgotten but I wasn't going to remind you."

Amin laughed, but I saw him glance at the bottle more than once.

Emotions are hard to give up, I know.

We reached the top of the town, where the last pitiful vendors begged bypassers to trade a bottle of happiness for one of their "famous fortune tellings."

"This is my stop," Amin said. He seemed a little sad that our walk was over. We stopped dead on the road to say our goodbyes, probably a stupid idea because the guards don't care about peasants like us and would run into us without a second thought if they wanted to. Or shoot us if we lingered awhile.

"What are you dropping off?" I asked.

Amin pulled a small funnel from his pocket. He gestured towards the baker whose stand was hopping with hopeful customers, wondering if their bread would be stale.

"Lucian needs a new funnel," he said. "He mentioned something or another about flour or salt but you know he's hard to understand."

"Good luck Amin." I laughed.

"Goodbye Ser, safe travels."

Everyone around here always told one another to have safe travels. Even if they were just going across the street to their house.

It's common here for people to die. Unexpectedly.

An Empath dislikes their tone, they laugh too hard and their happiness gets captured by a passerby, it's an endless cycle.

I learned not to ask questions when Dad died. We never knew for sure how he died but we knew he was searching for kindlewood by the Empathorium and never returned. It was about a year ago, but it's all foggy. The doctors who collected his body told us it was poison gas.

There was a quick funeral with lots of tears and we never brought him up again. Mom trained me, in increments, to be able to withstand poisoned gas. It hasn't come to use yet but I suppose it's a good skill to have if I ever get captured or something. It's impossible not to pass out, but it's possible not to die.

My father's hat still hangs in our room and sometimes if I come home early from work I'll see Mom gently touching it and crying.

I finally arrived at my neighbor's house and knocked on their door, *reluctantly*.

They opened it wearing the same fake smiles.

"Oh! Hello Seraphai!" Hennie squealed.

Drew clasped his hands together, his smile was so plastered and fake it was eerie.

"Oh! Wonderful! You made our chains?"

"Yes, that'll be one bottle of sorrow," I said, trying my hardest to remain sane and not knock them both out with the chains. A small cloud of fury puddled from my boot.

Hennie pulled a bottle of sorrow from some hidden place and placed it in my pocket.

She made me uncomfortable, the way her smile widened when she grabbed the chains. The way Drew's eyes flickered -for a moment- away from my face to look at the handiwork of the metal. I prayed to God they didn't see the marks, but they did.

"These marks, why are they here?" Hennie asked.

"I dropped it," I said, face solemn. "Whoops."

They tried to shut the door in my face but I blocked it with my foot.

"Company policy," I said. "We have to ask why you needed chains of all things. I mean, we understand swords for weapons and forks for eating but chains? The whole company was concerned."

The lie came out easily.

Too easy.

Drew's mouth twitched. Hennie's hands tightened and became a frightening shade of white.

"Oh dear, why don't you come inside and we'll tell you, it's our little secret," Hennie said.

Drew put his hand on my arm.

My gut screamed at me to run.

"No, I really shouldn't. I need to get back to work. I-"

"Dear," Hennie said. "Come. Inside."

The hand around my arm clamped, keeping me in place. I debated just running for it and dragging Drew with me but something told me he had a gun out of sight.

I opened my mouth to scream. Screaming for Titus, for Amin, for my mother, for my legs to move.

For help.

I managed to get the first part out.

"He-"

But the chains came at my head too fast and all went black in an instant.

The last thing I saw was Drew and Hennie's grinning faces, overjoyed with their actions.

Chapter 3

The cold ground felt good against my cheek.

My head started throbbing the minute I gained consciousness, it was revolting, the way I could hear, and feel, my heartbeat in every muscle.

I was in a different room than I found Grayce in, my hands and legs tied behind my back. My first instinct was to scream for help but I knew it would be useless.

If they heard me, they would likely kill me. Just like Grayce.

The door opened and Drew walked in, holding a gun like it was a child's toy.

"We won't be needing a child-proof lock on this one," he said. "I had no trouble letting the little girl go run around and play sometimes, of course when the windows were guarded, but you would get into trouble.

I glanced at the chains around my wrists.

The same handcuffs I made.

"Ironic isn't it?" said Drew. "The same handcuffs you made for some other little girl fit perfectly around yourself. Now why did you make them so big? So that a little child's hands could escape through them. We specifically ordered a small one, I remember, I placed the order."

"I don't give a damn about your order." I snapped. "My mother will be looking for me and your creepy-ass house will be the first place she checks. She knows all about your little scheme. We were going to notify the Empaths today."

Drew laughed. "The Empaths don't give a shit! On the rare occasion, one of them stops by, the kids act like gold! Nothing a little threatening won't fix!"

He leaned in real close. He smelled like smoke. Not the nice smoky smell of cooked meat or a running grill. The smoke of a fire, the smoke of a cigarette, the smoke of stolen emotions that would never return.

"Do you want us to deal with your mom?" he asked. His breath smelled like power.

I pinched the sides of my legs to prevent myself from exploding with anger, my useless guts getting all over Drew's freshly ironed shirt. God forbid the core of my fury got out, I would be screwed. Someone would find it.

"No," I said.

"No sir," Drew growled, he held the tip of the gun to my temple. My throbbing, aching temple.

It was cold against my head. My heart leaped.

"No *sir*." I managed through gritted teeth.

Hennie walked in and noticed the gun on my temple. She gave Drew a look that I could read like a newspaper.

Now?

"My mom will hear the gunshot." I gasped. "The other neighbors will hear it. You'll never be able to do this."

Hennie laughed as she placed a plate of mush at my feet.

"Oh honey, gunshots go off every other day. Everyone knows that those rich enough to *have* a gun shouldn't be questioned."

"Besides," Drew said. "Your mother is weak. She's feeble. She's tired of working trying to provide for *you*. Maybe she'll thank us."

"Not to mention the soundproof walls," Hennie said.

Drew noticed me glance at the window, the window that if made out of simple glass wouldn't be soundproof.

He finally took the gun off of my temple.

My breathing went back to normal. Drew looked at Hennie and glanced down at the mush. She nodded and smiled.

"How am I supposed to eat when my hands are tied up?" I demanded, breaking the silence.

Drew laughed. "Figure it out," he said. "That's not our problem. Some kids lapped at it like dogs, really hunger does terrible things to you."

"I'm used to hunger you bastards." I snarled. "I'd much rather sit here chewing on my spit than eat that mush you gave me. I'll get found soon enough. My mom will find me."

Hennie took the bowl and slammed it on the floor. Some of the "food" got in my eye and a shard of glass flung into my barefoot ankle. It quickly turned from white to blood-red.

"We're smarter than you," said Drew, as Hennie stomped away. "Your mother is simply a minority. She's well beyond taken care of already."

I stood up and strained at the chains, lunging towards his face which was smirking so terribly.

"If you killed her! So help me, I'll kill you! I'll bring you down to hell myself!"

Clouds of fury emerged from my mouth along with the words. I couldn't care less about if they took my last emotion or not. The thing about the emotions, they are unusual. It's when the whole room starts to fill with smoke, that's when you know you've messed up and it's time to say goodbye because then someone would notice and would come by to snatch up your core.

And I was close to that. Although it was obvious Drew and Hennie wanted nothing to do with my last emotion because my core was practically dancing in front of their faces, begging to be captured.

No. Capturing it would be too quick of a death, too painless. How funny to think fading away to nothing would be a good thing. At this point, anything was better than the torture that was sure to come with my future.

Drew walked over to the glass window and tapped on it. "Soundproof," he said, which I could barely hear him say over my blood-curdling screams. I yelled every horrible thing imaginable at him, disrespecting his shiny hair, his fake smile, his weak arms, and his unforgivable intentions. He batted at the core of my anger, smiling as it burned brighter. As long as someone didn't capture the emotion it could thrive, it could grow. But if it grew too much, the core, the depths of my anger, would find a way to escape and some passerby would snatch it up, snatch my life up.

And hell, my vexation grew.

Until the door was closed in my face.

I was trapped in the room for I didn't know how long. My throat was raw and yearned for water. A bucket in the corner was my only bathroom. I didn't use it much anyway since I barely got fed or watered.

The window was so tinted that I couldn't tell if it was night or day.

I didn't cry, forced myself not to because tears would do nothing but make me even thirstier.

I wasn't going to die from dehydration, I wasn't going to. Anything else but dehydration.

It was especially hard to calm down because I only had one emotion left. With three out of my four cores captured, all of my emotions were balanced onto one. The core of my fury. The depths of everything enraged and empowered inside of me. This only made staying calm and collected harder. It was the reason having one emotion was so dangerous. No one with lost emotions has lived to tell what it felt like, but I imagine it is painful. Fading away to nothing.

I inspected the bloody wall, the freshly made handcuffs, the chains.

The chains.

I made these chains. I made them.

Sure enough, the divots were still there. Small but perhaps enough so that I could yank them away from the wall.

I couldn't do it now though, all I knew for sure was it had been hours. I would need to wait until Drew and Hennie had just come into my room to make sure they wouldn't come back until after some time.

I took my mind off the blood drying on my ankle and the itch in my throat by staring at the ceiling fan. After a while it mesmerized me, I couldn't take my eyes off it. I laid down on my back and watched the thing.

The wind in my face felt so real, blowing away my sweat, and cooling me down from the awful heat outside and inside.

I didn't even realize I was hallucinating until Drew came to give me a small glass of water, commenting on the disgusting puddle of sweat I was lying in, considering moving me to a room with a fan so that I wouldn't sweat so much and ruin the floor. The shiny, pristine floor.

I knew he only said that to make me hopeful.

His comment was enough for me. The moment he left I started to strain, pulling the chain from the wall. It was bolted in there well, but I wasn't trying to pull the entire thing off of the wall, just break the chain in general.

It didn't seem to budge so I put my legs against the wall and pulled. I was so hot that my hair was sticking to the back of my neck and wouldn't fall even though I was nearly like a board, straight and pulling. Begging the chains to break.

The metal dug into my hands, I could nearly feel it against my bone.

A tear fell down my cheek and mixed with my sweat on the floor, I didn't even notice it was there.

The wall creaked, the chain snapped and I flew backward, hitting the floor with a thump.

I heard thundering footsteps, so I crawled back to my puddle and put my hands next to the chain hanging from the wall, hoping they would believe any lie I could muster up.

"What the hell was that sound?" Drew yelled, cocking the gun and pointing it at my forehead.

"I'm sorry," I said, my voice quaking even though I tried to stop it.

"What was the sound?" Drew said.

"It was my food bowl," I whispered. "I got so hot and frustrated that I threw it. I'm sorry Drew."

"Call me sir." he said, "Not Drew, not mister or asshole or whatever else it is you and your dirty mother call us."

"Yes sir," I muttered, trying to hide my freed hands under my legs. It was extra difficult since everything was sweaty and sticky.

Drew finally shut the door and left me alone.

My mind began to race, scanning everything in the room and analyzing how helpful it could be to me.

My first thought was the door since it had no visible locks. At least I thought. I racked my brain and thought of the night I had snuck into this very house.

Think, Seraphai, think. Did any of the doors have locks? Did this one have locks? Where in the house are you, come on. You need to think.

The heat didn't help, and it made my need to escape even greater because I found myself darting for the door even without having gotten a clear answer.

I couldn't wait until night, I just couldn't. I needed to get out as soon as possible.

I placed my fingertips on the door. It felt cool against my skin. The clay was smooth and soft, better than my sticky puddle of sweat and blood.

I pushed the door open with much difficulty, I hadn't had nourishment for so long that my muscles shook when I pushed. It was pitiful.

My fingers left grease and sweat marks on the clay.

A look out of the nearby window showed that it was nighttime.

I slipped inside the nearest room, trying not to make a sound with my footsteps.

It was a bathroom. There was a neat little sink and a neat little toilet and a neat little tub which had some questionable stains on it.

I turned the sink on and let the cool water run over my fingertips.

I started to gulp down the water and let it run over my face. The water started clear and cool but after it ran down my face it turned brown and murky, trickling down my chin.

I had just turned off the sink when I heard footsteps coming up the stairs. They weren't as bulky as Drew's so I knew Hennie was coming.

I wiped my face with my shirt so that the water droplets wouldn't drip on the floor and give me away.

The tub was the only place I could hide so I crept inside and tried to breathe as quietly as possible.

I heard Hennie's footsteps pass the bathroom but then she turned around.

I had turned the light on.

"Drew?" she called. "Did you leave the light on again?"

I heard Drew's voice from downstairs. "No, did you?"

Hennie's footsteps became louder. I silently begged her to turn around, to look away, to at least let me live if she caught me. I just wanted to see my mom.

Moments later a shiny face was above mine.

Hennie began to scream and wail. "Drew, she got out! Drew! Grab your gun!"

I stood up and the adrenaline kicked in. I grabbed Hennie's highlighted hair and banged it against the wall.

She folded like a banana leaf, her legs sprawled.

A couple of her beauty products fell on the floor, including makeup, cleaning supplies, and soap. Almost instinctively, I started filling my pockets with goods before the sound of thumping startled me out of my stealing spree.

Drew was coming up the stairs, and fast.

I ran into the room right next to the bathroom. It was a storage room. Boxes and bags littered the floor. Jars of emotions with labels on them cluttered the ground. I tipped over a cabinet in front of the door. The bottles on it broke and filled the floor with shards of glass.

I sprinted towards the window, Drew pounding on the door behind me. I kicked at any boxes in my way, shattering the jars of emotions. The emotions of kids. Just little kids' emotions.

That misery belonged to a little boy.

That anger belonged to a little girl.

I fumbled with the window and managed to fling it open. The cores of countless emotions burst through the gap and into the atmosphere. They curled and looped, flying around and through each other, rising higher and higher.

It was almost as if they were flying away to heaven, to reunite with their lost carriers. The depths of them burnt bright, making them seem even more alive.

Something sharp grazed my shoulder.

As if my feet weren't bleeding enough already from all the glass, my shoulder was now too.

Drew was shooting through the door, either trying to hit me or get in. I couldn't tell.

I forced myself through the small window and dangled from the second floor with my hands.

The drop was higher than I expected, even stretched out as far as I could. Even without both of my feet tattered and bruised, the fall would still do some damage.

Spatters of blood trickled onto the grass but I didn't even know where from at this point. My mind was only thinking of escape, no matter how painful.

This is going to hurt like hell.

I let go.

Chapter 4

As soon as my feet hit the ground they buckled and I started to roll.

The front door thrust open and Hennie, holding another gun, started to sprint towards me. She was squawking louder than our chickens, screaming at Drew that I was out here and he needed to hurry.

I scrambled upwards and leaped the fence, unfocused on the sharp brambles scratching my legs.

Hennie started shooting wildly, there was no way her eyes weren't closed.

A bullet hit one of my chickens.

Our window.

The side of our house.

I thrust open Mom and I's rickety gate and started to run in the street.

The moon made everything look shiny. My feet hurt like hell. They left bloodstains on the sandy road, there was no way that Drew and Hennie wouldn't find me.

I unconsciously was heading towards the Empathorium and I knew that was a terrible idea.

A bloody, scraped, starving girl running up William's shiny palace steps would get lethally shot almost immediately.

I stopped for a moment in the road to rip my shirt and tie the pieces around both of my feet.

It wouldn't only stop the blood but it would also stop my footprints. I heard gunshots in the distance and knew they had found me.

Asking for help would be useless, people hear gunshots and lock their windows. Close their doors. Hide.

If a bloody girl asks for help they don't give her an apple and hide her away in a closet. If anything they give the girl away so that the shooting can stop and their little one can sleep.

I was close to the Empathorium, hobbling as fast as I could towards the steep dropoff that led to the woods below.

The Empathorium was on the edge of the dropoff. It was built on a small bluff, overlooking a patch of woods. The whole rest of the city, and from what we could see outside the gate, was sand, dust, trash, and a few scattered trees. The Empathorium kept the whole glistening forest to itself, per usual. It was the end of our city, the finale of the race, the trophy of trees, the backyard of birchwood.

The gunshots got louder behind me. I could hear shutters being closed and doors being locked with whatever measly locks the people of the city could muster up.

Mom and I have a simple rope that we tie into a knot. I would make us a lock out of metal but to install it would cost too much. Besides, it would be easier to knock our door down than it would be to pick a lock.

Drew screamed horrible death threats at me, each one sending a nasty shiver down my spine.

"I'll kill you!" Heavy footsteps echoed behind mine, furiously gaining on me. "I swear to God, I'll kill you!"

I had to run down the dropoff, even though it was insanely steep and trees were growing up it and the bottom was unbeknownst to many of us. There were so many dangers but I just had to. I couldn't just sit there and die.

As soon as I took my first step I knew it was a mistake. My brain screamed at me to stop. To turn around. To find another way. But it was too late.

The dropoff into the woods was so steep that my foot could barely hold itself. The injury didn't help.

My knee buckled and I had to fight to hold back a curse. It would satisfy my built-up anger but it would only give away my location.

I started to roll down the bluff, scraping my knees on somehow every stray branch that lay in front of me. My head hit something sharp, a branch or a pinecone. Again, I struggled to hold back a curse.

One of my cloths was torn off, exposing my feet to the unforgiving ground.

I couldn't hold back an anguished scream but I did manage to keep my mouth closed so it came out as more like a grunt. A painful grunt to say the least.

I finally hit the ground but couldn't care less about getting up and hell, running for my life.

Death has to be better than this. I thought, unconsciously ripping off another piece of my shirt and tying it around my arm.

My shoulder was in the worst pain of all, some dirt must have gotten inside the wound and irritated the raw flesh.

I heard some footsteps above me. I tried to scoop some leaves over me with my free arm but quickly gave up. I just wanted to go to sleep, I didn't even care if they found me or not.

My sweat mixed with my blood and created this awful substance that dripped down my forehead and slid into my eyes.

"Some fabric!" Hennie yelped. "Drew! I think that's some fabric! There, on that stick, right there."

Her voice annoyed me and disturbed my painful slumber. I wiped the substance from my eyes.

My eyes were focused on the stars above me, those I could see through the foliage of the trees, that is. The problem was, I didn't know if I was hallucinating again. Just like the ceiling fan in the unbearably hot room.

"Get the flashlight," Hennie demanded. "She has to be down here somewhere. She couldn't have gone far."

A light shone on my toes. It traveled to my stomach and then my head. It burned my eyes. I couldn't close them though.

"I think she's paralyzed!" squealed Hennie. Excited was an understatement, she was practically drooling over the fact that I was too weak to run away from them anymore. Her eyes were alive as she smiled at Drew. He nodded at her, giving her the okay to come and finish the job.

I saw her put her foot at the start of the dropoff and then quickly pull it away.

"Just shoot her Drew, we can't get down there."

"Hon, she's lying down at an impossible angle covered by trees, how in hell am I supposed to shoot her?"

Hennie fell silent.

"Well you're a much better shot than me," she argued. "How else are we to reach her without falling?"

"I'll just go down there," Drew said. "It can't be that hard, she did it just fine."

"Tumbling down a hill half-dead would only be seen as an accomplishment in your eyes, wouldn't it?" I whispered to myself.

Drew carefully put his foot on the ground and his legs immediately buckled. I heard him hit a tree and groan as he slid further down the dropoff.

"Drew!" Hennie screeched.

I put my hands on the ground and forced myself to sit upwards. Drew's arms and legs were bent at impossible angles, his gun was still clenched firmly in his hand.

As he did a sort of roll, the barrel of the gun was pushed towards his abdomen. His index finger was squished against the ground shooting the trigger and killing him instantly.

A limp body crashed through a bed of branches and hit the ground just beyond my feet.

Hennie began to wail, shooting her gun down below at me wildly as if I was the one who had pulled the trigger. As if I was the one who had pushed him down the hill. As if *I* was the one kidnapping helpless children.

I stood up and stepped away from the body. A puddle of blood had already formed from Drew's injuries and was mixing with the blood from my feet.

Drew's legs were both broken and a few of his fingers as well, as far as I could see.

Before I backed away from the body for good I grabbed his gun. The barrel was sticky from ichor, the trigger was sweaty from weak fingers.

I knew Hennie had run out of bullets because she screamed and chucked the gun down below her. None of her bullets had even gotten close to hitting me, most of them had hit a poor tree a couple of yards up.

Although my feet ached and my shoulder throbbed I kept walking through the woods.

That's when the snarling started.

I knew the government had watchdogs. I just didn't know they were let out at night, especially not at this hour. It might have heard the commotion but if it did it would have probably alerted others or found some way to trigger the alarms or something.

A beast stood in front of me, spitting and growling, looking at me hungrily with a flame of anger in its eyes.

I couldn't shoot it, fifty more would be after me.

I couldn't go back up the slope either or a grieving Hennie would somehow find a way to kill me.

The beast had matted fur and teeth the size of my index finger. It eyed the blood spilling from my shoulder hungrily.

I didn't know if it was a dog, a lion, or even a bear, they all looked the same to me. It wasn't that I had trouble identifying faces or anything, I just never got the proper education to tell the difference between many animals. All I knew was that it wanted to tear me limb from limb.

I looked to my right, at Drew's dead body. The blood from his abdomen was fresh, it filled the air with a choking scent of rotten flesh and disease.

I tucked the gun in my pocket and tried to inch my way toward Drew. The beast watched me closely, growling and spraying the ground with flecks of drool.

I was so close, I could nearly reach out and touch Drew's hair. His skin was hard and yellow, sort of like the callouses I would get if I had to grip a tool extremely tightly to make metal bend. His eyes looked foggy and cold.

A single speck of my blood rolled down my arm and fell onto a leaf below.

I was barely able to chuck Drew's body in front of me before the creature pounced, snarling and ripping through flesh as though it was butter and he was a hot knife.

A tendril of blood and meat landed beside me. Specks of intestines rained down on my hair.

I was holding Drew's body up by his wrists, praying the thing would get full soon and leave so I could go somewhere, anywhere, where I wasn't being hunted alive.

I looked beyond the creature -who was nearly finished eating Drew's insides and looked starving still- and saw a whole pack of beasts, barking and running, crying for the raw flesh.

I dropped the body and sprinted deeper into the woods, blocking out the sounds of Hennie's screams, blocking out the sounds of what sounded like a million paws after me.

Some of them stopped to fight for a shred of Drew's muscle or a lock of his hair but most of them were after me.

A fresh reward.

Warm blood.

I must have stepped on a trick rock or a fake stick because I heard a clicking noise and sirens began to wail around the Empathorium.

Red lights flashed from the trees.

Guns protruded from the walls and began raining fire, shooting at anything they could.

Sick and delusional I began to shriek like a madman and sprint through the woods, hoping the trees would catch any loose fire. The guns were a dumb idea, bombs would be much more effective but I wasn't going to go and give them any suggestions on how to kill *more* people.

Trunks were ripped to shreds, bark flew through the air as if it were running through a woodchipper.

Since when did they add the guns? They didn't have these forever, people used to gather wood from down here. Oh God, what else could they possibly have added?

A couple of yards down the hill I was descending, I saw a concrete slab that stood out of the ground a good five feet. The bullets were deflecting off of the stone like it was rubber, bouncing into the mulch, defeated.

I slid down the rest of the hill and managed to roll behind the slab. The beasts' flesh was torn to shreds by the bullets. Some whimpered while they lay, dying, but most didn't even get the chance.

I could hear the sirens still blaring but someone must have woken up and found the off switch because a few moments later the bullets finally stopped pursuing me.

I was in agony. Every inch of my body hurt.

My feet were the worst, battered from the glass. I tried my best to stop the bleeding but it didn't stop the leaves below me from being splattered with blood.

My head felt too heavy for my body. My eyes started to blink slower.

I knew I was losing too much blood, it was inevitable. Although the bullets hadn't hit me they had slid past me and nicked my legs. For a moment I was confused about where I was, about to get up and walk home. That's when I knew I needed to stop all my bleeding because I'm usually not so stupid and reckless.

The door guarding whatever was inside the concrete had a simple lock but it had been torn to shreds from the bullets.

I knew they would replace the lock soon, maybe even that night because if something was important enough to be guarded in the Empathorium's backyard it wasn't something I should be messing with and I knew that.

I heard gears turning, mechanisms shifting.

I stood on my toes and peeked over the concrete. Sections of the walls were opened to reveal more creatures, except the other ones looked like ants compared to the new ones.

They had giant teeth which curled over their upper lip. One of them looked right at me, grunting and snarling trying to unclip the rope that attached them to the wall.

For now.

The rope unclipped and the things started to charge at me. They must have been over nine feet in height, roaring and spitting as they knocked down trees as a human would knock down a toothpick.

Out of fear or pain, I couldn't tell, my knees buckled and I dropped in the dirt, defeated.

I managed to stand up, grabbed the concrete, and made my way to the door. I had to go slow or else my knees would buckle again, I was sure of it.

An entire tree landed just inches from my feet, shaking the ground and causing me to stumble.

If my horror hadn't been traded a little while ago, the amount of purple-tinted fumes protruding from my body would have been enough to make the air unbreathable.

Just yards away a roar reached my ears. I could feel my stomach vibrating with the creature's emissions.

Behind the door was a flight of stairs, very neat, unlike anything in the city. They weren't covered in blood stains or had an odor of dead bodies.

The stairs led underground to what must have been a basement. There were colored lights down there, flickering and jumping. They littered the walls of the little concrete building.

I dove down the stairs, not even caring what other monster or creature or hell, gunman was down there.

Speaking of creatures, the brute chasing me had reached my hiding place. He thrust his head through the hole but couldn't fit the rest of his ragged body through. The concrete rumbled a little but didn't break as he bucked and roared.

Under any other circumstances, I wouldn't have been able to sleep. The roars too loud, the pain too intense.

But something was taking over me, something that seemed too strong to avoid. The smell was so familiar. I remember that same smell, with Mom.

The gas. The poisoned gas. Oh God. This is where Dad died. This is where Dad died. This is where... Dad...

My brain got too foggy, my eyes closed, and my wounds let out a final wave of agony.

I was almost relieved when my eyes closed and I was detached from reality.

I was so comfortable.

My wounds were cleaned, and there was not a speck of dust left on my face.

My hair had been washed and combed.

My body had been scrubbed down, and not with waxy rose soap, but with real soap. Empathorium soap.

I opened my eyes and touched the surface I was lying on. A soft, pillowy bed, the sheets tucked into the mattress so tight that not one crease would dare to show itself.

I was wearing a flowy white dress complete with white gloves that reached beyond my elbows.

My feet were covered in silky slippers which molded to them perfectly. My hair was put in a formal updo complete with what felt like a flower pin.

I sat upright and looked to my left. No one else was in the room with me except a couple of sleeping people who also had on white clothes. It was the Empathorium Infirmary of course but why had they taken pity on me? They were keeping whatever the colors were secret but then why not kill me on the spot?

I didn't want to disturb anyone who was sleeping and the door seemed closed and locked so I slipped out of bed and began rummaging through the cabinets.

If I was going to make the best out of this I could at least steal some things that Mom might need.

The cabinets didn't contain medicine or medical books. Not even some gauze or bandages. They contained lots of cleaning supplies and makeup. One drawer was miscellaneous, it had matches and balled-up papers. Scraps of metal. A shoelace. I ended up snagging a match in case Mom and I couldn't find firewood one of these days. A few of the closets had white dresses like the one I was wearing. It was pretty hard to breathe in with how tight it was around the waist. It was certainly a gown but not the hospital kind.

The ball kind.

Even if I did swipe some makeup it would be useless because no one goes out these days. I ended up stuffing my pockets with wipes and other small finds.

Hopefully, they let me keep the dress. It would make some good curtains.

I was rather hungry but there wasn't a button to call for the nurse and I didn't feel safe calling for anyone. I would rather just wait until I got home instead. Or maybe I should ask for food, I could steal some and take it home, maybe get a nice piece of fruit from William's finest stash.

The thought of getting something good to eat for once made me giddy, I had to resist smiling like a fool just thinking about the expensive fruits and meats the Empathorium would hopefully offer to me.

I started to look through another drawer when I heard voices and footsteps from a distance away. I closed all the drawers and repositioned my pockets so that it looked like neither a wipe nor a match had been stuffed into them.

I sat on my bed, hands folded in my lap, and put on my best innocent face.

"Oh hello, Mister. It seemed I woke up before the others." I muttered. "Seems... seems I woke up before the others, not seemed that's stupid."

A paper sitting on a table by my bed caught my eye. It had a picture of me on it. A picture of me down in that concrete basement. Bleeding out, lifeless.

The paper had only a couple of things on it. My name, date of birth, all of that. But one line caught my eye, right as the locks on the door began to jiggle.

"Disposal: Immolation"

Immolation?

Keys jingled from beyond the door.

Immolation.

That's what they did to Dad after the funeral.

Immolation.

They think I'm dead.

Oh my god.

It all made sense. My lifeless body. The wounds. The pristine, formal clothes, government clothes. Disposal by immolation. No one else in the room was awake. Of course, they weren't awake. They would never be awake. No one in this room ever was awake, the whole time I was in here.

My heart beat faster as my eyes glanced around the room. It was like they were open for the first time, noticing the lifeless bodies and dead eyes that stared into nothingness.

This isn't a hospital, this is a waiting room for the inferno.

They think I'm dead.

Oh God, they think I'm dead and they're going to fucking burn me alive.

Chapter 5

I managed to throw the paper back and reposition myself right as the door opened.

Two men walked in and they went to my bed first, of course. I don't even think it was first in line.

"This was the one who was in the stronghold." someone said. His voice frightened me.

"Trying to steal them no doubt." another growled.

They snatched my paper and it was silent for a moment.

"Death by immolation." one said. "Lives with just her mother, too poor to afford a burial of course."

"Are there any others who are the same?" the other asked. I heard footsteps stopping by all the bedframes.

"Just her," he said. "The rest could afford a proper sendoff."

Someone yanked me by my arm and threw me onto a different bed. This one had wheels and could be rolled down the halls. They weren't paying much attention to if they hurt me or not but that made sense considering I was supposed to be dead.

"She deserves to be burnt," one said. "She found the stash of emotions. *Somehow.* She knows too much- *knew.* Knew too much."

Oh God. I'm dead.

"Really?" the other asked. "Who found her?"

"The new guard, the nightshift one. Said he heard the gunshots. She was all bloody and battered, he said. Bet the kid almost threw up; he hates that stuff. I'm sure he sent for the body pickup right away."

They laughed as if this whole mess was funny.

As I was being rolled I opened my eyes just a crack.

Light flooded into my brain.

Why was everything here so bright?

The only colors they knew were white and gold.

After my eyes got used to the daggers they called colors I started to look around for any escape route. Anything I could use for a weapon.

The Empathorium dug their own grave, licking my wounds for me and letting me rest for a couple of hours.

My adrenaline felt like cocaine in my veins. I couldn't wait to get somewhere to slit some sorry worker's throat.

The hallway was filled with material crap. Expensive vases on expensive stands polished with expensive polishes and garnished with expensive gold.

Maybe I could hit one of them over the head with a vase but the other would pull out a gun and kill me.

And vice versa.

They weren't paying much attention to me, yes wheeling my bed but not facing my direction. One walked ahead, leading the other who pulled my bed as if I were a small baby doll in a little red wagon.

They were speaking but it was forced small talk, as friendly as you can get while you go to burn bodies.

I heard another set of wheels, heading for us from just beyond the hall.

"Oh, hello sir." someone said.

One of the men cleared his throat.

"Where ya headed Tommy?"

"William told me to sell this. Flour and eggs and stuff like that. The prices are all jacked up now that some people are selling fake emotions. We keep getting fear, it's outrageous and so common, practically comes from the dirt nowadays, with all these chickens, and-"

"It wasn't an invitation into your life story Tommy." the other man sneered. "And you forgot the fruit. Sell that for something big now, like joy or something."

"Shit! William himself got onto me last week for being late to the shops."

I heard footsteps sprinting down the hall.

With one eye open I could see that both the men's backs were turned, even though one was yards ahead of the other. They were both laughing at the man, but not in a funny friendly way.

I slipped my hand out of the bedframe and reached as far as I could. The only thing in reach was a small bag of flour so I hid it under my dress.

I hoped Mom was okay. That she wasn't getting persecuted due to fake emotion bottles.

William didn't even need all those emotions.

They had no value once they were traded, no wonder they were locked in a stash room somewhere.

My cart began to move again.

"Let's get going Joel." the man pulling it said. "We gotta get back to dig the graves." They pulled my cart into a dark room, a steaming hot, dark room.

The door slammed which ensured I was trapped.

"She hasn't turned yellow yet, Culley," Joel said. "Don't they, the dead bodies I mean, don't they get yellow? Because of the blood right, because they have no blood."

"What? Stop looking so far into it." Culley said. A bucket of gasoline splashed and the room got ten times hotter.

"And it's not because they have no blood, you dumbass. It's because their heart isn't moving the blood. What's the word, pumping?"

By God they were idiots. And if they worked at the Empathorium they should be rich enough to afford proper schooling.

"I dunno," Joel muttered. "The blood ain't there and the skin turns yellow that's all I know."

Cold fingers touched my temple.

Cold fingers felt my heartbeat.

Cold fingers tore away from my head with a yelp.

"What the hell? She's alive! Culley, she's alive!"

I sat up from the bed, wielding the flour like a sword.

"Hell yeah, I am."

The two men stood across from me in horror.

At least for a little while before all hell broke loose.

I had never seen their faces but I could recognize their voices to see who was who. They both looked the same anyway. Big burly men with unkempt hair. They were also both glaring at me intently which didn't help in the quest to match the face to the voice.

Joel hollered as he ran for me first and yanked me towards the fire by my hair. I tried to pull away but he was stronger of course. I sank my teeth into his forearm until I drew blood, dropping the flour sack in the process.

Culley grabbed me by my stomach which knocked the air out of me. I gasped as he flung me to the floor. He reached for my arm but I kicked his eye and scrambled towards the flour.

I ducked under Culley's lunge and elbowed Joel on my way over to the fire. I tore the sack open with my teeth and held it dangerously close to the flames.

"Take one step towards me and I'll dump it in," I screamed, my voice breaking.

Joel wiped blood from his arm, looking me up and down. He looked at Culley and laughed.

"What'll that do?" Culley yelled.

"Flour's flammable dumbass." I sneered, blowing and scattering the flour away from me and about the room, careful not to let a speck hit the flames.

"It carries the fire, explodes almost."

Again, I held the bag over the flames.

"If I were to let go right now, or hell, throw this bag and let the flour travel, what would start as a small blaze would carry until this whole room would catch fire."

The men stood, frozen in fear of what I might do.

"The fire wouldn't spread due to natural causes, it doesn't carry onto, what's this? Marble?"

My voice was calm as ever, I was in charge here. I knew it, and they knew it too.

"However, the flour drifting around in the air would become ablaze, cooking your sorry asses into something William would sell for a cheap jar of fear. So do yourselves a favor and stay quiet and compliant boys."

Fear was the word alright. I could see it in their eyes although they would never admit they were afraid.

They also knew I was right, that if I were to so much as drop the bag on the floor, the explosion of flour would become ablaze and travel across the room, burning away on the trail I laid out. It was a simply genius plan but also a plan that could very well end in me being killed if these brutes didn't cooperate.

One reached for the door but I stopped him with just a glance. He put his hand back by his side, slowly, shooting daggers at me through his eyes.

"I want you to walk over to me," I said. "Slowly. One sleight of the hand and I'm dropping this thing."

"We get it," Culley said. "You have flour kid. Congrats. Someone will walk in here soon enough with a gun and you'll be blown to smithereens you little brat."

Nevertheless, they walked closer to me, stopping about a yard away. I told them to go stand next to the fireplace and they obeyed, luckily, or else I would have to follow through on my promise to blow up this room.

I wasn't bluffing, I would blow up the room if I needed to. At least die with glory, taking out some Empaths while I could. But of course, I didn't want to. Mom would be devastated, heartbroken. She would probably be proud of me for what I did, I'm not one to lay down and die, but the thought of leaving her all alone put a lump in my throat that I didn't like.

I slowly backed away from the fire, leaving a trail of flour on the ground. The men stayed standing, they were still afraid but they put on brave faces.

I knew that the moment I opened the door and ran down the hallway they would follow me, screaming no doubt, leading more soldiers after me.

And they would probably catch me, two tall athletic men against one girl in a ballgown.

My arm stung from where one of the men had scratched me, a streak of now-dried blood lay staring at me. It seemed so out of place next to my white dress and the powdery trail of flour at my feet.

I could clean the wound later, of course, with my spit and thumb or I could be bougie and use my wipes.

My wipes.

The match.

I have a match in my pocket.

My mind started racing at a thousand miles a minute. I continued laying the trail of flour though, acting as if I didn't know what I was doing. As long as they had the illusion they were in control, they wouldn't make any sudden moves or scream for help.

I retrieved the match without them noticing and held it in my fingers, still sprinkling the flour. If I could only reach the door I could get out of this whole mess practically unscathed.

That's when they started to sprint at me, knowing I was too far away to successfully throw the flour in the fire. Thinking fast, I ran to the wall and lit the match, throwing the flour behind me in the process.

It landed on Culley but floated over to Joel, covering them both in an explosion of powder. Joel started to scream, seeing the match, and sprinted toward me.

I threw the match toward the line of flour, leading to the furnace, and slammed the door behind me.

I heard them scream, wail in agony, and beg for forgiveness before it all went silent. I was drenched in a cold sweat, which was ironic because the room right in front of me was probably still ablaze. I touched the door timidly but pulled away. It felt warm, a little too warm for comfort.

Culley and Joel were dead, they had to be. Or at least dying, still on fire. The floors might not have been flammable but their shirts were. They were.

I shook all thoughts from my head and sprinted down the hall, trying to find my way out of this maze.

I took a left and then a right, ducking into a bathroom when I heard footsteps. They didn't go down the hallway I was in though, *luckily*.

Three rights and four lefts later I wasn't getting anywhere. Frustrated, I turned back around in a huff. At this point, it would just be easier to run into someone and force them to tell me where the way out.

I took a left and ran into a dead end so I decided I would turn around and make my way back to the furnace. I could find my way to the kitchen from there and maybe ask a chef where the way out was and they wouldn't think anything was suspicious.

I went back the way I came until I was in the hallway with the vases, the same vases that blinded my eyes when I was getting rolled away to the fiery inferno.

This meant a left and a straight led me right to...

The storage room?

No, this is supposed to be a kitchen, I went to the vases. The vases that were in this hallway as well. The vases that were... *everywhere.*

Okay, okay. I needed to calm down and find a way to mark where I'd been. I could shatter a vase and use the glass shards to mark my path but the sound would be heard. That's when I remembered the wipes in my pocket. I only grabbed a handful but maybe I could tear them in two if need be.

I grabbed four and made a left from the hallway I was in, carefully placing a wipe down in the corner between the two hallways.

Another left, another wipe.

Another left, *another* wipe.

Then a right, to make sure I didn't make a square and end up where I came.

I wasn't led to a door but I was led to a window, which when looking out of humbled me since the drop would surely kill me. Or at least break both my legs and then kill me.

I could have sworn I was on the first floor but I didn't realize how massive William's mansion was. The whole time I was wandering I didn't even see one flight of stairs. I also didn't see any clocks which made me even more scared because I didn't want to end up going crazy in this place.

It was Hennie and Drew's house on steroids, so bright and fake and shiny.

God, I hate rich people.

I looked around for anything I could use to get out of the window safely. On each window, I noticed there was a giant white curtain with a gold border.

I tore one from the wall and started frantically tying foot knots into it, trying to hurry before someone found me, found my wipes, found Joel or Culley, or found any evidence I was ever near this building in the first place.

The fabric was insanely hard to tie though, it was so thick and tough that I had to use damn near all of my strength just to get a mediocre knot into it.

After three I got impatient and started to think of a way I could tie the curtain somewhere safe.

The window didn't have any ledges or anything, not even a pole that I could wrap the curtain around. I was running out of time, someone was bound to come around the corner at some point.

Some guard, some maid, some chef, some someone.

Suddenly, an alarm began to blare around the mansion. It jolted me from my thoughts and made me jump a little. I held the curtain tighter in my hands as if it would act as a weapon.

"Intruder." said a voice. It was a woman's voice that blared and echoed around the corridors.

"Intruder. The palace is on lockdown. Intruder."

My heart started to race. I looked side to side frantically, praying that no one would run down the hall. It was obvious someone had found evidence that I was here and they were looking for me.

And this time they would make no mistake if I was alive or not. Either they would shoot me or they would torture me *and then* shoot me and I would bet on the latter.

I scanned the window again, hoping that maybe something showed up that wasn't there before, even though I knew it didn't.

That's when the metal gates began to come down. One started to cover the window. It was descending slowly but that didn't stop the panic from increasing.

I had to think. And fast.

My instincts kicked in as I opened, and threw myself out of the window, carrying the curtain in my teeth. My fingers grasped the ledge, my feet slipping on the walls, fighting for a crack to stand on.

There was a lamp, about a foot to the left and on the same level as my foot.

I stretched the leg to the side, straining to get even just a toe on the lamp, some sort of dominance.

Finally, I managed to get a foothold on the lamp, breathing a short sigh of relief.

With one hand, I took the curtain out of my mouth and placed it inside the maybe three inches of window space left. I made sure to place at least a yard of the curtain inside the window. That was how much I needed if my plan was going to work. The metal barrier continued to fall as the voice inside continued to drone and the sirens continued to wail.

I waited until the barrier was just centimeters from my finger and then took a final breath of safety.

Well, as safe as you can be dangling from a ledge fifteen feet off the ground.

I grasped the curtain with my free hand as the hand keeping me alive slipped off of the ledge.

I held in my scream as I began to fall.

About two seconds into my fall the curtain stopped abruptly and my hand was luckily tight enough around it to stop my fall.

I looked up to see that my plan had worked, the barrier had closed on top of the curtain, securing it in place.

I looked down and my hopefulness faded when I saw that a fall from this height would still leave me pretty injured, no matter how I tried to avoid it.

The curtain was about ten feet long since the ceilings at the Empathorium were freaking humongous. But they still didn't reach the ground safely.

I would have to fall a good four or five feet. I'd been through worse but it wasn't ideal.

I climbed down the curtain, taking advantage of the pre-tied foot knots to keep me balanced.

I passed another window and could still hear the faint voice of the loudspeaker. Letting the whole palace know that an intruder was in the building and was to be caught.

When I reached the end, I didn't even think about it, I just jumped. Hoping I could get to Mom before an Empath did.

I had disobeyed them.

And I had disobeyed them well.

I had killed their guards. Stolen their curtain. Broken into the Empathorium and then broke back out. But worst of all, I had found their stash of emotions. Their basement filled with discarded dreams.

I landed on my feet which sent a jolt of pain through them, reaching my ankles and causing the breath to escape my lungs. It didn't help that I landed on the concrete slab that the Empathorium was built on. Maybe that was a stroke of luck though, because if I was climbing down the curtain on the front of the Empathorium, the side that faced the neighborhoods, someone would have spotted me.

I shook both of my feet, hoping that would shake the pain off before starting to sprint home.

I didn't even make it to my street before the loudspeakers went off. Blaring that an intruder had escaped and everyone needed to get inside their houses immediately.

They announced that houses would be searched and that if anyone knew anything about some intruder they should tell the Empathorium immediately.

Everyone started sprinting to their houses and locking their doors. Kids picked up their mud pies and ran to their mothers. Parents locked their doors using pieces of tape and discarded scraps of twine. The rich kids piled their colored pencils and papers into their arms and ran into their two-story houses. The rich parents pushed their clay doors shut and sent their kids into the safe rooms.

Mom was waiting for me outside. Her face lit up when she saw me, in my battered ball gown, sprinting down the dusty streets to get to her.

"Mom, I'm sorry." I sobbed. "I'm so sorry, I don't know what to do anymore. They're going to kill us, Mom."

I saw tears run down her face as well but she quickly wiped them away. She simply cradled my face in her hands and smiled.

"I didn't think you were alive," she whispered.

She took me by my shoulders and led me inside the house, sitting my sobbing self down on my bed. Not an ounce of despair came from me. It had been traded a couple of months ago, I think it was for some berries but I don't remember. I don't remember much about my childhood. The memories are there but they're all hazy.

While I regained my composure, Mom started packing us some bags. She filled one with the scarce food we had. A little bit of nuts and some cans of mush. With the food went the clothes. While she packed I changed out of the ballgown. It would get asked questions since it was from the Empathorium.

In a separate bag, she placed our emergency emotions, plus the ones we had lying around. I don't know why we did because if the plan was to leave the city then the emotions would surely be useless unless we came upon another town.

Outside, the alarms continued to blare but the sound of shuffling feet was gone. Everyone was safely inside their homes, draped in the comfort that the intruder was not them and that in a few minutes, this whole mess would be over.

However, instead of throwing the bags over her shoulder and running out the door, Mom stashed them and the ballgown into the loose floorboard under our bathroom sink. We had dug a hole under it a while ago, to keep things that we didn't want the Empaths seeing.

"Mom, what are you doing?" I said, blinking back tears. "We need to leave, right now."

"I want you to tell me what happened," she said.

"No, Mom, we don't have time. All I know is that they're after me and they know where we are Mom we have to go right-"

"They aren't saying your name," she said, interrupting my rambling thoughts.

"Yes, but that doesn't matter does it?" I asked.

"They don't know that you did it," Mom whispered. "If they knew it was you, they would be blasting your name. We have some time Ser. We have some time, hopefully, this will all blow over."

I knew it wouldn't but Mom sparked some hope inside of me. She was right. The only people who knew me by name were Culley and Joel and they were dead. I had spoken to no one else in the place. Even if someone did find their bodies and activated the alarms they would check the *palace* for that intruder. The only place that had any record of me was the place with all the dead people and if they were looking for an intruder that was alive and well the last place they would check would be the room with the corpses.

For now, all the Empathorium knew was that there was someone who didn't belong. Someone who murdered two of their top morgue employees.

For all they knew I was dead. Burned by the same fire that killed Culley and Joel.

Mom sat on the bed next to me and gave a timid look around the room. "We have about five minutes before the Empaths come and interrogate us. Tell. Me. What. Happened."

I had just finished explaining everything to Mom when there was a knock at our door. She nodded at me. One motion that spoke a thousand words.

She was right, as she always is. There was no way for the Empathorium to know I was the intruder at the given moment. They would have listed me by name.

We were safe, for now. As long as I could get past the daunting questions and the lie detector.

"Hello, sir." Mom said, putting on her best pleasant voice. I peeked around the corner from the doorframe of our bedroom.

"There is an intruder currently in the Empathorium." a man said. He ignored Mom's welcome and walked right past her. Peering into the bedroom, he wrinkled his nose in disgust.

"There are supposed to be three people living in this..." the Empath looked around, disgusted. Taking a mental note of our sagging paint and cracked bed frames. He didn't dare say house. We weren't worthy of such a luxurious word.

"My father died getting kindlewood," I said. "We don't know how but we assume it was poison gas. Poison gas created by the Empathorium to kill common folk like him. Now why would-"

"Ser. Why don't you go get this nice man a drink?" Mom said, still smiling big. But her tone wasn't smiling. Her tone suggested that unless I wanted to die I should go get him a drink and shut the hell up.

"I'll administer your questions first." the Empath said, strapping a device to Mom's arm.

I heard them continue to talk as I huffed my way to the kitchen and filled up a glass with some water. I held back the urge to spit in it, or poison it, or make it the most disgusting water the Empath had ever had. Not that the water we got was great anyway. It was lukewarm and uncomfortably thick.

I knew he wouldn't drink it anyway. They never accept anything from us. And not because they're nice and want to save us our hard-earned winnings. No. Because they don't want to consume the same filth that keeps us alive.

I placed the water down on the table and stood next to it. Impatiently waiting for my turn.

We'd have no trouble getting past the lie detector test, learning to lie out of a test was something that was a standard practice here. More people knew it than not. It was all about keeping a steady heartbeat and a calm composure. The fatal flaw people made was trying to provide too much evidence. All that did was make the lie stick out.

The Empath walked into the room I was in, eyed the water, ignored the water, and then strapped the device to my arm. I sat down in a chair and put on my best calm face.

"Where were you when you first heard the alarm go off?" he asked, not taking his eyes off the screen in front of him. His gaze was cold and menacing. It chilled my spine.

"I was here," I responded.

"What were you doing when you heard the alarm go off, and why were you doing it?" he asked.

"I was outside, collecting eggs from our chickens. We were going to make fried eggs tonight for dinner. I had to get to the eggs before the chickens squashed them or a hawk stole them." I didn't hesitate or stutter. I gave him no reason to believe I was making up a story on the spot.

"Mhm," he said, glancing up at me for a second before re-fixing his eyes on the screen. "Do you know anyone that has talked about or planned breaking into the Empathorium before?"

"No."

"That's no sir to you. And the final question: Why have you been lying to me this whole time, Miss Vane?"

Chapter 6

My heart wanted to leap into my throat, skip a couple of beats, or start hammering out of my chest but I stopped it.

"I have not been lying to you... sir." I said.

The Empath glanced at the screen before looking back up at me. He slowly removed the device from my arm. I looked up at Mom, praying that he had simply asked me a trick question. I remembered the tactics, honestly, I had. I pleaded with my mind praying that something would go in my favor for today.

Slowly, the Empath took his gun out of the holster.

I took one last look at Mom, at our house, at the unforgiving eyes of my condemner.

But he didn't shoot me or hit me over the head. He simply gestured towards the door.

"You need to get yourselves a proper lock. Intruders are running around these streets wild. William's done enough for you, providing you with this house."

Oh, now he calls it a house.

"Yes sir." Mom said, waving to him as he walked away. "We will do just that sir. Thank you for caring."

When she closed the door we both took our first real breath since this whole mess started.

"He's going to Hennie's house next," I whispered. "I don't think she saw me since the incident. I mean, if you thought I was dead, maybe she does too."

"She came over." Mom said. "She told me you had killed Drew. She said that there better be at least fifty happiness bottles at her doorstep before she even thought of forgiving you. I told her you were dead too, and it wasn't even a lie. I thought Ser, I thought you…"

She held back more tears and took a couple of sips of the water I had gotten for the Empath. Her face twitched slightly, upon tasting the water, but she continued to drink it, placing the finished glass back onto the table.

"Anyway. She probably does think you're dead. She isn't that bright. She wouldn't have connected any dots that you could be the intruder. I didn't either."

"But you were waiting for me when I was running home," I said. "I saw you, waiting at the doorstep. Why would you wait if you thought I was dead Mom?"

"The just, wise person in me thought for sure that you were gone, one way or another. But the mother in me hoped that you weren't. She knew that you weren't. And she was right, as always."

A tendril of glee arose from her fingertips and swirled around the room. She quickly waved it away and cleared her throat, keeping her face calm. It was too dangerous to lose control of an emotion with Empaths running wild in the streets. Not to mention Hennie, no doubt watching our every move to see what she could do to make our life harder.

Rather, Mom's life harder. I hoped that to her I was dead. Just a thought. A bad memory.

I watched as Mom's wisp of joy tried to escape, bouncing off the walls and searching for any openings before it finally found a crack in the door and set off for a life of adventure.

One could only hope.

The next day, I woke up late. I had to hurry if I wanted to make it to work on time. Mom was already gone, probably out shopping or 'borrowing' from gardens.

I pulled on my clothes and my boots, hurriedly ripping through my hair with the brush. I didn't have time to eat breakfast but we didn't have a great selection anyway.

When I finally pushed open the giant clay door and got to my workstation, no one asked me why I was late or why I hadn't been to work in a couple of days.

Since we didn't get paid due to hours, no one cared who was there and who wasn't. We got paid by the families we made the creations for. We could clock out whenever we wanted, honestly. The families could reject our welding though. If it wasn't good enough. At first, everyone sat and sorted through the cards for hours, trying to find a family with the highest pay. If someone got lucky they would find an order card straight from the Empathorium. Now we don't care as much. I'd make more doing four cards instead of spending four hours finding the highest pay.

I pulled an order card from the table and nodded at the Empath watching us. He didn't nod back.

The order was for a new lock. Pretty common these days, and probably especially after that mysterious intruder broke into the Empathorium. I honestly wondered what brilliant criminal mastermind could attempt to break into the Empathorium.

The lock was fairly easy to make, as many things were. It was just melting and pouring. The hardest part was waiting for the scalding hot metal to harden. The rules were that we couldn't get started on another project until our first was finished. It was set in place to prevent people from getting distracted and wasting metal by attempting to complete four or five different projects at once. One time someone made a crack on William's order. Their body was found in a ditch near the Empathorium.

I messed with my shoestrings while I waited for the lock to harden. The Empath stood as still as a statue, except for the occasional turn, watching our every move.

Suddenly, there was a scream from outside. Everyone rushed to the door, but the Empath reached it first. He pulled it open and ran outside. The rest of us held it open and watched from the doorframe.

A man was lying on his stomach in the dirt, pleading for the Empaths not to hurt him. There were five surrounding him, including our guy. One woman whispered to the rest, probably informing them of the crime he committed.

"Please." the criminal begged. "Please I didn't mean to. I have kids, and they were hungry. I needed to feed them. They-their names are Cardin and... and Merit." His eyes searched the crowds, begging for someone to help, and we locked gazes. He started to scream at the people watching him.

"Please! You would want help if we switched places wouldn't you? Help me dammit! Somebody please he-"

One Empath with shaggy hair that covered his eyes placed his boot on the condemned man's head and shoved it into the dirt so that he couldn't breathe. The criminal resisted and squirmed but could not overpower the Empath. His hands started to scratch at the boot and the Empath's ankles but didn't do any real damage.

"This! This is the consequence of stealing from the vendors!" one Empath screamed. She raised her gun in the air as she looked around at the crowd. It was almost as if she wanted us to throw stones at the criminal and agree with her.

"The man shall be killed. For we spare no cheat. We spare no liar. We spare no fugitive. We give no warnings, no second chances. For if we did the streets would run wild with fugitives. We are doing the people of our town a favor. By Willilam's decree, this criminal shall never see the light of day again."

She looked at the Empath with his boot on the criminal's head and nodded.

"Binigo ka ng iyong emosyon." she uttered. The same words are spoken to every criminal. Every thief. No one knew what they meant but one thing was for sure.

Those words meant that you were dead.

The barrel of the gun rested on the back of the criminal's head. He screamed a muffled scream that couldn't carry through his sandy grave.

I turned away as I heard the gunfire. There were plenty of whispers and murmurs from passersby and crowds that gave me the idea of how gruesome his wound was.

All I could think about were his kids. And his wife. I had seen plenty of deaths, dozens and dozens. But seeing more deaths didn't make witnessing them any easier.

Everyone else scattered from the doorway and resumed working as if nothing had happened. The Empath returned after a short while and resumed his post. Also as if nothing had happened. He didn't even seem upset.

When my lock had dried I took it out and grabbed the order sheet. I walked over to the Empath and showed him my work.

"The house number is 056," I said. "Just down the street, so I won't be gone long."

He nodded at me, but even as I turned away I could feel his eyes staring into the back of my neck.

I passed the place where the man had been shot, and even though body pickup had come already there was still an abundance of his blood. Just laying, pooled, and worthless on the road. My heart shattered for him but there was no more sadness in me to give.

After what felt like an eternity, I gained the strength to step over the pile of ichor and continue on my route.

The death threats from the Empath, who screamed for me to get going unless I wanted to die the same way, only helped.

The walk wasn't long, but it was frightening.

Usually, people line the streets, asking to trade or trying to create a childhood for their kids. After the gunshot, everyone boarded themselves up and decided that they wouldn't be outside anymore. Besides me and the Empaths, the roads were practically empty.

They must have noticed it too, because one Empath stepped in front of me, blocking off my path.

"Where are you headed?" he asked. "There were just gunshots, it is not safe to be out at this time."

"Oh, I work at the blacksmith sir," I said. "We do deliveries. I'm headed to 056."

The man inspected my lock and scoffed.

"Return to your workplace immediately. Orders are shut down until body pickup comes."

"It did come." I insist. "Right outside of our workplace. Sir, this is the only way we get money. Have a good one."

I shouldered past him, ignoring his scoffs of disbelief and disapproval. It was obvious what he was doing. They don't like when we make money. It makes them feel like we are doing something right and that's not okay here. How dare we try and survive.

Luckily, no one else bothered me until I got to the appropriate house. It was a house like Hennie and Drew's, a big clay one with some glass windows and a small garden out front. That was stupid of them. I'd have to remember to snatch some carrots or something on my way out.

I knocked on the door but before I could even pull my hand away it flew open and a hand grabbed me.

"You need to get inside. Gunshots. My husband hasn't returned yet. Hurry."

The woman yanked me inside the house and shut the door, pressing her back to it and looking side to side frantically.

"There's nothing out there anymore," I said. "Body pickup already came. It was just me and the Empaths."

"Body pickup?" the woman whispered. "Someone died? And no, it couldn't have just been you. My husband is on his way home right now. He was just out shopping."

"I have your lock," I said, ignoring her invitation into her life story. "That'll be one bottle of fear please."

The lady straightened her hair and wiped off her clothes. She walked to one of her cabinets and pulled out a jar. "Yes... um. Do you accept... debts? This is our last bottle."

"Debts?" I laughed. "In a place like this, with a garden out front? A big clay roof over your head?"

"Yes, we have a garden but you can't get emotions from plants." the woman murmured. "My husband, I sent him with the last bottle of sadness. He was gonna try and bargain. I told him, just don't steal. Just don't. But he was determined to get us food and I'm afraid..."

Before she could finish her sentence, a little girl ran into the room, her hair as wild as her expression.

"Momma. Cardin's losing his anger. Can we use it to buy chickens?"

The woman sighed. "No, no dear. We couldn't keep those bastards alive last time. It's too expensive. And no, don't you ever even think about extracting your brother's emotions."

Cardin?

Cardin.

The man. The man in the street. He had a son named Cardin. And a daughter named...

"Merit," I whispered.

"Yes?" the little girl asked. She looked at her mother, eyes filled with confusion.

"I didn't tell you her name, did I?" the woman asked.

"Look, I'm sorry Miss," I said. "I am. But your husband... the gunshots... the body pickup just came. He stole from the vendors."

It was quiet for a moment. Merit broke the silence with a wail, screaming and crying. Blue, red, and purple tinted fog shot out of her. I saw the cores, thick and bright. I almost thought about grabbing a cup or a jar and capturing them but I quickly stopped myself from thinking such horrible things.

The mother slid down to the floor with her back against the wall. Sorrow protruded from her heart. The tendrils swirled around each other before the core emerged. It slowly rose, the depths of her sadness so silent, yet so deafening.

I quietly placed the lock on the table and then left. I knew I was better than most people. Almost anyone else would have hurried to capture the four free emotions while the cores were out and strong. I guess that made me feel a bit better about myself.

By the time I made it back to the blacksmith, the blood was cleaned off of the road. It was a sight to behold. A patch of fresh road while the rest choked in the dust. They never cleaned the whole road, just the parts with blood on it, so they always left funny little circles of cleanliness.

Well, as funny as something can be in a living hell.

The next morning, I didn't go to work. I stayed up until almost midnight making and delivering things. I had gotten three bottles of fear and one bottle of sadness. One lady even gave me a tip, a sack of the imperfect potatoes from her garden.

When I got up, Mom was making potato pancakes. She called them that, but I know they are just fried mashed potatoes with some flour. Back when Dad was alive, we had a small garden with all sorts of fruits and vegetables. She would make the pancakes every Saturday, and sometimes Dad would get some maple syrup if he got lucky at work.

I sat down at the table and ate breakfast, scoffing at the Empaths that walked by. They were doing daily neighborhood checks now, patrolling every street.

They were still trying to figure out who could have broken into the Empathorium, but by some stroke of luck hadn't figured out it was me yet. The only other person who had even seen me was the chef but he most likely thought I died in the fire that killed Joel and Culley.

Most likely.

"I'm still trying to get us out," Mom whispered, blowing on her still-hot potatoes and sitting down next to me.

"It's these mountains," I whispered back. "Or cliffs, or crags, I don't even know anymore. Either way, they're *everywhere.* Even if we could get past the gates and the guards there's no way of knowing how tall they are or how steep."

Mom sighed in agreement.

"Why build a town surrounded by cliffs?" I sneered, picking up a newborn chick and shaking it violently. Purple smoke swirled around my body as it shivered and squeaked.

"I mean, I guess for protection. But it's more dangerous here." Mom said, grabbing a jar.

The core of the chick's fear escaped from its beak and Mom snapped the jar's lid around it. It grew brighter and bounced against the walls, looking for any escape but it knew it was trapped.

"Oh, I get it," I said. "If we manage to escape we'll still be trapped. Not by the guards or the gates but by the cliffs. Can you imagine? Being out there all alone and vulnerable?"

"They'd rather come back to the city than die in the heat, unable to scale the cliffs." Mom agreed.

The rest of the terror started to fade from the room. The chick was still as scared as he could be but there was nothing to show for it.

I tried to grab the fear from Mom but she pulled her hand away. "I'll go to the markets from now on. Too risky," she said. "For all we know..."

"I know," I muttered. "Just... just make sure you go to Mortia's booth. If she's there. We need some more flour and some more water. And tell her that's happiness. Oh, and if Atlas is there..."

"Compliment his outfit and he'll give some discounts. I know Ser. I've gone to the markets too, you know."

"Yeah, and you always come back with some stupidly low amount of food that Atlas talked you into buying," I muttered under my breath, turning toward the kitchen.

Mom walked out without another word, so I didn't know if she had heard me or not. She always had a way of making me feel bad after arguments, even small bickers or just disagreements.

I went outside to grab whatever eggs the chickens laid and was disappointed to see that there were none. Usually, the chickens gave us two or three eggs. One if we were unlucky and four if we were really lucky.

But none were unusual. Someone had to have stolen them but who? Hennie was rich enough unless she had done it out of spite, and since the shooting, a lot fewer people roamed the streets. Most people had a daily routine of going to the market but that was it. Especially since the Empathorium was getting frustrated that they hadn't caught this intruder yet. I knew they hadn't thought of expanding their search anywhere useful which was calming to me since Mom and I-

A high whistling sound shattered my thoughts. I turned around and had just enough time to scream before the bomb made contact, blowing my house to smithereens.

I woke up sprawled against the fence. A few chickens were exploring the remains, but most were balled up in clumps.

I stood up and examined the house. Most everything was done for. The walls and roof were gone, and only a few patches of the floor remained. Our cabinets had nothing in them anymore, although there were some charred potatoes flung around the house. They stuck to the walls and littered the floor.

Mom and I's bedroom was a mess. Our beds had disappeared, replaced with piles of splintered wood, still on fire.

The bathroom was worse, the shower head was bent at an unimaginable angle. Rusty water started to pool on the floor, but no amount of water would be able to fix the inferno our house had turned into in a matter of seconds.

They had to have found out it was me. My heart started to race, my breaths became short and quick. I collapsed against the sad remains of our bathroom wall and ran my hands through my hair. I had been tricked by false hope and now nowhere was safe. As long as the Empaths were alive I wasn't safe.

As long as *I* was alive I wasn't safe.

They would be coming any second, flocks of them. Guns held high, waved around like a trophy.

I scrambled to the bedroom and stomped out a small fire that was blocking where Mom had put our bags. The floorboard under my foot splintered and revealed that the bags had been severely burnt. Any food or clothes inside were done for. For the first time since I'd lost it, I was glad I didn't have my fear. If I did, the emotion would just be one giant smoke signal. Letting all the Empaths know that I was here and I was alive.

I looked up and saw Mom running towards me. She was near the Empathorium, all the way down our street, but just the sight of her made me want to cry.

Suddenly, a flood of guards swarmed from the doors and two went after Mom. They grabbed her by both of her arms and yanked her away. She kicked and screamed but my sight of her was soon lost as they carried her into the crowd and through the doors, swimming through Empaths like a salmon fighting its way upstream.

I wanted to scream, cry, or wail, but I knew that if I was going to help Mom in any way I needed to get out of this mess alive.

Our house was a big, bright, burning target on my back. And if I wanted to get out alive and have even a chance of saving Mom from the Empathorium's grasp, I needed to leave it behind.

I stepped over the burning remains of our bedroom wall and took one last look at the house I grew up in. Now I was thankful I had lost my sorrow too because if I didn't I would be screwed once more.

The sounds of the stomping Empath boots got louder and I took that as my cue to leave. I left my jacket behind, to both mislead them and as a little gift.

Maybe William could hang it on his wall since he's so obsessed with me.

I started to sprint away from my house and towards the Empathorium, using the houses of my neighbors as cover. There was a small patch of land between all the houses on my street and the gate, which was pretty useful if we ever wanted to get somewhere without using the main road.

Who knew that 'if' would become a reality so fast?

The more I ran, the more my anger grew, but I had to stop it before my core came out or before it became noticeable.

I kept a small bit of fury though, just enough to make me passionate but for no smoke to come out. No matter how much Mom tells me that getting mad doesn't solve anything, I believe that without it no one would ever taste the sweet juices of revenge ever again.

I stopped behind a house that was just a couple yards away from the Empathorium, a house that had a very pleasant view of the dropoff that Drew and I battled on.

I caught my breath and ran my fingers through my hair, pulling it into a quick ponytail and using the hem of my shirt as a hair tie.

The shirt was old and battered, so it ripped easily.

I peeked around the corner and peered up at the balcony. Two people were up there, but I couldn't see them very well.

Suddenly, alarms started to blare. It wasn't the hide-in-your-house alarms but the alarms that meant William had an important announcement. People started to peer out of their doors and cautiously gathered around the Empathorium, staring straight up at William on the balcony.

When the family that lived in the house I was hiding behind exited, I took my opportunity and slipped inside their house. I grabbed the first thing in reach that could cover me, a tattered blanket lying discarded on their patchwork couch, and followed behind them, pulling the blanket over my head to disguise my face and features.

I elbowed my way through the crowd until I was snug in the center, certain that no guards would be able to spot my face. I knew that William was going to do something with Mom, maybe banish her or perhaps warn everyone about her. My heart was trying to beat its way out of my chest but I kept a calm composure and kept my eyes fixated on William. Just like everyone else in the crowd.

Yes, I was just like everyone else.

Maybe if I believed in that fantasy hard enough it would come true.

After a couple of minutes of waiting for his people to gather, William started to speak. There was a microphone attached to his ear and secured at the cheek, blaring his voice probably beyond the cliffs.

"As you know, someone broke into the Empathorium. News has now been discovered that they killed two of our top guards, Joel Meridus and Culley Grant."

The crowd started to whisper and shove, pointing and mumbling. There were a few cries of family members or friends but I couldn't care less. Culley and Joel deserved what came to them and I didn't feel bad.

"This worthless bastard is the murderer's mother," William announced, silencing the crowd. "Her daughter broke into the Empathorium and killed two of our guards. We can not let the blood relatives of a criminal remain unscathed can we?"

There were more whispers as Mom was forced to her knees. My mouth opened as I saw the Empath behind her start to tie a noose around her neck. The end of the rope was then tied to the balcony.

There were a few protestors, all of whom quickly got removed from the crowd by armed Empaths. I couldn't move, I couldn't scream or protest or even breathe properly.

Two Empaths grabbed Mom and forced her on top of the balcony, holding her there while she wobbled on top of the railing. She looked around in fear but made no sound.

William nodded at the guards who let go of Mom, leaving her to balance on her own. She looked down at her feet, and then at the rope. Her face crumpled in despair.

An Empath started pushing through the crowd. I went stiff as he elbowed me in the ribs, forcing his way past me and running up the stairs.

He was carrying the jacket I left at the house.

William saw the commotion and paused, waiting until the Empath burst through the door to the balcony. He thrust the jacket into William's arms and whispered something to him. William's fists clenched around the jacket and turned white.

"News has been spread," he announced through gritted teeth. "That although the criminal's house is now demolished, she remains alive. There was no body at the crime scene."

Again, waves of whispers and murmurs crashed through the crowd. I heard at least five rumors, in the time that the chatter lasted. Spread between families and friends about this mysterious murderer.

William walked up to Mom and held up the jacket, spinning it around in his hands.

"I'm going to make one final offer with you, sweetheart," he said, looking Mom square in the eye. "You tell me where your daughter is, and I'll let you go. Free. Unharmed. Your house, rebuilt. Big clay doors and big clay walls and hell, I'll even throw in some bottles of terror to get you started."

Mom looked at my jacket and shook her head. She turned to face the crowd and screamed for the whole city to hear, face streaked with tears.

"Agreeing with the Empaths doesn't provide an escape," she screamed. Her voice broke. "They will torture us, kill us, and steal every last of our emotions. And for what? Not for peace or justice. Just to aimlessly pile them up in their little hideou-"

William threw my jacket over Mom's head and mouth, muffling her last words and causing her to slip, her legs and torso dangling off of the balcony while her hands held onto the railing for her life.

Her head was turned towards the crowd, away from William, allowing him to tighten the grasp of the jacket and suffocate her. I could do nothing but sit frozen in horror as I watched my mother dangle feet first from a balcony, hands white-knuckling the rose-engraved railing.

She tried to turn herself around, the muffled sounds of her screams echoing through William's microphone.

He leaned his face down to the railing and near hers, smiling at her demise.

"You can't outsmart the Empathorium." he snarled.

He let go of the jacket and Mom plummeted to her death. The crowd applauded as her neck snapped and she swung from side to side. The creaks of the rope matched the painful beats of my heart until all went silent.

Every ounce of me wished my heart would go silent too.

Chapter 7

Shortly after the scene, the crowd began to clear out. They treated it as if it was a movie. Some people walked away laughing, some people walked away crying.

I sat, stunned for a while. The body pickup came right away and chopped down the rope from the balcony. Mom's body dropped into the sand.

I couldn't bear to watch anymore, so I took my first step. Then another. And another. I kept the blanket pulled over my head as I followed a crowd heading down one of the streets.

They dispersed into their houses, but I kept walking, unsure of where to go but persistent to get somewhere.

A hand grabbed my shoulder, startling me. I froze in place, trying to turn my head in the opposite direction so that they couldn't see my face.

"Ser, I know it's you. Get inside."

I turned my face to see Amin, brow crumpled in worry. He grabbed me by my shoulders and forced me inside his house, turning to smile at the Empath patrolling the roads a couple of yards away.

"Get her in here." Amin's mother said, hustling me into the bedroom and sitting me down on a bed.

My face crumpled as I started to sob, pulling my shirt over my face in embarrassment. Amin started to fill me a cup of water while his mother comforted me. I started to choke on my sobs, tears streaking down my face and wetting the collar of my shirt.

"They... she... I..." I wailed, voice heaving with sorrow. My breaths were quick and deep. Amin ran his hands through his hair. "Ser, I.. we're so-"

He didn't finish his sentence, instead choosing to take a deep, shaky breath.

"They, they blew up... house.." I whispered, gulping in the air before sobbing into my shirt again. Nothing was left for me here. Nothing. The only reminders that I even had a life were what memories were left of me and the clothes on my back.

Amin exited the room to keep an eye on any upcoming Empaths, but his mother stayed with me. She let me collapse in her arms and sob, saying nothing.

Somehow silence was the best thing she *could* say.

I don't know how long it took me to stop crying but I do know that I somehow shifted from the bed to the floor, the stolen blanket wrapped around me like a hug.

Like a hug from the mother that I'd never see again. And I didn't even get to say goodbye. The last she saw of me was when she was captured by the Empaths. Her legs kicking in the air, her hair wild, her face twisted in concern and confusion.

And I just stood there... I just stood there and watched. I didn't scream or run after her, or beat up the Empaths. I didn't plead or give myself up in exchange for her life when she was on top of that balcony.

I didn't and I could've.

Amin's mother brought me a plate of some bread with butter. She even took the time to peel me an orange, so I choked it down, even though I felt like I wanted to explode.

Amin came to eat with me, sitting on the ground beside me. Back against the bed. We sat in silence for a while. I stared at the closet in front of me, my under eyes coated with dried tears.

"I never knew the term heartbreak was real," I muttered. "Until now, I mean."

"Do you feel it?" he asked.

I tapped on my heart. "It hurts," I whispered. "It physically hurts. And not in a heart attack way, it just... hurts."

Amin nodded, silently eating the rest of his bread.

He seemed pretty shaken up as well, barely blinking and staring off into space, the same as me. I was about to ask him why they decided to help me, I didn't think we were that close of friends when his mother came into the room. A panicked expression filled her eyes.

"There's an Empath. Checking all of the houses. Just procedural questions, I think. But they are still looking for you Seraphai."

Amin took my empty plate and ran to the kitchen to put it away. His mother checked under the bed and nodded at me.

"Do you think you can fit?" she asked.

I peeked under the bed and nodded, squeezing into the small space in no time flat. I couldn't take a decent breath under there, which only made me more anxious.

Amin and his mother ran to their closet and started pulling out boxes and handfuls of clothes. They started to stuff the items under the bed with me, creating a sort of barrier.

"I'll continue covering her up, start putting things under your bed so that there's no suspicion," Amin ordered, throwing a blanket under the bed with me.

I used the blanket I was already wrapped up in to cover any parts of me that could be seen from a glance under the bed. They were still stuffing items next to me when we heard a knock at the door.

"Shit," said Amin.

His mother hurried to answer the door.

Amin dropped to his hands and knees and looked at me through a crack between a box and a pile of shirts. "Pull the blanket over your head if they check." he hissed. "They'll have a flashlight and-"

"Hello sir!" his mother said in a shaky, yet calm tone. "What can we help you with?"

"Mandatory house check." the Empath grunted. I heard his footsteps approaching and pulled the blanket over my head, trying to slow my breathing.

I heard him check in the closet, shuffling things around. He started to pull the covers off the bed and open all the drawers. As if I could fit myself into a drawer.

He reached into his belt and grabbed a flashlight, kneeling to check under the beds. He checked the one I was under first. I saw the shimmer of the flashlight from under the blanket.

By some stroke of luck, he didn't see me, but instead moved over to the other bed. After shining the flashlight under it and heaving himself up, he grunted out of disgust.

"Keep your shit in the closet. Not under the bed."

"Yes sir," Amin said.

I heard him walk around some more, opening all the kitchen cabinets. He took out a plate, probably the one I had been eating off of, and scoffed.

"Do you not clean your plates?" he asked.

Amin cleared his throat sheepishly. "We were trying to save water, sir. Someone in the street told me there was a drought coming. And... well... I figured in a drought the Empathorium would raise the prices of..."

His voice trailed off. I heard large footsteps.

"The Empathorium raises prices when we see fit. We are very generous to you." the Empath snarled.

Amin cleared his throat. "Yes of course... *sir.*"

"And don't listen to people in the street." I heard the click of a gun reloading. "We kill those people for a reason. Rules are rules."

The door creaked open.

"If you hear or see this 'Seraphai', let us know. She's dangerous. Her last emotion is anger. We recently disposed of her mother and her house is gone, so we assume she is running wild somewhere. Keep that in mind."

"Yes sir." Amin's mother whispered.

The door creaked shut.

We waited until it was dark to get me out.

The rest of the time we spent sprawled out on the ground, thinking of a way we *could* get me out.

"They swap out," Amin said. "There's one guard in the morning and then another at night. I think they swap at midnight."

"What do the night guards wear?" I asked.

"The same uniforms as any Empath," Amin said. "But maybe in the dark, they wouldn't be able to see very well-"

"What if you pretended to be a guard, Amin?" I muttered. Thoughts ran through my mind at lightning speed. A plan was slowly but surely forming. It was dangerous, and we relied mainly on hope, but it was the only plan that involved even a chance of me getting out of this hellhole.

Amin changed into pants and a long-sleeved shirt while I explained the plan to him.

"You're going to go up to the nightguard, and you're going to say that it's time to swap out."

"And what if he politely declines?" Amin asked, slipping on a green jacket. The color was hideous and didn't match the Empath's uniforms at all but I hoped the dark would be enough to cover it. "Or, you know, gun to my head declines?"

"Just say that it's William's order," I responded, absentmindedly folding the stolen blanket into a small square. "Tell him... tell him he needs to go speak to William. All we need is five minutes anyway. Then you can hoist me over the fence. By the time anyone comes back you'll be gone."

"Just hide your face." Amin's mother said. "And then once Ser is out, run back home."

Amin turned to me and wrinkled his brow in worry. I was about to reassure him that he would be safe but he was worried about me instead.

"How will you get food?" he asked. "Or... or water? Nobody knows what's out there. How will you even make it?"

"I'll be fine," I said, trying to smile but it was hopeless at this point. I didn't even believe myself no matter how hard I tried to.

Amin nodded as he walked to the kitchen and handed me a bag of dates.

"Here, at least you'll have something to keep you going."

"Thank you, Amin."

I tucked the dates into my pocket and stood up, blinking away the forming tears and heading for the door.

"Be safe. Both of you," said Amin's mother. Her voice broke but she cleared it quickly. Amin smiled at her and opened the door, making sure it didn't creak. Before I could leave, Amin's mother pressed a small handgun into my palm and closed my fingers around it. The look she gave me said everything that needed to be said.

"Thank you." I said, "I'll make sure to give it back to Amin before he leaves."

It was pitch black outside, a few scattered street lamps provided bubbles of light but they didn't do much for vision. Amin placed a hand on my back and led me through the street, pausing if we heard a branch crack.

"These damn chickens," he whispered. "Always stepping on something."

"At least they cover our trace," I muttered back. "If an Empath were to hear anything they'd think it was a chicken. Not a criminal and a common boy trying to break out."

We continued creeping along the street, which was dangerous because we were out in the open. We had decided, however, that creeping in or behind people's backyards was even more dangerous. Some animals would freak out at the sight of us, and the road was sandy so it covered our footprints. Most people's yards had at least some grass or one bush that would drop leaves and pollen.

We had almost reached the gate, stepping more carefully now. Amin gestured to a house only a few yards away from the gate. It was a small wooden one, just like Mom and I's.

Well, just like *mine* is.

Was.

I swallowed back my feelings and strayed from Amin's side, taking shelter behind the small house. They didn't have chickens or anything, not that I could see at least. I stood behind the house and watched from the corner as Amin approached the night guard, whistling calmly. As if this was *his* territory. As if *he* had the power (and the weaponry) here.

I heard a gun click and a woman's stern voice. An Empath began to emerge from the darkness, walking closer to Amin. Her boots were loud, even in the dust.

"What do you think you're doing here?"

Amin raised his hands and chuckled. "Woah, woah. I've come to take over your shift. William's orders."

The Empath paused. She checked her watch and scoffed.

"It's not time yet. Come here, let me see your watch. William should have put his signature for approval."

My heart began to race. I knew the Empaths communicated and lived on their high-tech watches but how were we supposed to know that William put his signature of approval on them?

Amin hesitated before walking towards the Empath. I could see her, squinting in the moonlight, trying to get a good look at him. A plume of fear emerged from each footstep that Amin took. It gave him away, *shit.*

The Empath's eyes widened when she saw our makeshift uniform and the painfully obvious fear that accompanied it. Her gun was aimed at Amin's heart. He put his hands up and tried to back away, pleading with her.

"No, you don't understa-"

The gunshot echoed and made the crickets fall silent. Amin toppled to the ground. His horror began to swarm his body, swirling around him, terrified.

The Empath began to approach him, still aiming her gun at his head. She smiled. *Smiled.* A strand of anger emerged from my fingertips and darted around the gun in my belt pocket.

I leaped out from the side of the house and aimed my handgun at the Empath's head. She noticed me too late. My trigger was pulled and her skull was fractured. She crumpled to the ground, her body bent and twitching. Blood poured from her mouth and stained her uniform.

I had only a few minutes before a whole army of Empaths approached, so I had to hurry. I grabbed the Empath's hand and placed the barrel of my gun on the end of her thumb.

One pull of the trigger blew it clean off.

I left the gun in the dirt, not intentionally but the adrenaline fogged up my brain and left me to regret my horrible decisions.

I sprinted to the gate and pressed her thumb to the fingerprint recognition, breathing my first sigh of relief in ages when the light blazed green and the gate began to creak open.

As disgusting as it was, I saved her thumb in my pocket, in case the fingerprints would come in handy some other time.

I backed out of the gate, about to make a run for the hills, when I heard a small voice.

"Ser..."

It was Amin. He lay curled up on the ground, hand covering his abdomen. He reached a hand out towards me. "Ser..." he cried. "Please, help me."

I heard the doors of the Empathorium swing open and saw an army of Empaths begin to run towards us. From the back gate, they looked like ants but they were approaching fast.

The gate squealed to a stop but I knew it wouldn't stay that way forever. I also knew that they would kill Amin, if they found him alive, and anyone else that tried to help him. Whether that was his unassuming mother or me.

At the last second, I gave in to his cries and sprinted to him, wrapping my arms around his chest and dragging him through the already-closing gate.

As the Empaths came closer, I could see their flashlights and hear their screams. They ordered civilians to stay inside, yelling that there was an emergency that would soon be dealt with and they could all go back to sleep in a moment.

Amin tried to help me drag him by frantically kicking his legs, which only knocked me off balance. The gate squeaked closed as we backed away, hopefully out of sight from the flashlights. There were a few scarce trees and hills of sand leading to the mountains, but nothing big we could hide behind.

Amin gasped for breath and pointed to our left.

"The tree," he whispered. "The tree. The tree."

To our left, a skimpy ironwood tree stood as tall as it could. From what I could see it had a pretty decent-sized trunk but not nearly as many leaves or branches as we needed. Leaves and branches were what kept us covered, what kept us alive.

I gritted my teeth and continued to drag Amin towards the tree. The Empaths had reached the gate and were inspecting the dead body and everything around it. I prayed that they didn't notice the thumb was missing. I prayed that they didn't connect the dots. I prayed that Amin would stay alive. I knew not everything I prayed for could come true but that didn't stop me from pleading to the stars.

I heard lots of terrified screams and cries. Doors were knocked down. Families were frightened. Little kids wailed as their happy dreams were crushed by the harsh reality of guns and torture. Families got forced into the street and interrogated. Amin's mother was likely one of the bunch.

My muscles started to burn, and Amin sensed it. He grabbed my forearms and heaved himself up, still keeping a hand on his abdomen. He started to limp to the tree, clinging to my shoulders and back. This was probably slower than me dragging him but I would try anything because I couldn't drag him forever and it was too late to leave him behind.

I looked behind me to see flashlights swirling around the crime scene. They would be a comforting source of light if they weren't searching for us. The Empaths hadn't thought to check outside the gate yet, instead, they scavenged backyards and tore apart houses, looking for two certain children that would probably never return.

When we finally reached the flimsy little tree I propped Amin against the trunk, and immediately dropped stomach first in the dirt, watching the Empaths carefully.

"Thank you, Ser," Amin whispered, trying to catch his breath and very obviously gritting his teeth due to the pain. "I-"

"Shut it."

"If I don't make it, I want-"

I clamped my hand over his mouth to make him stop talking, but not because I thought he *was* going to make it. Not because I didn't want him to jinx it, not even because I wanted him to stop putting himself down for once.

The Empaths were on the prowl and any sound would be heard. Usually, Amin would know this but with the shock and distress he was in plus the actively bleeding gunshot I knew he wouldn't and couldn't think straight.

I tore off the jacket, which was already blood-soaked from his wound, and tied it around his abdomen. He winced in pain but didn't resist. When I had finished and laid back down in the dirt, my hands had a red tint to them.

I continued to watch the Empaths, and for a while, they didn't leave. Amin ended up falling asleep and it scared me half to death when I turned my head for the first time and saw him slumped over with his eyes closed.

One Empath ventured outside the gate but only once, he barely even left, just walked a couple of steps into the night before turning on his heel. The Empaths had never been outside either. They would always talk about it, in the conversations I could hear, but they never went outside for good.

I wondered if it was against William's laws. I hoped so because then we would be safe. We would be free. Free.

The word sounded weird on my tongue. I imagined what freedom was like, beyond the mountains. I pictured green grass and a babbling brook. Butterflies and lots of lush trees with juicy fruit on them. I didn't even realize I had fallen asleep until Amin woke up, disgruntled and frightened, which woke me up.

His wound had stopped actively bleeding, which was good. But it was still severely damaged. He instinctively placed his hand over his stomach, either trying to hide the damage or mask the pain.

It was still dark out but the crickets had started back up and the families had been moved back inside of their houses. A couple of Empaths were still there though. Body pickup had removed the corpse and cleaned the blood leaving the stupid little patches of un-dusty street again.

Three Empaths remained, clutching their guns and standing guard against the gate. They didn't talk or even move. They looked like three statues, keeping watch for a girl that wasn't in their labyrinth anymore.

I leaned close to Amin.

"We need to move now. The sun is going to come up soon and they'll be able to see us. We need to get to the cliffs. Can you get there?"

Amin looked beyond me at the cliffs. I don't know what I imagined for them, since they were mostly made of tan and beige rocks. The hope in me thought maybe there would be grass or something beyond them but hope can only get a person so far.

They weren't too far away, less than a mile but far enough so that it would be quite a difficult journey with an injured partner.

Amin nodded.

"Yeah, I think I can get there."

As quietly as we could, I helped him get to his feet. I expected him to grasp on to me for support but the couple hours of sleep must have done him good. It would have been a lot worse if his leg got shot.

I kept checking behind us, in case the Empaths turned around. I knew they wouldn't, they had no reason to believe...

But something kept me turning around anyway.

We had moved only a couple of yards towards the mountains when Amin began to slow. His breathing was shallow. His face was crumpled in fear.

Clouds of horror began to emerge from his cheeks which were quickly turning white.

We were out of earshot from the Empaths, but if his fear grew they would take notice eventually. He knelt to the ground, quaking a little bit.

"Hey, hey. What's wrong?" I asked, my voice shaky. I knelt beside him and placed my hand on his back, not sure what to even do with him. "No, you're okay Amin. It's all okay. You're safe now."

That was a lie.

"I know," he murmured. "I know. I just… I don't feel well. I got this… this rush of… bad feeling. All nauseous and nasty and now look at me. Down on the ground like an idiot."

He quickly picked himself up, obviously ashamed. He pulled his hands away from his abdomen and continued walking, shaking his head.

"Amin, give yourself a break. You just got shot."

"I almost got us caught, that's what I did. I can't control my fear and it's obvious Ser. And it's even worse, knowing I left Mom behind and she's probably dead."

A lump formed in my throat. The words 'Mom' and 'dead' weren't ones that I wanted to hear. And to think I had almost forgotten about it. To think I was ever even close to thinking another thought besides the one screaming that my Mom was dead.

It was a relief and a tragedy at the same time, almost forgetting about Mom's death for even a second.

We walked the rest of the way in silence.

When we reached the scattered boulders just in front of the cliffs, the sun had begun to rise, making the beige rock look even more orange.

The city looked small but the Empathorium still looked huge. I didn't think anyone would be able to see us, and even if they did would they even bother coming to get us or just let us die of natural causes?

Amin kept walking until he reached the rocky base of a boulder. He leaned against it panting. His hands covered his wound but were shaking a little bit.

"Move your hands," I said. "Let me see how bad it is."

Amin looked up at me and shook his head.

"No, no I'm fine Ser. I promise I'm okay. I just need a little break, that's all."

I didn't know if he was trying to convince me that he was alright or convince himself. Either way, I needed to see the wound so I could see if he even stood a chance at making it.

I placed my hands on his and removed them from the jacket, taking a mental note that it wasn't as bloody as I thought it would be. That was good, but it was a gamble what lay underneath.

Plumes of fear surfaced from Amin's stomach as I unwrapped the jacket. His shirt was still over the wound, covered in thick, hot blood.

I peeled the shirt away from his skin. It made a disgusting squelching sound as it separated from the gunshot. Amin kept his face angled towards the sky, not daring to take one look at the situation he was in.

The wound was covered with blood and dried pus while the skin around it looked reddish-brown and swollen. The gunshot itself was barely distinguishable. There was blood and ripped skin everywhere. The blood was congealed and sticky from being half-dry, but I knew one wrong movement would start the whole wound up again. Every time Amin took a breath, some of the blood and ichor would pile to the surface, before returning when he exhaled.

I resisted the urge to gag because that would only make Amin feel worse and then his terror would start up.

"How is it?" he gasped, still staring straight up. "Tell me the truth, how bad off am I?"

"Not bad," I said, lying through my teeth. "You heal up great, you're going to be just fine. Just a little blood, but we knew that. We just have to keep something on top of it and don't stretch or anything, it might rip."

Amin started to breathe a bit slower. I hoped that he believed my lie and would calm down a bit.

"We need to wash it," I said. "And get water."

"I can walk a bit more," he said, placing the shirt back over the wound and shakily standing up.

"If I can get you out of sight I can search for water," I said, placing my hands over his shoulders and leading him up the rocks. There was a giant cliff, a few yards ahead, spanning across the sand for what seemed like an eternity. I knew there was no way in hell I could get Amin over it, but I could at least shelter him in the rocky crags and bluffs that littered the ground just below it.

I led Amin up a pile of rocks and helped him back down them. There were lots and lots of boulders littering the fluctuating surface but there were a few spots where he could lay down. There was no water in sight though, which troubled me.

I set Amin down with his back against a rock, pulling the dates out of my pocket and giving them to him. I heard him crinkling the bag while I set off to find anything edible.

It was mostly sand and rock, those were the only things that were visible anyway. I heaved myself over a giant boulder and stared up at the multitude of crags and rocky bluffs that were too far down for me to go around. I couldn't pull myself up either, they were too steep and too rocky. One wrong move would leave me impaled and bleeding out, leaving Amin as good as gone as well.

I looked behind me to see him, sprawled out against the rock, his hands clenched around his wound as they had been ever since he got it. He had placed the jacket back over the gunshot though, probably to distance himself from it in some way. It was weird to see Amin like this. It was even weirder to know that it was all because of me.

I kept exploring the rocks, traveling along them instead of beyond them. From the looks of it, all that was beyond the strip of rocks was sand and dust and a few of those useless trees.

I yanked myself up a boulder and slid down the back, my shoe splashing into something. A small trickle of water was forming a small pool. It was a tiny little thing, only a bit too big to be called a puddle, but it was enough to get us going until Amin was healed. Especially if the trickle was continuous.

I cupped my hands and drank a bit, letting the water run down my chin and clean my face.

Before I could fully drink my fill, I hoisted myself up the boulder and sprinted back to Amin. The bag of dates was next to him, only a few taken out. I poured them into my hand and brushed away a layer of sand from the rock Amin was lying on. All I cared about was the bag, not the dates, so the freshly cleaned-off rock would have to do for them.

"Wha? What are you doing?" he groaned, propping himself up and looking at the dates on the floor. His expression changed from confusion to accusation, scooping up the dates in his hands and staring at the bag in my hands.

"I found water," I said, eyeing his uncleaned wound and chapped lips.

He nodded, a quick nod filled with hope. I grabbed the bag and sprinted to the pool, almost spraining my ankle ten times along the way. When I got to the giant boulder blocking the way, my adrenaline-filled, energetic body nearly hurdled the thing, which definitely would have sprained my ankle then.

I dipped the bag into the water and twisted the top of it shut. I resisted the urge to drink it all by myself; Amin needed to be cleaned and hydrated first because he couldn't take care of his needs to save his life.

Literally.

When I got back, I handed him the bag to drink from before I started to clean the wound. He spilled the water all over his face and it dribbled down his shirt. He handed me the bag back though, obviously before he got his fill, but that would have to wait.

Amin lifted the blood-soaked jacket and winced, staring down at the bloody shirt for the first time. Plumes of fear emerged from the wound, blocking my view.

"Amin, you have to calm down. It's going to be okay." I assured, waving the fog away.

He started taking some deep breaths while I peeled away his bloody shirt. The wound looked about the same, but even *I* was afraid of what lay beneath the dried blood and purulent discharge.

"This is going to sting a bit," I warned, picking up the jacket and pouring some water onto the exposed flesh. It didn't do much to the already dried blood, hence the jacket.

Amin sucked in his breath when the water made contact, but winced whenever I dabbed the jacket around the lesion. I tried to be gentle but I knew it still hurt him.

The jacket was a hard tool to wipe with but it did clean away some of the blood and pus. I never wiped his injury, only dabbed. It was disgusting, seeing the congealed blood stick and slide around like jelly. I resisted the urge to gag because I knew if I did Amin would freak out and I wouldn't be able to see again.

"It's not bad at all," I said.

"Don't lie to me, I'm looking right at it," Amin said, running his hands through his hair and staring at the injury, wide-eyed.

"It looks... all these hunks of my flesh sticking out and then... there's this hole."

"No, I'm being serious. It just looks bad because you've never been injured like this. My friend, she got shot. And, you know, it looked worse than this and she was fine."

The lies came a little too easy. I didn't have one friend besides Amin. And I didn't know if I could call him that before. I could now though, after risking our lives for each other. After kneeling and dabbing at his gunshot with an old jacket.

Yeah, we could call each other friends.

After a couple more minutes of pouring water and dabbing with the jacket, Amin tapped out.

"We can try again tomorrow." he huffed, placing the shirt back over the wound. "You need water. I need water."

The bag was nearly empty so I gave it to him to drink and then set off again.

"Turn your shirt around," I said. "Put a fresh cloth on it, not the bloody side. You might get an infection."

Amin nodded as I stepped over the rocks to get to our puddle. I prayed that the trickle of water kept steadily flowing, or we wouldn't survive much longer. We also couldn't stay in the rocks forever, once Amin was healed we needed to get *out.*

As far away from the Empathorium as humanly possible.

I cupped my hands and drank my fill, pouring some water over my hair to wash it. The crystal clear liquid that poured over my hair ran down my neck grimy and sweaty.

I was careful not to sit in the water or get my sweat in it so that it wouldn't become contaminated. Amin was waiting. He was sitting on his deathbed, we both thought so, but he was still waiting.

The greedy part of me inside thought that maybe I shouldn't give him too much water. If he was going to die anyway. Why waste it? But the empath inside of me -the sympathetic one, not the bloodthirsty one- pushed that horrible thought deep down inside.

I filled the bag and hurried to Amin, letting him drink. He nodded at me when he was done.

"Thank you."

"Of course," I said, picking up some dates and devouring them. Now that we had water, food would be a struggle. Any wild animals learned long ago never to come anywhere near the Empathorium unless they wanted to turn into a steak or extracted of all emotions.

Amin placed his hand back over his wound.

"Where are you going to go?" he asked. "I mean, when you find a way out."

"When *we* find a way out." I reminded him.

"No," said Amin. "When *you* find a way out. It's obvious Ser. I'm not making it past this. I'll only slow you down."

"Shut up, you'll be fine," I said, lying on my back next to him. "And that's a promise."

A promise that I couldn't keep.

Amin grabbed a date and chewed on it, real slow, either absorbing the flavors or thinking. After a while, he extended his pinky to me.

"*You* promised," he muttered, smiling bashfully.

I extended my pinky and interlocked with his.

"A pinky promise can't be broken. Right?" he asked.

"Yes, that's right," I said.

My heart broke for him. I honestly didn't think he would make it past tomorrow, with the fact that he could barely stand up. Besides, how long can someone survive, sprawled out over a rocky bluff like a sitting duck?

It was unbearable to watch. To see him sitting there so helplessly, trying to make the best out of a situation that would never go right for him. Unless he made it back to the city, which would never happen.

Not with William being such a damn dictator.

"I'm going to go look for fruit trees or something," I said, getting out of Amin's eyesight before he saw me cry. He was dead, I knew it, he knew it. I couldn't bear to sit there and watch it, watch him die.

But I also couldn't leave him. I couldn't sneak off in the middle of the night, put him out of his misery, or try and help him back inside the city just for him to get shot.

I was better than that, I was better than them.

I needed to stay with him for his last days, and if that meant only moving a couple of yards every day I was fine with that. There was the gnawing feeling that we could run out of water or food but I couldn't leave him nevertheless.

I hoisted myself up a ledge, placing my hands and feet inside any small crevices or crannies that were available.

The rock was pretty smooth but not impossible to climb. I hadn't climbed much in my life, we didn't have rock walls or even many trees. It was a pretty natural instinct though, that must have kicked in, in that very moment.

I tried not to look down but I did anyway. My stomach dropped when I saw that if I fell I would most likely break a leg and be more useless than Amin.

My palms were sweaty by the time I reached the top and pulled myself up, sitting at the top for a moment to recollect myself and my thoughts.

There were no fruit trees, I knew there wouldn't be, but there was *a* tree. It was another small ironwood, with hardly any leaves but an abundance of branches. I snapped a few off and threw them down the bluff, starting a small pile.

When I looked ahead of me, I saw the city and the Empathorium. I could barely make out a few people, coming out of their houses and crowding the vendors.

They looked like ants.

Desperate little ants that had nowhere to go and nothing to live for but wanted to live nonetheless.

From what I could see, there were two guards now, in front of the entrance we had escaped from. The houses nearby had no little ants running around. No kids outside playing, no parents tending to the gardens.

I hoped they were still alive, that they were okay, that they weren't killed because of me.

It was all a blur, everyone who had died or gotten injured because of me. And the part that made me angry was that it wasn't even my fault. It was Drew's. And Hennie's.

I was only saying that to make myself feel better, but at least it helped with the panging guilt that twisted my stomach into knots and took up a large amount of space in my mind.

When the pile of broken branches got pretty big, I started the climb down the crag. Down was easier than up, once I got close enough to the ground I could just slide down. That was a mistake though, my leg hit a stray rock that ripped open my ankle.

"Shit," I whispered, wiping away the blood that started to flow down my foot.

I pulled the leg of my pants down farther to cover up the already-throbbing wound and limped towards Amin, holding the sticks in my arms.

"Sticks?" he asked.

"To make a fire," I responded. "But we have to go somewhere else, where we're covered. If the Empaths see the fire they'll know we're here instead of dead."

"Okay, I can make it somewhere else," Amin said. "Not far right? Just behind a rock or something?"

"Yeah, probably behind the one I climbed, that's big enough," I answered, shifting the sticks to one arm and helping Amin up from the ground.

He tightened the jacket around his waist, walking with me to the bluff I had just climbed. It was in the direction of the towering cliff, which wasn't a big step towards scaling it and getting out but it was something.

"You climbed that?" he asked, eying the bluff.

"Well, yeah, it's not that far," I said. "It just looks like it to you, because, well..."

Amin sat himself down, moving some stray rocks out of the way. I placed the sticks by his feet.

"You break these," I said. "I'm going to go look for a starter rock."

I heard the sound of Amin snapping the twigs as I walked away. I found a rock that was the right size pretty quick, a smooth, flat, stone. It wasn't hard, the whole place was rock and sand and rock and sand and rock and sand.

When I returned, Amin was beaming at me proudly, ecstatic that even the simplest task of snapping twigs was accomplished. After hours of laying on a rock, useless, I couldn't help but give him one win.

"Do you know how to light a fire?" I asked.

"Yeah," he said. "Who wouldn't?"

"Oh. Well... I dunno."

I didn't want to say it was because he lived in a richer house and usually people who lived in richer houses didn't need to light fires from scraps. Usually, they could afford matches or ovens that worked well and could light roaring fires with the click of a switch.

I handed him the rock and sat beside him, watching as he placed a stick vertically to the rock and began rubbing.

Quick, sharp movements downward that soon created a flurry of smoke and then a spark that spread to the other sticks.

It took a couple of attempts, due to the small flame that we would produce blowing out, but we soon had a fire. Amin rubbed his hands near the flames, watching the sparks and smoke that flew into the night sky.

My stomach grumbled, and Amin heard it. He pulled out some of the dates from his pocket and gave them to me.

I chewed on one carefully, savoring the flavors. I had learned to savor everything I was given to eat early on. It made you less hungry and tricked your stomach into thinking more food was being consumed.

I placed the rest of the dates Amin gave me on the floor, not caring about dust or crap like that.

I thought about Mom and Amin's mom. I thought about being free and where we might end up. Cities with lots of technology and gadgets and-

"Ser," Amin whispered.

I glanced at him and he gestured to my dates on the floor. A mouse was inching towards them, sniffing and wiggling its ears. I nodded to Amin, pretending like I didn't notice the creature. It soon approached my dates, sniffing them cautiously.

Either it wanted to die or Amin and I were master hunters. Either way, catching it was all too easy.

The thing cooked better than expected, with crispy edges and juicy meat. Even though it was a small little thing, just a taste of meat was enough to satisfy my cravings.

Amin and I each had a leg and he insisted that I eat the rest, practically begging me to eat it.

"Are you not hungry?" I asked, pulling off a hunk of fur.

"You need it more than I do," he said. "I doubt I'll need it soon. It's not getting better, Ser."

"No, it is," I demanded. "I promise. You're going to be okay. I pinky promised, didn't I?"

"I guess," Amin muttered.

He removed one hand from cradling his wound to grab a date and then placed it right back over again. The shirt had been re-bloodied, not as bad but not a great sign either. He noticed me staring at his wound and pressed his palm more firmly to his stomach.

"Save some dates," I said, trying to change the subject more than warn Amin about wasting food. "Tomorrow I'll try and catch more mice."

"I guess mice are too poor for William," Amin said, glancing behind him at the lights of the city. "Bullshit."

"Can you imagine him eating a mouse?" I laughed. "He wouldn't know where to begin. All he knows is turkey and steak. Caviar and coffee."

"Ham and oysters." Amin chuckled, joining in. "The finest pigs, freshly caught seafood."

"And wine. Lots of wine. He's probably always drunk, hence the *great* decisions he makes."

"Ooh. And um... what're they called again? The truff... truff something. The bakers made them one time."

"Truffles?"

"Truffles!"

"He probably loves truffles."

"They just sound rich."

We both laughed, hearty laughs. They weren't the fake ones that emerged when company was over. They weren't nervous laughs in the presence of an Empath either.

"It feels nice to laugh for real," Amin said, apparently reading my mind. An array of coughs followed, which worried me. He keeled over and spat across the rocks. The puking came next.

"Are you okay?" I asked, crawling over to him while he gasped and regurgitated.

It smelled horrible, mixing with the burning smell of the fire and causing me to hold back a gag.

Amin sat back up, wiping his mouth and shuddering, still gasping for breath and spitting out any excess.

"I'll get you some water," I said. "Just... get away from the fire for a bit okay? And your... that."

I grabbed the water bag and sprinted to the puddle of water, hurdling jagged rocks along the way. I could hear Amin coughing; gagging and sputtering on his vomit.

When I returned there were small clouds of terror surrounding him, his core hadn't escaped but I could tell he was close to that, as he glanced at me with helpless eyes.

"Drink this," I demanded. "And calm down, you're okay Amin I promise. You probably just choked on your food or something."

Amin tried to drink the water but in between coughs it only ended up spilling all down the front of his shirt. In some way it was a good thing, it would clean the wound and a little bit of Amin.

The water must have helped because he stopped coughing pretty quickly, taking sips of the water and breathing deeply. His fear scattered nervously around the fire before fading away into the night.

"I'm sorry," Amin whispered. "I'm sorry, I'm useless and I'm going to get you killed. We've gotten nowhere in the past two days except from rock face to rock face and it's all because of me and the fact that I can do practically nothing."

His self-loathing went from whispers to snarls in only moments.

"No, Amin."

How was I supposed to do it?

How was I supposed to convince him that I wasn't waiting for him to die before continuing the long trek myself if I couldn't even convince myself that I wasn't doing that?

Deep down I wanted Amin to make it. I wanted to bring him somewhere with towering fruit trees and a dense jungle. Somewhere with big houses and friendly faces no matter where you turned but I knew it would never happen because each day that he sat on that rock was another day he was slowly dying.

And I couldn't push him to the finish line of the pinky promised land and I couldn't leave him to die on a rock all alone in the heat.

All I could do was continue to protect him and lie to him that no, I was not waiting for him to die, I was just waiting for him to get better.

We both knew I was lying because we both knew Amin wasn't making it to the pinky-promised land.

I threw another broken promise on the fire but this one hurt a little more.

Maybe a lot more.

Well...

It hurt like hell.

It was around midnight that Amin fell asleep, with his head drooped over his shoulder and his hands in their new favorite position, over his abdomen.

Even when he slept he looked as if he was in horrible pain. His face was twisted and he twitched more often than not. I told myself he was just having nightmares, so I didn't obsess over the fact that Amin was in agony and I couldn't do anything to help him.

I couldn't sleep if I tried so I stayed awake, lying on my back. My eyes were fixated on the stars.

I never understood those constellations anyway; there was no way that a clump of white dots looked like anything other than a clump of white dots.

However, Mom still taught me the constellations.

She pointed out the one that looked like a spoon, the smaller spoon, the man, and the fish. She loved the things, probably because they were something to take her mind off of the suffering happening down on earth.

I hoped that she was up there with her favorite ones, free from the conflict and agony.

Free from the damnation and wrath of William.

William could reach the city but he couldn't reach the stars. Not like my mom could.

Chapter 8

I don't remember falling asleep but I must have. I woke up with two arms around *my* arms, dragging me across the rocks. My hair got caught in snags, and my arms and legs got cut up by the shards of rock that lay askew.

"Wait, what's going on? Stop!" I shrieked, trying to claw at my kidnapper from behind.

Amin was getting dragged across the rocks and screaming as well, but from what I could tell no actual words were coming from his mouth.

"Be careful with him! He's hurt! Do you hear me? He's hurt! Let him go, take me but let him go!"

I tried to turn around to get a look at the person taking me but they had no distinguishable features with only the stars as my light and I couldn't turn my body at such a weird angle anyway.

The man lifted me over a large rock and started dragging me through the sand and dirt. I kicked and screamed and dug my heels through the ground to create resistance but they continued to take me towards the city.

"You're an Empath," I whispered. "Please, please listen! You killed my mother, it was the only way! You were going to kill me too, I knew that!"

I started to cry, pleading with the Empath as I heard the all too familiar sound of the gate opening. My sobs echoed around the sleeping city. Amin was being dragged on his stomach, head limp in the dirt.

"Amin?" I screamed. "Amin, wake up! Dammit Amin, wake up! Wake up!"

People started to come out of their houses and point at me. They whispered to their spouses and applauded the Empaths that tugged my helpless body through the streets.

Amin was unresponsive, his body bending at impossible angles whenever he was pulled across a loose rock or a clump of dirt. People pointed at him too but they didn't whisper about how he was a convict and should be killed. They knew as much as I did that he is innocent.

He *was* innocent.

My tears streaked the sand as I sobbed for the life of Amin. I didn't even know if it was because of his wounds or if he suffocated in the dirt but all I did know was that he was gone and it was my fault.

"Please, please help him." I sobbed, my voice hiccuping and cracking as I searched for even an ounce of remorse in anyone's face that was watching me.

Some people laughed.

Some cried with me.

Still, no one helped.

"Someone help him, he has a chance. Why will no one help him? Someone please, it's my fault, not his! Please!"

Tears stained my shirt as I neared the Empathorium and the parade of watching my helplessness neared its close.

"I pinky promised," I whispered, voice quivering in despair and desperation. I stared each passerby in the face, hoping they would help me. Stand up for me. Or at the very least help Amin. He did nothing wrong.

The Empath yanked me up the stairs, adding new patterns of bruises to my already battered skin. He let go of me at the top, gun aimed at my forehead.

"Please," I whispered. "Mom? Mom help me. Mom help me, please. Where's my mom? I want my mom." The words flooded from my mouth nearly as fast as the tears.

I lay a crumpled mess atop the Empathorium stairs, begging to a man who would rather kill me than see me alive any day of the week.

A small crowd formed to watch the execution. Amin got dragged up the stairs and laid to rest beside me.

"Oh God. Get up, Amin. Please get up. I'm so sorry. I pinky promised Amin. I'm so sorry, I pinky promised." I wailed, burying my face into his shirt and soaking it with tears as well.

The cold barrel of the gun rested on my temple. I could hear the Empath speaking some words and I could hear the crowds murmuring with agreement but all I could focus on was the silence coming from Amin's heart.

His skin was becoming cold and hard, more so by the second. I took his pinky and interlocked it with mine, whispering to him.

"I promise I'll find you in the afterlife. Wherever we go anyway. You deserve an apology. I pinky promise. I pinky promise. I pinky promise."

The gun clicked, pressing deeper into my temple.

This was it, this was it.

I was dead.

I didn't have anything to live for anyway. Some part of me didn't even care while the other part burned with anxiety and terror of what was to come.

"I pinky promise Amin, I pinky promise."

My soon-to-be-silenced heart made up for all the beats it was about to lose, rocketing out of my chest at a million miles a second.

The Empath spat the criminal's imprecation at me.

"Binigo ka ng iyong emosyon."

"I pinky promise Amin. I pinky-"

Bang.

I woke up screaming and drenched in sweat. The fire had diminished to barely a flame, waving around the sticks pitifully.

Amin launched up, fear in his eyes.

"What? What happened?" he asked.

I wiped the incoming tears from my eyes and took a shaky breath.

"Nothing. I'm sorry. Bad dream. We're okay."

"Are you telling me that?" Amin asked.

I stared at him in curiosity.

"Or are you telling yourself that?"

"Myself. I think."

Amin started to cough, doubling over and nearly putting his scalp right into the fire. I blew out the flame and reached for the water bag that Amin had tied off last night.

I ripped open the knot and handed him the bag, forcing him to drink. His face was somehow a mixture of red and pale nothingness, turning him an almost pink color.

His eyes were filled with fear. Fear that surrounded me and circled the rocks. His cough was getting worse; it went from something that someone would hear and maybe wash their hands one more time to avoid to something that someone would hear and immediately call body pickup.

It was useless trying to get anywhere with him anyway. We couldn't get past the small patches of crags and bluffs let alone the daunting, rocky cliffs that lay behind them.

"I'm sorry," he said. "I think it's getting worse. I don't understand Ser."

"Don't apologize," I said. "You're okay. It's because of the food. Your stomach is what got shot so it's just doing too many things to focus on digestion right now."

"Yeah, the two dates and half a rat took a toll on me." Amin scoffed, repositioning himself.

My stomach gnawed at itself, irritating me at even the slightest mention of food. I grabbed a couple of dates and set them next to me. I wasn't going to get much sleep anyway, and Amin needed food to heal.

I knew the mouse was most likely just some dumb stroke of luck but I hoped that I could catch another one all the same. I also hoped that there was something, anything beyond the cliff that could support life.

The cliff wrapped around the city, even to the back of the Empathorium. There were only a couple of yards separating it and the city gate, but a whole lot of yards separating from where we were and the city.

"I wish there were more trees," I muttered, lying on my back next to the dates. "There aren't a lot of trees in the city. I hope we reach a forest one day."

"I hope we reach a beach," Amin whispered.

"Really?" I asked. "More sand?"

"Yes, but the ocean," he sighed. "You can just swim and swim and no one can stop you. And it must be so... free. So full of life. The sand is different there."

"How so?"

"The sand and dust here, it's not sand. It's pieces of dead bodies... and glass from jars that once held stolen emotions. The sand on the beach is different. I bet it's soft."

"I'll take you to a beach," I whispered.

"Pinky promise?"

My mind flashed to my dream. With Amin's lifeless body facedown on the Empathorium's steps. His lifeless pinky interlocked with mine while I sobbed and awaited death by a cold bullet.

Every promise I made to Amin was another burden to uphold that I doubted I could uphold in the first place. It was only sensible to just deny it, to save myself in the future from the heartbreak of lying to him.

"Yeah, I pinky promise. You and me and the beach."

Screw sensible.

One mouse came that night, and it practically crawled *on* me before I noticed it and bashed its head with a rock.

Before Amin even woke up I had relit the fire and was smoking the thing as if it was a kebab. The smell must have woken him up because he sat up quicker than ever and stared at the fire, famished.

"How many dates do we have left?" I asked.

Amin pulled some out of his pockets and counted the ones on the ground.

"Not enough," he said.

"For what?" I asked.

"To keep us alive for long. We should keep using them to catch mice if there are any more. Besides, are there any cacti or something we can eat?"

"Do you see any cacti?"

Amin looked around and sighed.

"I guess not. It was just a thought."

"I'm sorry. I'm just stressed."

I broke off a piece of the mouse and gave it to Amin, wary of how much he ate because I didn't want him to eat a lot just to barf it all up again.

On the other hand, he probably needed food to heal which left me stuck in a solutionless problem.

"Do you think you can walk to the big cliff?" I asked. "We don't have to try and climb it, today at least, but I could make the trips to get water. And then we'd be farther from the city, you know?"

"I think so," Amin said. "I just feel horrible. Leaving my mom behind. What kind of son leaves his mother to die? Can't we stay a little longer? Can't you go back for her? I can try to help but I probably won't get far."

"Go back for her?" I scoffed. "Amin, I went back for *you*. And it's been hard enough having to lug you around like a piece of crap. Feeding you and watering you and watching over you."

"If I'm such a burden for you then leave me behind why don't you? If you're leaving my mom behind too?"

"Do you hear yourself?" I started to scream, pointing and gesturing wildly. "You want me to go back for your mom? My mom is dead and so is yours Amin. Accept that. We don't have enough food to support us, let alone her."

Amin glared at me as he stood up. It was with much effort but he still managed to do it furiously.

"And where do you think you're going?" I screamed. "You can't get two steps without collapsing!"

"I'm going towards the cliff," he yelled. "Then, even though my intestines are falling out of my shirt as we speak, I'll climb that thing. You know what? How about I carry you while I do it? How's that Seraphai? Does that fulfill your needs? Does that make me less of an object to you? Less of a burden?"

"You could have done nothing without me!"

"Maybe you should have left me to die then! We both know that's what you're doing. You're waiting for me to die. Maybe I'll climb that cliff and make it faster for you, Your Highness. I see you, you know. I see the way you roll your eyes when you see me struggle, I see the way you hesitantly share your food. And I'm sorry that I'm not as strong as I hope I can be but... but..."

He turned around and leaned close to my face, his eyes filled with equal parts rage and sorrow.

"You know," he whispered. "Maybe the reason William is always after you is because you guys are pretty alike. Deep down inside you hope I die so you can get your pretty little self to safety faster, don't you?"

He started to walk towards the cliff, clenching the water bag in his fist. It had just a couple of sips left but he still held it with intensity.

His words cut into my soul like a hot knife through soft butter. I stood by the fire, my insides worming up inside of me like a ball of pythons.

I didn't want to think about Amin dying faster so that I could get myself to safety but the thoughts just appeared. I guess I didn't realize that Amin could sense that.

"I'm sorry," I whispered, but Amin was too far ahead to hear me. I doubt he would have cared anyway.

I didn't know what to say or do besides follow him in silence, hoping that he could forgive me before it was too late.

The day droned on in a boring way. I explored what I could but all I saw was sand and cliff, sand and cliff, sand and cliff, and some dust.

There were a couple of trees but none of them had anything of use. Only dead branches and a trunk that was infested with beetles and ants. There were hardly even any leaves and not enough to make anything with.

Amin sat in silence, hand over his wound, face scrunched in a permanent frown. I had tried to work up the courage to apologize but some part of me burned with rage and was waiting for *him* to apologize to *me.*

I did work up the nerve to talk to him, once the sun went down and he couldn't see the embarrassment on my face. I never was good at apologizing.

"We'll go at your pace from now on," I said, sitting next to him and running my hands through my hair nervously.

"No, no, that was stupid of me," Amin said. "You weren't rushing me to do things I couldn't. You weren't waiting for me to die. You wouldn't do that."

He looked up at me with his big doe eyes. Eyes filled with a childish flicker and a broken past.

"You're not William," he said. "You aren't."

"Thank you," I whispered. "We will climb the cliff when you are ready. When you are healed."

"I'll try tomorrow," Amin said.

I pointed to our left, where in the fluctuation levels of the cliff a small section was lower than the rest. It would still be a dangerous climb, a gamble, and a choice, but it was our only chance of getting somewhere high before the Empaths raided our makeshift campsite.

Amin drifted off pretty fast, his breathing ragged and shallow. He even coughed during his *sleep*, ragged painful coughs that caused him to wake up and grip my arm with fear.

I stared up at the stars again, whispering to myself. And maybe Mom, if she was listening to me.

"My name is Seraphai. Not William. My name is Seraphai. Not William. You are not waiting for him to die. You are not waiting for him to die. Amin is going to make it. Amin is going to make it. He's going to make it and you are going to help him make it."

I chiseled the information into my brain as if it were a block of stone. I chipped and chiseled and drilled until what I was repeating wasn't a wish but a fact.

It was a long night but I finally fell asleep, pleased with my new statue of truth.

I woke up late, with the sun scorching my face. My eyes took ages to adjust to the light and I was angered to find that over the night, the bag had leaked and only a couple of drops of water remained.

The rest turned the sand into silt, collecting in a leaky pile by Amin's right hand. Amin had shifted to his side, cradling his stomach and struggling with each breath.

He was still asleep though, so I took the water bag and made my way to the puddle.

The city was awake and alive, bustling with little worker ants. I had to sneak behind rocks and crawl through the sand to stay hidden.

If I could see the people in the city as ants they could also see me as an ant. And an ant didn't belong in the freedom of the cliffs. All ants belonged to William, working and providing for what little sliver of paradise they could get their hands on.

When I reached the water pool, I was pleased to find that it was not dried up but I was anxious to find that it wasn't exactly growing either.

A mouse was drinking from it when I got there, getting its grubby little whiskers and paws all over our only hope of clean and drinkable water.

"Get out of here!" I yelled, stomping my boot next to its ear and causing it to scurry away. Plumes of anger fogged up the water and started chasing the mouse. It squeezed its chubby little body into a crack of a rock and disappeared.

I should have caught it when I had the chance. Built-up frustration took over and led me to scare it away instead. As far away from me as possible.

I was used to it.

But with people more than mice.

When I returned Amin was still sleeping.

I tapped him with my boot and rolled him over.

"Amin, wake up, do you feel like traveling?" I asked.

I got no response. His eyes stayed closed and his neck bent with each roll and shake.

My stomach dropped into my shoes and my heart started to pound even faster.

No. This couldn't be it. It simply couldn't. He wouldn't die. Especially not at night. He was doing so good yesterday, he walked and talked and barely coughed. He ate and drank and fell asleep. At least it was a quick passing in his dreams. Painless. What if he felt pain but I wasn't awake for it? What if he tried to wake me up? Remember Seraphai remember. Were you woken up?

I dropped to my knees beside him and threw my fingers over his wrist to check for a pulse.

There was silence, silence that lasted a second yet an eternity all at the same time. I held my breath and placed my ear close to his arm as if I could physically hear any heartbeat that would appear.

It's been too long. Has it? What if he's in a coma? How slow does a heart beat? Why does my *heart hurt? Oh God this is it, he's gone and we just fought and-*

Something vibrated under my fingertips.

A pulse.

A thump.

A *beat.*

I held my breath and waited again just to be sure.

Another thump followed, after a few moments.

I heaved a sigh of relief and observed his chest, waiting for signs of breathing. Turns out he *was,* but at such a slow pace he might as well be declared dead.

I ran my fingers through my hair in a frenzy of anxiety and relief. Amin was alive but at what cost? Was he in a coma?

I didn't know what the humane thing was to do anymore. I couldn't wait too long, there weren't enough resources, and if I left out of hunger or thirst I would never forgive myself. I couldn't heave his lifeless body up the cliff either, it would be a struggle for us to climb even with him awake. And if I were to drop him or injure him in some other way I would never forgive myself.

I couldn't leave him or put him out of his misery because that would be what William would do. Even if it was out of pity and grace I would never forgive myself.

Yet at the same time, I couldn't venture out beyond the cliff because then I had no idea if I would ever come back. My greed and hunger for freedom would drive me to leave Amin in the dust, staining it red with his innocent blood.

And I would never forgive myself.

I caught as many mice as I could during the day, using the dates and small leaves from the trees.

It was boring, sitting behind a rock and waiting for an unsuspecting mouse to come before bashing its skull in with a boulder.

I ended up catching three and eating two before realizing that I should save one for Amin, if-

No.

When.

When he woke up.

I finished off a mouse and threw its carcass to the side, watching Amin. As if he would move or anything.

The sun had moved again, falling on his face and burning it to a crisp, no doubt. I glared up at it, angry that it kept making me move camp to avoid hurting Amin more. It retorted by blinding me, causing me to curse and rub my eyes.

"Here we go again," I grunted, standing up and grabbing Amin's ankles. His head outlined the dust as I dragged him along the outline of the cliff, seeking shade.

I tried to keep my thoughts cheery. Think about how much he was resting and how good that was because bodies repair themselves when they are resting.

He'll be up soon. He just needs some extra sleep. He's so heavy, I can't do this all day. And to move all of the supplies too. The damn sun, casting all these different shadows. I miss Mom. I miss the company. I didn't even say goodbye to her. Did his head just hit a rock? Good, maybe it'll wake him up.

I stopped dragging Amin's lifeless body when I was a couple of yards into a patch of shade.

"There." I sighed, dropping his ankles and repositioning his body so he didn't look so... dead. "I'll be right back," I said. "Don't go anywhere. Ha ha."

God, I've gone crazy.

It was quite the opposite because I was trying to distract myself from going crazy by talking to both myself and Amin who couldn't respond.

I headed back to where we were to grab the rest of the dates, the leftover mouse, and the water bag. While I walked, I glanced at the city.

It stood tall. Not a soul seemed to miss us or care about all the deaths the Empathorium had caused.

I snatched up the water bag causing it to fling out of my hand and lose all but a sip of survival.

"Crap!" I yelled, snatching up the empty bag and leaving behind a ring of rage in its place.

Every step I took left behind a cloud until I made it to the puddle, splashing the bag into it and impatiently waiting until it filled up.

I tied off the bag and splashed some water on my face to cool myself down. Literally and figuratively.

I wiped myself off with my sleeve but stopped when I heard the sirens coming from the city. They weren't the sirens that meant there were bombs or a fire or anything, it was the announcement sirens.

I squinted and could barely make out a little blob standing on the Empathorium's balcony. Lots of small blobs crowded the street below him. Even the guards were gone, probably outlining the crowd of people. They couldn't escape without a thumbprint anyway.

I felt the Empath's thumb in my pocket. Sure enough, it was still there, bloodied and hard. At first, I didn't even recognize it, I thought it was a stone or a date.

I crept towards the city, quickly making it to the tree that once housed a bloodied Amin and me. There were still imprints in the dust that I quickly wiped away in case they decided to check outside.

I told myself I would only go a couple of feet closer but that didn't work because I soon found myself pressed up against the gate, straining to hear what the announcement was about.

"We didn't want to do this again," William said. His voice echoed around the city, booming and powerful.

Do what again?

"It was just a couple of days ago that we had to kill... *her* mother. We pray that... *she* is dead now. But the damned are still alive, still walking the streets. Much like this one."

William didn't dare mention me by name. It was an endless string of 'her' and 'she' and 'that girl' but never my name.

My name was a curse.

A disease.

How dare it come out of Willliam's mouth. No. William was too almighty. William was too powerful for a name like mine. Shame on me for being born. Shame on me for protecting myself from Hennie and Drew. How selfish of me. Yes, William, I should have let myself get shot instead of stumbling upon your stash of emotions.

Sincerest apologies.

The question lingered in my mind. If not me, and if not Amin, who was William hanging? No one else had helped me, no one else was alive, no one else cared...

Except...

Oh.

Oh.

"Where is your son?" William yelled, and the crowd chanted in agreement.

"I don't know. Honest, I don't know. My son is dead!" Amin's mother cried. I could hear her sobs even from where I was. The lump in my throat expanded.

"Liar!" William screamed.

"I don't know!" she yelled, crying harder now. "I don't understand. I don't know what happened! His blood... you found his blood... but I don't know where the body is. I don't understand! He's dead, he got shot!"

Her voice turned frantic as she started to screech. No matter what sensible thought came out of her mouth it sounded absurd, as she shrieked at the crowd and bawled to people that would never save her.

"He's dead! He's dead! I don't know anything! The girl is dead too! There's nothing out there, there's nothing out there! Please! I did nothing wrong! I did nothing wrong, please!"

Her voice broke and quivered as she yelled. The tears started to form in my eyes but I blinked them away. She was as good as gone and even if I tried to stop the execution it would only end up with me getting shot.

"Please, please William. Sir. Please you don't under-"

Her words turned to screams as she fell until I heard the crack. The creak of the rope swinging came soon after.

Cheers erupted through the town as William announced that all of the criminals were either dead or on their way to being dead. He beamed as he ordered everyone to go about their daily lives. He laughed as he talked about me, starving and hot on the mountaintop.

"She wasn't going to last long anyway." he chuckled. My blood boiled at the sound.

He said nothing humorous but the crowd laughed right along with him, shouting words of shallow encouragement and agreement to his statements.

"Oh, but of course... poor Mrs. Hypeir. She couldn't give us the details we asked for. Look where silence led her."

The crowd laughed, yet again, and shouted chants of agreement, yet again.

"I don't know! I don't know!" William said, mocking Amin's mother. He broke his character and started laughing. But not a laugh that caused others to smile because it filled them with happiness, a cruel, cold, evil laugh.

The flood of fog that followed poured out of me with importance. I didn't even try to stop it until the core of my anger emerged, darting around me with stupid bravery.

I looked up and saw my anger rising, creating a smoke signal that I couldn't let happen right now. Everyone was gathered in one place, a surprise smoke storm would draw attention. Would draw attraction. Empaths would swarm me before I could get anywhere near the rocks and the tree wouldn't be enough to hide me in broad daylight.

I always hated being afraid but at that moment it saved me. As my anger was replaced by fear all the fog, including my core, disappeared. My core floated towards me and disappeared into my abdomen, rather slowly.

I breathed a sigh of relief and waved away the remaining fog before it disappeared on its own. William cracked a few more jokes about all the deaths he had caused and then told the crowd they were free to return to their daily lives.

I forced myself to back away from the gate, sprinting to the rock and diving behind a small boulder. My shoulder hit the ground first, knocking the air out of me. I lay on the ground for a while, waiting for anything.

I didn't hear any footsteps of Empaths who saw me or any screams of a pedestrian who noticed me. All I could hear was my heartbeat, which somehow pounded through my ears more than through my heart.

William didn't know exactly where we were, which was good, but Amin's mother was dead. And if he woke up, how was I supposed to tell him?

He wanted to go back for her, after all.

I started the trek back after a couple of minutes, staying hidden behind both boulders and bluffs.

A wisp of anger floated away from my shoulder when I returned and saw that the sun had covered Amin once more.

Chapter 9

My anxiety grew with the night. The darker and later it got, the slimmer the chance that Amin would ever wake up.

He kept breathing, and sometimes he would twitch but it was all a false hope.

Maybe I'm imagining that Amin is alive. Have I been dragging along a dead body this whole time? Grief and sunstroke got the best of me? What if Amin never made it out? No. No, he's still here and you're doing just fine.

I laid back in the sand and listened to the sounds of my heartbeat.

"That's not fair," I whispered to the sky. "How come I still get a heartbeat but everyone else doesn't? Mom and Amin's mother? And maybe Amin?"

It wasn't the survivor's guilt that hurt the most, it was the silence. I hated silence. Ever since I was little I hated silence because it was too empty. It meant I was alone.

I wasn't used to being alone, unlike the many orphans and homeless children who littered the streets of the city and filled up the shelters. I always had Mom, even though I had no siblings and Dad met his unfortunate end. She would always talk with me and then when she died I could talk to Amin.

Never about grief though.

Never about the real stuff.

I never talked to anyone about my raw, deep emotions.

Not even Mom. She would have understood though, if I wasn't so scared of vulnerability.

Funny, how all of my emotions could stay bottled up inside of me just to remain bottled up if they got captured.

They would eventually leave that bottle, and make it to the bigger bottle of William's basement but they would never be *truly* free. Able to express themselves.

I dreamt about being captured again because dreaming about being free would only make reality hurt worse.

"Ser?"

My eyes fluttered.

"Seraphai?"

I shot up as fast as I could, staring into the eyes of no other than Amin himself. His eyes were baggy and his face was pale but he was awake. He was alive.

"Water," he said, voice raspy and breaking.

I untied the bag and handed it to him, still in utter awe that Amin had woken up in the first place. I didn't want to admit that I was thinking he would die because that would bring us back to our argument again but I didn't know if he would ever become strong enough to wake up.

"Are... are you okay?" I asked, picking up two rocks and getting a fire started. "Here, I'll cook you something to eat."

"What happened?" he asked, laying back down and placing the water bag against my leg.

"I- I don't know," I responded, simultaneously tying the water bag and blowing on the fire to grow it. "I woke up... and you were just... out."

"For how long?" he asked.

"About two days," I said. "But... William... he hung..."

Amin started to cough violently, clutching his stomach. It cut me off from horribly trying to explain to him that his mother was dead, hung by William for the crime of simply knowing me and helping me.

"Oh God..." he whispered, lifting his shirt and checking the damages of his wound. Thick tan drainage covered the face of it with a puffy red exterior. Dried blood caked the skin around his stomach and stuck to his shirt. A red streak climbed up his stomach towards his heart.

"It hurts Ser..." Amin whispered. "It hurts. And it's not getting better... it's not... it's not..."

"Shhhh... I know."

I helped him lay down and repositioned his bloody jacket over his injuries. He repeatedly whispered how he was afraid, staring deep into my eyes.

My heart broke.

His fright clouded around him. I waved it away, speaking softly, frantically trying to get Amin to calm down while remaining as calm as possible. He grabbed my arm and gripped it tight, breathing shallow and rapid.

It was torture, for both me and him. He hadn't asked me to kill him but was he thinking it? Did he feel that he was only living to be tortured some more?

I let him hold my hand while I cooked the last mouse. My stomach twisted in knots at the sight of it but I gave it to Amin with a forced smile. I was not going to turn into them. I was not going to turn into them. I was not going to turn into them. Sure, they're well-fed and powerful but I would rather be hungry and weak and powerless than ever turn into an Empath. I would rather die.

Amin sat up with much difficulty to eat his mouse but took only one bite and gave the rest to me.

"I'm not hungry," he muttered.

"No. Neither am I." I said. "I promise. I just ate. I caught like five mice before. You will eat this because you need it."

"I'm not a child," Amin said, placing the mouse on the ground next to me. "I will not eat it because I am not hungry."

"Amin, come on, you need to-"

"I'm. Not. Hungry." His tone surprised me. It was powerful and sure of itself. I hadn't heard *that* Amin in a long time. I was used to fragile Amin. Glass skin Amin that relied on me in dozens of ways. My eyes widened as I turned to him. It was almost relieving to see him with power and grit. But of course, he started to cough soon after, falling back to the floor and curling up into a ball.

I finished off the rest of the mouse and waited for the fire to diminish. Amin was facing away from me, breathing shallow. He swirled his fingers in the dirt.

"Do you dream about being free?" I asked, sitting beside him and facing the city. The gates seemed short from here. As if they could be cleared with a single bound.

"Yeah," he said. "I mean... of the beach mostly. But you know that. It's kinda hard though, to dream of something you don't know anything about."

"I dream of being captured," I said. "Not because it's my dream or I like it, I just know it's reality. All I know is reality."

I glanced down at Amin. He was shivering even though it was scorching hot. Fever no doubt but I didn't mention it in fear of making him more terrified.

"Do you live by that one rule?" he asked.

"Hm?"

"That one." his voice was shaky from shivering. "You know, if you don't get your expectations up you can't get let down when things don't go your way?"

"Yeah, something like that," I said.

"I don't like that," he muttered. "You could at least try, you know? Try and dream. Tonight I want you to try and dream. About freedom. You liked the forest, right?"

"Yeah. That or a jungle. Can you imagine it? Trees upon trees upon trees upon trees and the sun hardly reaches you. Not hot but not cold either... cool and fresh. Not here, where we're drowning in William's hot breath."

Amin laughed but stopped abruptly to wince.

"What was the Empathorium like?" he asked.

"Oh... I dunno. Long story. Lots of bright colors."

"Please talk," Amin whispered, turning his head as far as he could to face me. "Talking distracts me from the pain. I'll just listen though, maybe try to sleep."

He untied the jacket from his chest and placed it over his eyes. I didn't try to stop him. The bleeding had stopped, but losing blood wasn't the dangerous part anymore. It was the infection. How sick it was making him. A jacket couldn't stop that or help us in any way.

I cleared my throat nervously.

"Well. Um. I woke up and thought it was a medical room of some sort. There were all these people and I was dressed in this fancy white dress. They had me all fixed up and brushed my hair and my teeth and everything. It was nice."

Amin's breathing became slower. It was still raspy and sounded horrible and he was still quaking with fever but it was a start. The quick, fearful, shallow breaths were replaced by deep, calm ones.

"So I did some exploring. I filled my pockets with these wipes and a match I found. Crazy story about the match. Anyway, I looked at this paper by my bed and it had all these things on it like my name and stuff and I was thinking how weird that was but I didn't think *much* about it."

It was hard, reliving the story, but I did it for the sake of my friend, who was dreaming in the jaws of death.

My voice hurt after only a few minutes of talking but I carried on anyway. I made it through the whole story of escaping the Empathorium, stopping once I got to Mom's death. I could relive lots of things but I couldn't relive the only moment that ever made me feel a wave of suicidal thoughts.

After a while I wasn't telling the story, it was telling itself. Words flooded out of me that I never thought I would be saying. I talked about how I felt and how I hated to feel. What reassured me about becoming so vulnerable was that Amin was sound asleep.

I fell asleep too, the sun scorching my face, the bugs swarming my neck, and the fear of losing my only company filling up my heart faster than I could comprehend.

The heat and the bug bites were temporary.

Losing Amin was forever.

Amin woke me up when the stars were out. Part of me was agitated that I slept through the daylight but the other part was relieved because that meant I wouldn't have to deal with the heat or fear of being seen anymore.

"Is there any more food?" he whispered, voice hoarse and fading. For the sake of myself, I made myself think that he was only losing his voice and not being drained of it through death.

"Um. Yeah. Here." I handed him a date and what was left of a mouse. He nibbled on them whilst staring at the stars.

"I think I see the spoon one." he croaked out, pointing to a jumble of stars just above the city.

"Oh. Yeah." I said. "Yeah, I think that's the big spoon one. The little one is kinda under it."

Amin nodded, placing the mouse on the ground away from the water and the rest of the dates. It looked horrifying now, just a clump of bones with hunks of meat sticking to it.

Amin reached for the water bag, groaning. His teeth were clenched and his brow was rumpled. Plumes of fear swirled around his stomach as he groaned in pain.

His fingers fumbled to untie the water bag. He pressed it to his lips but inhaled sharply and dropped it, flinging his body to the ground in agony.

"Oh God. Oh God Ser. It's happening." he gasped.

I crawled beside him and watched in horror, not knowing what to say or do that could help him.

"No. No Amin you're alright. Please. You have to be alright. Do it for me Amin."

The words came flooding out of me. Tears streamed down my cheeks and soaked the collar of my shirt. Amin grasped my hands and clenched them as tight as he could.

His fright grew and grew until it surrounded both him and me. It was horrific. The cloud of worry left me anxious and overwhelmed, trying to help Amin as he writhed and whimpered in both pain and terror.

The core of his fear emerged from his wound, circling his head. Amin's rapid breathing was the only thing I could hear, as he pleaded with me through his eyes.

"Oh God, Amin." I sobbed, holding his hands tighter. "I promised I'd take you to the beach. I promised."

Amin was struggling to breathe now. His eyes were popping out of his skull, mortified and affrighted. Tears streamed down his cheeks as well but I doubt as fast as mine.

I couldn't do anything but hold his hands and sob, whispering to him to focus on the stars.

"You see... you see the little spoon?" I whispered, trying to calm myself down for the sake of him.

Amin jolted his head towards the sky, gripping my hand even tighter. Any breaths he could take were raspy and rapid, fighting for oxygen.

"The three dots in a line." I gasped, blinking away my tears. "Those make up some man. He guards the sky. He guards heaven from William. William isn't going to reach heaven Amin. He isn't, I promise."

The struggling breaths got slower.

There were fewer of them.

The grip on my hands loosened.

The writhing of a boy's body in pain slowed down to only a few twitches here and there.

"And..." I struggled to continue instead of breaking down. My voice shook with each word. My hands started to shake as well, gripping Amin's tighter as if to make up for the lifelessness of his.

"And..."

I hadn't heard a breath in a long time.

The hands that once clenched mine lay defunct in my palm. I slowly turned my head away from the sky and cast my eyes on the body of Amin.

His eyes lay open, fixated on the stars. There were no movements. No breaths.

"Wake up," I whispered. "Wake up now." It was more of an order than a wish. I figured that if I didn't believe he was dead, he wouldn't really be gone.

There was no response. I would never hear his voice again. He was as dead, the same as practically anyone I knew these days. The pinky promises I once made would be buried with him, suffocated and diminished in the unforgiving sand.

My body shook with sobs. I buried my face into Amin's bloodied chest to block out the sounds of my wails before they reached the city.

I never got to properly mourn the loss of Mom, so I took the opportunity of being so far away from the city to do it. My tears flooded Amin's shirt but they would never outnumber the amount of blood shed.

"I'm so sorry." I spluttered. "I'm so sorry. Oh God. I pinky promised. Please wake up Amin. Here's the beach. The sand. Oh God. This sand is different, I pinky promise. It's soft. And your mother is here. She's... she's here. I pinky... I pinky..."

Oh God.

Oh, Amin.

The clouds of his fear became thinner and eventually disappeared into the night. The purple tint that hovered in the air disappeared with it.

His core remained, drifting down to him and heading for his heart. It tried to return to him but couldn't. It couldn't sink into him anymore. Confused, it kept trying, sinking halfway into his chest before springing out again. It hovered near his injury for a while before floating back upward and heading high into the stars.

It was free.

Free to fly without fear of capture.

Amin never had that privilege.

And he would never have that privilege again.

I stared deep into his wound, the rage building up inside of me. Wisps of anger projected from my fingertips and circled his injury.

Circled his heart that was too big and too forgiving for the nature of the world.

Circled his eyes that would never be able to look at the smiling face of his mother again.

Circled his fingers that would never be able to feel the soft sand that made up his dreamt beach.

I stared back at the city, right at the Empathorium. The blinding gold and white stared right back at me, still as shiny and fake during the night as it was during the day.

All those little ants. Working their lives away to die. Their wasted emotions bottled up in a concrete jail. Their screams of suffering and agony overlooked by the very leader they relied on.

I didn't ask for a plan to form, but it did.

A plan that would avenge Amin.

And Mom.

And every other blind sheep that ever had the burden of being injected with William's poisoned ideas.

"You didn't die for nothing," I whispered, closing Amin's eyes and intertwining my pinky with his. His fingers were cold and limp which only further ignited the fire that burned inside of me.

"I pinky promise."

Chapter 10

Within the hour, I placed the bloodstained jacket over Amin's body. I couldn't bear to walk away from it if he was still there, eyes open, staring at the constellations.

I scraped away at the dust until I had collected a handful of the softest sand I could find. It was warm and airy.

I placed the sand in Amin's palm.

"I'm sorry I couldn't take you to the beach. And I'm sorry that I'm the reason you couldn't go yourself."

I took one last look at the only person I had ever considered to be my friend and set off towards the city.

I kept myself from looking back because I knew that if I did I would turn around and die next to him. Probably dehydration, from crying and the inability to move and get water. Or suicide, from survivor's guilt and the horrible feelings bunched up inside of me.

With every step I took, the city got closer and closer. The guards got closer and closer. The Empathorium. William.

If I managed to get inside without anyone noticing there would be no one there waiting for me. There would be no mother that could hold my face and tell me how sad she was that I was gone. There would be no friend, or rather a coworker, that could express how happy he was that I was back at work so that we could chat. Ironically, the only one truly waiting for me was William. And it wasn't to bake me cookies and throw me a welcome party but rather to slit my throat and cheer as my blood ran through the streets.

I had a vague idea of how I could convince the guards to leave the gate's entrance for a few seconds, long enough for me to sneak in but it was insanely risky. A risk that could kill me. A risk that could destroy me.

I stopped by the puddle of water to wash myself off. I nearly filled up the bag but ended up tossing it. It was useless anyway, Amin was the only reason for the bag due to his injury and inability to walk and...

That wasn't a problem anymore.

I drank my fill before scrubbing blood and dust from my hands. The water became a murky red with sand and dirt particles floating around in the mix.

I continued my journey to the gate, making sure to walk quietly and hiding behind any rocks or trees that I could. I made it to that same tree Amin and I had hidden behind in no time.

I touched the bark gently. The sounds of Amin's pained grunts and stifled sobs replayed over and over in my head. If only I had done something different to help him. Cleaned the wound sooner or tied the tourniquet tighter.

If I hadn't been so greedy about his death and had made sure he ate and drank a little more...

Maybe he could have helped me in more ways than I helped him. I was only waiting for him to die anyway, wasn't I?

"Maybe we *were* alike," I whispered, staring at the blinding infrastructure of the Empathorium. William was probably feasting inside of it, wandering his indoor gardens and slaughtering animals on his farm.

Waiting for the sick or injured to die so that he could have more precious resources to himself. Limiting them so that they would die faster.

That sounded more familiar than I liked.

The more I thought about it, and Mom, and Amin's mother, the angrier I got. Which was a good thing. It's what needed to happen.

I crept closer to the gates and the guards turned their backs until I could just about reach out and touch their spotless uniforms. They were insulting the poorer citizens, waving their guns and laughing. It burned, how angry I was feeling. I had to bite my tongue before my smart mouth got me killed.

Fog swirled around my boots and my arms but I waved it away. I was waiting for one very important thing. Something valuable. Something that could be captured and sold for gain at a market.

My core.

It emerged soon enough, circling my head and drifting down the road. One guard nudged the other. They began to walk towards my fury, pointing their guns at any spare citizens wandering the streets. It was mainly the homeless, out at such an hour, so they were just as interested in my anger as anyone else.

Anger was expensive.

Anger was powerful.

Anger was rich. Anger *meant* rich. Just below happiness, of course.

The guards would never leave their posts for a crying baby, or a dying citizen. They wouldn't bat an eye at a struggling elder or a lost child. But anger?

Anger was fought for. Anger was worth it.

They didn't get paid much more from William than regular blacksmiths or farmers did. Most people became Empaths for safety. For the power. The guns and the steel and the protection. No one could resist the high of capturing an emotion.

Once they were a good distance away, I took the thumb out of my pocket. It was still disgusting, bloodstained, and cold, but fingerprints were fingerprints.

It had to work, it had to.

I squeezed my fingers through the small gap between the gate and the fence and pressed the thumb against the fingerprint recognition. Nothing happened at first, which made my heart drop. The fear and misery took over, which made my anger begin to slow and head towards me again.

No. Please open. Please open. Please open.

The gate stood still.

My anger began to head my way. The guards would turn around and see me. It would drop lower and be able to be captured. It was all going wrong.

No. No. Think of Mom. He killed her. He hung her from yet another one of his balconies. He didn't think twice. He didn't even think twice. That asshole didn't even think twice.

My core began to glow brighter and head farther down the street. The Empaths loaded their guns and followed it.

I repositioned the thumb and held my breath yet again, hoping with all my heart but still believing that the gate would stay silent and still yet again.

Something vibrated against my fingertips.

My heart began to beat faster, with a new cause other than survival. With *hope.*

The gate, slowly but surely, began to swing open. As soon as it was somewhat wide enough, I squeezed through and sprinted towards the first house I saw.

I slid behind it, dropping stomach-first into the dirt. The thumb was still clenched in my palm.

Sure I was inside the city, but my anger was still drifting around into the night.

The gate squealed to a close, letting out a rather loud creak as it repositioned itself back into place. A creak that would be heard by the guards.

I heard their boots thumping against the road as they sprinted to the gate, shooting wildly. The bullets ricocheted off the metal, clinging to the dust below.

"What the hell?" one shouted.

"Did something get in?" the other yelled.

"Stay here, I'll check the perimeters." the first one ordered. I could hear him reload his gun.

Something flickered in the corner of my eye and startled me, causing me to whip around. I let out a breath of relief when I saw the core of my anger. I thought only of positive things until it disappeared, sinking into my chest.

From the other side of the road, I heard a chicken squawk. It was followed by a gunshot and several scattered screams. Lights, candles, and lanterns began to flicker on following the gunshot.

"Clear?" the guard standing in front of the gate asked.

"It's another... *chicken.*" the other guard responded, obviously fuming.

"Careful Pluth. Your anger."

"Don't act like *you* wouldn't be the one taking it Reeve." Pluth scoffed. His comment was followed by silence, which was somehow scarier than if the Empaths were talking.

He would search the other side of the road eventually. He would search behind the houses. Behind the house I was by, specifically.

"Should we look inside the houses as well?" Reeve asked.

"Did you hear a door open?" Pluth inveighed. "If someone got in, they're out here. We weren't that far down the road. We would have heard."

"At least check through the windows," Reeve said with much apprehension. Pluth let out a frustrated sigh but all the less I heard the click of a flashlight.

I looked up, inspecting the house. Maybe the roof? There was a window right above me, maybe I could use the ledge to climb up and-

"What are you doing out here?" someone whispered.

I looked up, eyes wide with panic. My gaze softened when I saw who it was, a little girl, sticking her head out of the window above me. I hadn't even realized it was open.

I stood up with caution and looked her in the eye, trying to smile but it was near-impossible.

"I'm hiding from those mean men," I whispered.

"They killed Daddy." the little girl whispered back. Her little fingers gripped the windowsill a little tighter. "With the guns. In the street. He didn't do nothing."

She looked at me with curiosity.

"Did you do nothing?"

"Yes. I did nothing and they want to hurt me badly."

The little girl looked behind her in her room. She looked me up and down, thinking hard.

"This side's clear," Pluth yelled.

The girl moved to the side and waved her hands wildly.

"Come inside of here. Hide and seek from the mean men. They won't find you like Daddy. Pinky promise."

I didn't think twice before diving inside the window and shutting it behind me. I closed it as slowly and as quietly as I could. I could hear scattered conversations between Pluth and Reeve, including the stomps of boots and the click of guns.

The little girl's words echoed through my head.

Pinky promise.

Amin.

Oh, Amin.

I positioned myself under the window, trying to squeeze my body as close to the wall as possible. If Pluth were to look through the window he would see me, out in the open. But not if I was directly under him.

"Pretend you're asleep," I whispered to the girl. "He's going to come and shine a light through. And... and if you're awake the light will turn red and a big monster will come and take us away from here."

The little girl hid under her blanket and pressed her face against her bed.

"Maybe away from here isn't so bad," she said, her voice muffled from being pressed against her mattress.

I heard a motion from outside the window. Pluth's flashlight shone through the window and landed on the little girl. I could hear her suck her breath in and hold it, terrified.

The flashlight shone onto the floor, and the ragged pile of clothes in the corner, but it never fell on me.

After a little longer than I hoped, the flashlight finally tore away from the window and the boots stomped along to the next house. I let out a breath of relief.

The little girl jolted upward, beaming.

"We did it!" she whispered. "The mean men never caught you and they never caught me!"

"Yes. Good job." I sighed, sitting up with caution and peering out of the window. It was a gamble on how long I could wait in this house without the little girl's mother finding out and either giving me away or shooting me herself.

"My name is Flair." the girl whispered, climbing off of her bed and sitting next to me on the floor. "What's yours?"

"Um. Azalea." I whispered.

I knew she was just a little girl but who's to say her mother didn't warn her about the deadly thief Seraphai that should be killed immediately?

"Yeah, I'm really good at hide and seek," Flair said, drawing circles on the floor with her finger. "I hide from him all the time, at school, ya know?"

"Who do you hide from?" I asked. My mind began to spiral, thinking of the worst. I knew it would be something horrible but that didn't stop me from asking.

"Teacher!" Flair said. "He keeps taking the kids into the closets and sometimes they don't come out. But sometimes we do learning like math and read and crafts and-"

"What does he do to those kids?" I asked in terror. The horrible thoughts kept clouding my mind. Nowhere in the city was a safe place but to kids? Not returning? Do the parents know about this?

"Well, I dunno," Flair said. "Mommy said never go into the closet ever ever ever. Sometimes the kids scream and then sometimes they laugh. They also cry. And get all mad too."

He was harvesting their emotions. That was the first horrible thought to come to my mind because no matter how horrific it was it was also the most sensible option as to what a teacher would be doing to a kid.

"Why does your mother send you to school?" I asked.

How could she? Knowing what the teacher did? Living with the fact that one day her daughter could not return because her childish laughter was bottled up and traded?

"She's gotta," Flair said. "Or the mean men come by. I gotta learn about numbers and stuff I guess. But we don't really do a lot of numbers. Most of the kids play hide and seek from the teacher."

I sat on the floor in disbelief.

"Yes," I said. "You should listen to your mother."

It took me a while to even remember that I had a plan and I needed to follow it. After a couple of minutes, Flair went back to her bed and fell asleep. She handed me her pillow before she returned to her bed and smiled at me. A plume of joy danced from her fingertips and swirled around the pillow.

I thought about what the next step should be. I needed a shield to get past the bullets. Not getting shot the first time was a stroke of pure luck that I didn't think I could have again.

I could send in an order for the blacksmith but I didn't know how I could come up with the emotions to pay them with.

I couldn't... *wouldn't* steal any emotions from anyone, let alone a small child like Flair. She was too innocent. Too young.

That left me with having to sneak into the blacksmith and make the shield myself. No one worked there at night, everyone went home around midnight at the latest, but Empaths guarded the streets and the gates, even more so because Amin and I had escaped.

I stood up and placed the pillow back under Flair's head. She woke up with a jolt but calmed down once she realized it was just me. She smiled at me and sat up in bed yet again.

"Are you going?" she asked.

"Yes," I replied. "I'm going to go show those mean men that they can't keep us here forever. After a while they'll run out of emotions to steal, they'll scramble for each other's. And there's no point in taking ours anyway if William's just going to keep them locked up in-"

I stopped myself from saying it. Flair was just a little girl. She didn't need to hear about the issues of the world any more than she already was. Besides, anyone who knew about the secret vault of emotions was dangerous. And even though to Flair I was Azalea, it was too dangerous to trust such a little girl with such an exorbitant amount of information.

"It's nothing," I muttered. "Adult stuff."

"They all tell me that." Flair sighed. "Mommy won't tell me why I can't let the teacher catch me. She teaches me hiding spots but she has scared looks on her face when she does so it isn't as much fun."

She flopped back on her bed and began to pick at a loose thread on her blanket. I slowly opened her window and crept out of it, placing my feet as carefully as I could so that I made virtually no noise.

I knew Flair would tell her mother that a girl named Azalea snuck into her window last night and slept on her pillow but that was the least of my worries. And based on what Flair had told me about her teacher I knew it was probably the least of her mother's worries as well.

I began to creep around the houses, making my way to the blacksmith. The problems started when I had to cross the street since Empaths were everywhere. Besides, the vault of emotions was on the right side of the city and I was creeping behind houses on the left side.

I couldn't possibly cross that many roads without being seen, it was impossible. Even with the shelter of the tightly packed houses, it was too risky.

I ran my fingers through my hair in a nervous fury.

"Make the shield tonight," I whispered to myself. "Stay the night in the blacksmith. Move when everyone's walking around. You'll be fine."

I peeked around the corner of a house and saw no guards but I knew that just down the road were Pluth and Reeve, already on edge from the whole sneaking-in thing. I didn't know what to do. I couldn't let my anger loose again, that was a one-time thing and this time I was sure someone would capture it.

I heard footsteps to my left. They startled me but my gaze softened when I saw that it was just a beggar. They littered the streets, asking for any spare bottles of emotions but no one ever gave them any. The best they got was some leftover food or various pieces of trash.

The lady I saw was wrapped in an old cloth. She hobbled down the street, mumbling to herself. Several stains fell on her clothes but that was common to me too nowadays. I was sure I still had Amin's blood on me somewhere.

I peeked down the road to see Pluth and Reeve's reaction to the beggar. They looked disgusted by her. They couldn't even look at her for more than three seconds without turning their heads away and laughing.

They fell silent and Reeve muttered some things to Pluth that I couldn't hear but it must have still been making fun of the poor lady because Pluth cackled and reloaded his gun.

He wasn't going to shoot her. I knew that. Empaths knew their guns meant power. They would reload them and point them at people and show them off but most of them rarely used them unless it was for an emergency.

Others made it a goal to shoot someone every day. Those kinds of people didn't shoot to the head or the heart but rather to the leg or the arm so that they could inflict as much pain as possible on whoever did them wrong.

Right before the lady wobbled her way across the street to the next row of houses, I leaped out from my hiding spot and followed after her. I copied her mannerisms and movements, shuffling across the street, and staring at my shoes.

I heard Pluth and Reeve laughing again, which was a good sign because it meant that they weren't suspicious of me. The lady didn't even realize I was following her, she was too starved and too crazy to notice let alone care.

She began to hobble across the next road so I followed her there as well. Luckily, no Empaths noticed me.

She continued muttering to herself and walking down the next road and the next but I was already on the strip of houses where the blacksmith was.

I turned left and began to creep behind houses, careful not to step in their gardens or trip over their makeshift fences.

I was more in the open now since I wasn't behind any houses close to the gate. There were roads on either side of me. Not many Empaths were night guards since it was mainly the gate that needed to be watched over but there were still too many for comfort.

I had nearly reached the door to the blacksmith when I heard the click of a gun. I froze in place, preparing for the worst. They had found me. This was it. They were going to kill me. At least I would be with Mom. And Dad. And Amin. And Amin's mother. And poor little Grayce.

"Turn around. Slowly." a voice boomed.

I obeyed, opening my mouth to plead my case but that's when I heard a different voice. It was shaky and scared, quivering with each word. I slid to my knees and bunched close to the blacksmith's wall, straining to hear the conversation.

"I didn't steal nothing. I swear. Please, sir."

"How could we believe you when we calculated the prices?" the Empath snarled.

I could see a good bit of the road, from the space between the blacksmith and the building next to it. A frail shadow was the only view I had though. It looked so familiar.

"I work. I work as a trader. Well... until William fired me. For no reason. One of you ass-kissers musta reported me."

"We counted missing bottles and suspected *you*." the Empath said. He stepped closer to the woman. I could now see both of their shadows. One was weak and frightened. The other held a gun with power.

"Well... I..."

"You tried to hide from us because you knew we were after you. Pluth and Reeve found you wandering the streets." the Empath said. "You can act crazy and act like one of those homeless bastards all you want Mortia but we know it's you. The *nerve* of you. To steal from the Empathorium? You can't hide from us."

Mortia?

The trader?

The one that you can lie to and get more for less? What could *she* have possibly done to the Empathorium? She's as blind as a bat and wouldn't hurt a fly.

"I told you. I didn't steal anything." Mortia spat. "You must have counted wrong. I told people the prices and they handed me the bottles. I don't understand. Besides, the only reason I felt the need to hide as a beggar is because of *you*. Hunting me down and I don't understand why."

The Empath laughed.

"Oh, you forget dear Mortia. We have eyes on you all the time. All earnings go to the Empathorium and we give you your fair pay. Dresses and necklaces and boxes of food left your stand day after day. All those things are worth *happiness* Mortia. *Happiness*."

"Yes I know," she said. "I know... I told the customers and they handed me the bottles. And I put them under the booth just like I was supposed to. In the box. To be collected."

"But there were never enough happiness bottles to make up for the lost inventory." the Empath said. "In place of them, there were extra fear bottles and extra sorrow bottles. Those are what *you* get paid, are they not?"

"Well... yes but I-"

"So are we not to believe that you took the customer's happiness bottles and exchanged them for what *we* paid *you*?" the Empath screamed. His voice caused chills to run down my spine. And I wasn't the one at gunpoint here.

It was because of us. Mortia did nothing wrong. Mortia believed the lies we told her. She didn't steal the happiness at all. The extra bottles were from *our* lies, not hers. Any ethical person would leap in front of the Empath and plead for Mortia's life. Explain to the Empath that it wasn't Mortia who tricked the Empathorium but the common folk.

Even though my fear was captured, terror was what stopped me from telling the Empath, and Mortia, the truth.

"I don't know what happened sir," she whispered. "But I didn't steal any joy. You can check my house. All I have is sadness and fright. What I get paid from you."

"William's orders." the Empath said. "You need to be dealt with before the Empathorium gets tricked anymore. Through the procedures, you shall be terminated before any more damage is dealt."

"No. No please." Mortia cried. "I did nothing. I don't understand. The prices... I didn't dabble with them."

"Well, we'll never know for sure. It's a safety precaution I'm sure you'll understand." the Empath continued.

"I just don't understand." Mortia wailed. "Atlas was always just a couple yards away. Everyone... they always came and asked for the expensive stuff but I can't really see the bottles and I get nervous asking them to clarify..."

"Binigo ka ng iyong emosyon." the Empath sighed. He spoke as if he were inhaling the words. It was pleasing to him, to be able to speak such words. I held my breath, accepting that Mortia was damned. There was no turning back after those words.

"I'm sorry," Mortia said. "I just don't underst-"

The gunshot pierced my ears and left them ringing.

Mortia's shadow was replaced by her body. She was killed immediately, by the cold bullets made in the very blacksmith I hid behind. The very blacksmith that I hid behind in *fear*, too afraid of repercussions to save her life.

The Empath typed some letters on his watch and spoke into it. His voice was calm as if this was all a game. Or a dream.

"I need body pickup over here. Job center. Yes, Mortia. Yes sir I found her. I'll go let Pluth and Reeve know. Yes sir."

He stepped over Mortia's body and headed towards the gate, not looking back once. I would have cried if I hadn't been through the loss of anyone I had ever considered family. I had shed all the tears I could.

The only guilt that piled up was the worthless feeling of survivor's guilt, tearing apart my insides and filling my brain with horrible thoughts.

I stood up with much difficulty and crept over to the door of the blacksmith, shoving it open. I tried not to glance at Mortia's bleeding body on my way in but it was inevitable. She was old and that was both good and bad in their ways.

She lived a long life but was it a good life? A life deprived of joy? A life where one's only purpose is to work and obey and please just to be condemned in the end anyway?

I slid against the door and waited until I heard body pickup come and drag Mortia's body away. The smell of her blood still lingered, although there were also my bloodstains and Amin's bloodstains on my shirt so I couldn't really tell anymore.

Even long after the body pickup had left I sat there.

I wasn't in shock or anything. I knew what I had to do. I just couldn't get myself to move. What if they heard me? Making the shield. Every Empath was surely on edge tonight, after me breaking in and after Mortia getting shot.

"You need to make the shield," I whispered. "You promised Amin. No. You *pinky* promised Amin. He is up there with Mom and Dad and *his* mother and they all died because of William. They all died because of this... this *place.*"

A thin veil of anger emerged from the very pinky that interlocked with Amin's and drifted across the room. With only the moon as my light, it was hard to see but I followed the swirl of fog nonetheless. It weaved around the forge and moved to the anvil. As I calmed down it began to fade away, taking the red tint that it brought to the dark room with it.

I froze when I heard footsteps outside. Heavy footsteps. Empath footsteps. My mind raced to the worst as I searched for places to hide and weapons to use that could possibly get me out of this situation.

They passed soon enough but that was enough proof for me. There was no way I could create anything close to a shield without people hearing. My hearing was out of shape from relentless bombs and gunshots yet I could *still* hear any slight footsteps from outside.

The walls of the blacksmith, while a *little* thicker than usual to block out as much noise as possible, were still just clay.

I didn't think there was anywhere in the city that I could make noise in at night without being heard. And I couldn't sneak back in here during the day either because people would recognize me and turn me in. I thought about the last time I had worked at the blacksmith. When I pulled the ticket for Hennie and Drew's order for shackles. I had tried to warn everyone and I had tried to get people to agree with me. Maybe if someone did, Grayce would still be alive.

Maybe if I had pulled a different ticket, things would have been different. I wouldn't have been captured and put in that room. That horrible soundproof room that no one could hear me yell for help in.

That...

That horrible... *soundproof room.*

Hennie was useless at shooting a gun anyway. Drew was long dead, mauled, and ripped to pieces by crueler beasts than he was.

To forge, we didn't have ingots or blocks of metal. We had sheets. They were pretty thin, for the most part, but it was to ensure that no metal was wasted.

To make things like knives or silverware, all we had to do was cut the shape out of the metal sheet and then polish it. If our job wasn't done correctly, the Empath monitoring us would pass our ticket on to another person and more or less fire us.

There were barely any jobs available, other than Empaths but the sane would never. It was the starved and deprived *insane* who squabbled for a chance to get any emotions from William. Or the power-hungry control freaks, who drool over the chance to hold a gun and enforce the rules.

I could only take one trip to Hennie's. Two were too dangerous and even one was one too many.

I grabbed a couple of metal sheets and a blowtorch to mold with. I rummaged around in a couple of drawers for the best hammer, to flatten and shape my shield with the best I could while it was semi-moldable.

I stood by the door, breathing heavily. Earlier, I had followed Mortia and acted like a beggar to get past Pluth and Reeve but I couldn't do that anymore. Not with my hands full of expensive blacksmithing tools. They would think that I stole them and shoot me on the spot.

Or they would toy with me first, as they did Mortia. They would recite that horrible oath that filled them with such ecstasy and pull their trigger, giddy to call body pickup. Giddy to report to William that they were a good Empath and shot another person.

"They'll guard the gate more," I whispered. "The gate is where you broke in so the gate will be guarded more than the streets. The one who killed Mortia... he was only there because he got called by Pluth and Reeve."

My mind was still swarming with horrible thoughts of torture and murder, but I gathered the strength to push open the blacksmith door and walked down the street in a hurry.

I kept my head low and my pace brisk until I was safely in the shadows of another row of houses. I held my breath and crossed the next street, again only stopping when I was safely hidden in between clay or wood walls.

Hennie's house was on the next strip of buildings, right next to my house. Or at least where my house was. The remaining infrastructure had been torn down and construction on a new clay house was starting. White and gold tools littered the ground and glinted in the moonlight.

It was the trademark of the Empathorium. Shiny, fake, white and gold. Somehow, it seemed as if they never got dirty. The whole Empathorium brand, that is. Everything was always there and always shining. It would be comforting, a guiding light in such a dark and dusty city, if they didn't have such a horrible reputation for killing little boys and little girls for simply trying to survive.

I poked my head out and examined the street. Left and right and then left again. There were no Empaths, for now. I swore that I heard boots in the distance but my hearing was bad anyway. The fear of getting caught didn't help my anxious ears.

I darted across the street and sprinted inside Hennie's yard. I didn't even bother to run all the way around to the back, I just dropped stomach-first in the dirt.

I didn't hear any gunshots or outrageous screams from Hennie, so I assumed I was safe. I had my tools still clenched firmly in my hands, but I placed the metal sheets on the ground next to me.

I heard nothing from the house, but I guess Hennie had no one to kidnap children and belittle anymore. I listened for any sounds that she was even inside the house, water running or footsteps, but my ears were met with silence.

I left my sheets and my tools and crawled over to the front door. I tried to push on it, but it wouldn't open. I should have known. They were on the richer side, so of course they could afford a simple door lock.

We make them all the time, at the blacksmith. Usually, we only charge two bottles of fear, one for the lock and one for the key, but sometimes we'll get lucky and just get a bottle of anger instead.

I crept back around to the side of the house and began pressing on all the windows. No one had window locks, it was way too expensive. Most people just slept with a gun nearby and crossed their fingers.

And that was the exact problem with using the window. I could maybe sneak past Hennie if I used the door but climbing awkwardly through a too-small window would certainly get her attention.

By the time the frightening thoughts formed, it was too late to turn back. I was already halfway through the window. Hennie hadn't come running yet and there were no traps set off or anything. It should have been reassuring but it only made the whole ordeal more suspicious.

I slid through the window and landed in the kitchen. Stray cups littered the countertop. The precious and coveted strawberries that were the highlight of this household were smashed on the walls and stained the counters.

All the silverware was either on the floor or stabbed into the cabinets. There were knife marks everywhere, on the walls and the chairs. What was left of the chairs at least. Most of them lay smashed to pieces.

I ventured upstairs and took a look in the bathroom. The mirror was smashed. The faucets were stained with thick, hot, blood. The shower curtain had streaks of blood on them as well. The floor was completely stained, puddles upon puddles.

Dark red footprints and handprints lay splattered across the walls and the floor. They ultimately created a path to the bathtub. I placed my hand on the shower curtain and hesitated.

Did I want to know what awaited me?

Whoever did this could still be inside the house. The blood wasn't fresh but it wasn't over a couple of days old either. A beggar could have broken in, crazy with hunger, desperate to live somewhere besides the unforgiving streets.

I hesitantly pushed the curtain to the side and nearly gagged at the gruesome sight that awaited me.

Drenched in her blood, Hennie lay. She clenched a knife in her hand, a big kitchen one. Stab marks covered nearly every square inch of her body. Her throat was slit, probably as the final blow, causing a thick red waterfall to run down her chest and pool on the tub floor.

Her once pristine hair lay snarled and matted. Some parts of it were ripped out in chunks while other parts were stuck and hardened together from old blood.

She had been dead for a couple of days, based on the way she looked. Her skin was hard and cold. Her face was nearly unrecognizable, with how mutilated it had become. Chunks of flesh lay everywhere, making up the bloody hunk of raw meat Hennie had become.

"Who did this to you?" I whispered. My fingers began to tremble. Who would have such motives? And why? Was I next? I couldn't leave without the shield but was it worth it anymore?

A piece of paper lay next to Hennie, propped on the side of the bath. I reached to pick it up and my arm brushed against hers, leaving congealed blood sticking to my skin.

There weren't many words on the paper, but it told me everything that I needed to know about what had happened to Hennie and the danger level I was in.

The note being covered in blood didn't help, but I could still make out the five words, scrawled in rushed handwriting.

"I'm coming with you, Drew."

Chapter 11

I wasted no time but gathered my supplies and made my way straight to the soundproof room. They had tidied it up, but there was still no fan. I began to break out in a sweat just thinking about working with a blowtorch inside of, more or less, a sauna.

The shield was pretty easy to make. All I needed to do was melt the two metal sheets together and pound them flat. The shield would be made out of the same metal we make bullets out of, which gave me hope.

The sounds of the blowtorch and the hammer pierced my ears and filled me with terror.

What if someone heard?

What if an Empath heard?

Would they come to investigate? And if they did, would they recognize me? There weren't many portraits of me or anything, and no warrants outside, that I could see at least.

The blowtorch was hard to work with, with how much I was sweating. If I dropped it, it would either burn me or my shield. And ironically, my shield was more important.

My legs could only do so much to protect me from bullets. Nothing more than sprint for my life and hope for the best. My shield would be the only thing that could get me to and from the emotions alive.

I finished pretty quickly but was still dripping in sweat. When I took a step back to look at my work my stomach dropped down to my boots.

I had forgotten to grab an extra sheet of metal to make the handle. I could grip the shield by the sides but if my fingers got shot there was no other way to hold it. My mind raced as I tried to think about what could be made out of metal in this wretched house.

Maybe the shower head but it was too bulky and could never be crafted into a handle, especially not with the slim pickings of tools that lay before me.

"Think, think," I muttered. "When you first came in... there was the broken glass and all the strawberries and all those knives stabbed into the cabinets..."

The knives.

There must have been dozens down there. Cooking knives and utensils and the knives that they used to inflict punishment on those poor children.

I ran downstairs and found the biggest one, which was dangerous because it was also the sharpest. I would have to move steadily, yet fast, to both make it to the emotions and not slice through my hands.

The handle was big, I had spent another ten minutes hammering and blowtorching, but it was sharp. I tried to torch the sharp edges, to melt them and round them out, but the metal was so thin that it melted immediately and dripped down onto both the shield and the floor.

"You are going to have to deal with it," I muttered, flinging the blowtorch and the hammer across the room in a fit of built-up fury.

Wisps of anger followed and darted around my shield. They cast a daunting red hue before fading away. It should have been an empowering red gleam but it wasn't. And it only reminded me how screwed I was if I failed.

William would have a field day if I got killed. Or even brutally injured, because then he could finish me off himself and ensure that I was dead.

I left the shield and pushed open the door, breathing in the cool air that met me. The heat hadn't helped in the battle to control my rage, but the sweet night air that cradled me outside the wretched room was everything I needed.

I wandered back down to the kitchen, gulping down a cup of water and rummaging in the cabinets for any food that Hennie hadn't destroyed.

There were cans of beans and a box of rice but no fresh fruit. No matter how coveted it must not have been important enough for Hennie to save when she demolished the house.

The only things she left untouched were the poorer items of her house. The juice bottles lay smashed but the tap water in the sink was untouched. The strawberries lay squished against cabinets and the floor but the can of emergency beans in the upper cabinet stood tall.

Only one stray bottle of sadness was left, laid under the stairs. The splinters of glass that littered the floor left me with the conclusion that any other emotions were set free. Ironically, their freedom came from the *wrath* of Hennie's pure rage.

I pried a spoon from the wall and devoured the can of beans, hardly even minding that they were lukewarm. After days of eating cooked mice and drinking puddle water, any food given from the Empathorium was a luxury.

No matter how much I despised them for even limiting our food in the first place.

I stumbled around the house, more tired now than ever. Adrenaline always took me far, especially at night, but now with no stomach nagging me for food or water, there was nothing to keep me awake.

I was...

Content?

It had been so long.

If I wasn't so tired I would have taken more time to wash myself and my clothes, but the moment I walked into Hennie and Drew's bedroom, I unlaced my boots and crumpled in their bed.

I dreamt that Hennie's ghost came to haunt me, and Drew was with her, still white-knuckling his gun. I should have woken up sweating and screaming, or at least rolled out of bed with a jolt, but it was the greatest sleep I had gotten in ages.

I woke up late.

It was a pretty good thing though, because I felt safest moving around with large crowds where I could blend in. I ate an actual breakfast, of some smashed fruit and some rice, with an actual cup of water.

Hennie had killed herself in the worst place for me because I wasn't comfortable moving her body, but I also needed to wash myself off.

Desperately.

I tried in the sink, and that got my body clean for the most part, but my hair was still nauseating, greasy, and covered in dust. It didn't even fall very flat anymore, it was just a tangled nest of split ends.

I got an idea but I pushed it out of my mind.

I couldn't. I just couldn't.

Not after growing it out for so long.

Mom used to braid it for me. I never learned how because she was always there and I thought she would always be there forever.

How naive. To think that in such a world my mother would always be there for me. God forbid William let one family live to their oldest days together.

I still couldn't. I wouldn't. It was too hard for me. My hair was the only part of the past I still owned. The ends that lay across my shirt were there when Mom was and it was too hard to let them go. It was a stupid thing to hold on to, yet I shuddered at even the thought.

No. I couldn't.

Please don't do this Ser.

They won't recognize you though.

It's the only part of you that is left.

It's too risky. Something to pull. Something to get stuck. Something heavy on your back.

Heavy on my back? Heavier than the survivor's guilt? Heavier than the weight of my dead family and friends?

I subconsciously rummaged through all the drawers in the house, looking for scissors. My mind twisted into pretzels and continued arguing with itself.

No.

Yes.

You wouldn't.

I wouldn't?
You wouldn't.
I wouldn't.

What did I do?

My eyes fell on the chunks of hair in the sink. The rusty scissors lay beside them. I couldn't even bring myself to look at my new hair in the mirror. I felt too disappointed in myself.

I felt it though. Much shorter. Was it enough to trick the Empaths? They would still execute me if I set the emotions free, no matter what my hair looked like.

Did I cut it to let go of the past or to create a new future?

Or both perhaps?

It was just hair.

A precious memory of what life used to be like, but just hair all the same. Just hair.

After ages, I threw on some of Hennie's clothes, grabbed my shield, and walked out the door. My head felt lighter but not my shoulders.

My shoulders still carried the weight of the world.

Even though most of my world was dead.

I tried my best to hide myself in the crowds, flocking to the trading booths. They kept their hands firmly against their bottles of emotions, ready to fight anyone who got too close.

The Empaths lined the streets, keeping an eye out for any suspicious behavior, and probably me.

I kept my eyes downward and tried not to hit anyone with my shield. It didn't get questioned but I caught some kids laughing at it and I caught some parents giving it weird looks.

I stormed straight ahead, not even caring about the bullets or the beasts. The Empaths could shoot my legs off, go ahead, I would crawl my way to that basement and rip off the door with my teeth if I had to.

I had a plan set in mind. It was risky but it could be worth it. It meant I had to be fast. And fearless.

I was fast but was I fearless?

I guess I was going to find out, one way or another.

There was an Empath by one of the booths, watching everyone's moves very carefully. He had a looser grip on his gun, which was just what I needed.

I took strides of importance toward him, weaving through whining kids and swerving around impatient shoppers.

I was a man on a mission.

A woman with a wish.

But most importantly, just a kid, who probably wasn't prepared to fight against her kismet.

The Empath locked eyes with me, probably because I was unintentionally staring him down. He took a step towards me, visibly annoyed.

"Hey, these people are waiting too, you can't just-"

I took a sharp step forward and snatched his gun before he had a chance to shoot me. I fumbled with the trigger while he yelled before shooting him square in the leg. He fell to the ground, screaming and trying to stop the river of blood.

For Mom.

People screeched and ran out of the way. I ignored the chaos and threw my shield down into the dropoff, followed by the Empath's gun. I wasn't going to have the same fate as Drew.

Empaths shouted behind me but I didn't listen and instead dove down into the unforgiving forest.

For Dad.

I grabbed the gun and my shield and began to sprint, clearing a fallen log with a single leap. The guns came out of the wall and a barrage of bullets began to ricochet off of my shield. The Empaths shot at me too but didn't dare come down the dropoff, where the endless bullets flew. They were just people after all. Instead, they pulled alarms. And yelled. And shot.

For Mortia.

The beasts were released next. It was stupid, releasing them while the rain of bullets continued. Most of them got shot but some of them got lucky, swerving around trees to get to me. But I was too far ahead for them to get me before I reached the concrete slab. I slid behind it and sent bullets ripping through the remaining beasts.

For Grayce.

I shot wildly at the door until it was broken enough for me to knock it down with my shield. I flew down the stairs and froze at the bottom.

Hundreds upon hundreds of cores. Raw emotion. Pure agony and pure bliss. Horrible despair and agonizing terror. They fluttered and flipped, gliding around my arms and making their way to the exit.

"Go!" I screamed, trying to shoo more towards the exit. I became dizzy, stumbling around, tripping over nothing. I needed to get out of there while I still could before the poison left me useless on the ground.

And I had a feeling they would make sure I ended up in flames, dead or alive.

Some of the emotions darted in the opposite direction, while others were more interested in me. I was close to giving up, about to stumble up the stairs to get some fresh air, when one finally flew up into the sky.

Followed by another.

Three or four more took their chance.

Dozens followed.

In a matter of seconds, hundreds began to pour through the opening. They filled the dull sky with color. Color that was bright and full of life.

I followed them up the stairs and stopped at the very top, still cautious of the bullets, but eager to breathe fresh air and regain my strength. The emotions began to race into the sky, floating towards the city.

They were free to return to the bodies that had lost them. Most would be dead but some would find their happy ending. In their lost oasis. I took it all in, before a bullet met my skull or a beast tackled me. Swirls of colors and orbs of passion blew past me and sent breezy waves through my hair.

Heaps of happiness. Clusters of rage. Bunches of fear. Groups of misery. They were all for him. All because of him.

For Amin.

"Shut the bullets off!" I heard a voice bellow. "Send the beast! All units to the south wall!"

Another voice followed behind it. A child's voice. She wasn't scared but she was curious.

"Hey! Mommy! Those are our emotions!"

Those six words were all it took.

Those six innocent words, of an excited child.

No one could have guessed they would be the reason for the death of dozens.

Upon hearing the child's excited words, crowds of hundreds began to push past the Empaths and head for the clouds of cash. They cared more about the chance of getting something worth trading than their own lives. The bullets sensed the motion and triggered, blowing dozens to the ground.

The Empaths were shouting to turn the bullets off and trying to stop people from falling down the dropoff, but no one stopped running. A few turned around and tried to climb the dropoff to escape the shooting but were pushed back down by mobs of power-hungry citizens.

A man reached where I was first and beamed at the abundance of happiness above him. He reached up to capture three cores inside of a single jar before being pummeled to the ground by a giant beast.

I took the gruesome sound of his screams as my cue to leave. I grabbed my shield, and my gun, and began to push my way upstream. I used my shield to protect myself from the bullets, and the gun to shove people out of my way.

A woman with her leg covered in bullet wounds tried to grab my shield, sobbing.

A father cradled his daughter in his arms, pushing past the mob of people and attempting to climb the hill with only his legs to help him. His daughter sobbed in his arms, screaming louder and louder with each body that fell.

A man lay dead on the ground, his hands clenched around three empty jars.

A boy no older than sixteen stood frozen in fear, back against a tree trunk. He locked eyes with me, before getting knocked down by an older woman trying to escape. Her hands were full of jars, each stuffed with joy and fury.

A core of sadness returned to its owner. A young woman frantically trying to claw her way through the crowd and up the dropoff. I watched as she lost her grip and tumbled down, hitting a tree with a horrible crack on her way.

The closer to the city I got, the more I heard the Empaths. They were frantically trying to control the citizens, with no results. They sounded scared themselves too, with no instruction on how to deal with such chaos like this.

They *were* people like us until William hired them and they became all high and mighty, barking orders at us and each other.

"Turn the guns off, we're losing dozens!"

"The beast is already out, they shouldn't have ran!"

"William's got the bomb ready! We need to clear out and rebuild from there!" one yelled.

I reached the dropoff and ditched my shield, throwing the strap of the gun over me.

I used the trees and the arms of other people to hurl myself up, wincing at each body that dropped down into the backyard of the same Empathorium that turned them into emotion-hungry slaves. Most people had made it up the dropoff and were helping others reach safety.

A few people still pursued the emotions, but the mob that had run down had turned tail and were now clamoring to get away from their cold deathbeds.

I didn't have time to make it fully up to safety before I heard an all-too-familiar whistling sound. The same sound I heard right before my house got blown to smithereens.

Right before Mom had gotten...

I needed to get out of there, and fast.

A man had his arm extended near me, helping others reach the, ironically, safe streets. He was one of the only ones still left, all the other people helping had started to sprint towards safety after hearing the Empaths mention bombs.

I had time to grab the man's arm, clenching his hand for dear life, but not time to pull myself up before the explosion ripped through the forest and sent me flying.

Chapter 12

I woke up to my ears ringing.

I had landed straight on my gun, which sent a horrible pain through my stomach and my chest. It was a blessing within itself that I hadn't been shot by it.

Dozens of other people lay beside me, all groaning and patting out fires near them or on their clothes.

Sirens wailed from the Empathorium. The excruciating cries of injured citizens down in the dropoff would surely haunt my nightmares for the next few weeks to come.

I grabbed my gun and limped over to the edge of the dropoff. My heart sank at the horrible sight.

Empaths dragged dismembered arms and cold bodies into big piles. Fires sent the once beautiful trees ablaze. The trees couldn't be found anywhere else in the barren landscape that seemed to go on for miles.

The people who were still alive wailed and begged, pleading for the Empaths to save them. They were answered with a bullet to their head, which was both cruel and merciful, as many were left without bottom halves or multiple limbs. Raw hunks of meat left to bleed out. Unanswered cries aimed towards the heavens, forever lost in the sky.

An Empath jabbed me in the side with her gun, causing me to fall over completely.

"You aren't supposed to have that gun," she said.

"I'm sorry," I said, trying to hide my face. I handed her the gun and stood up, facing the town instead of the warzone behind me.

The Empath jabbed me again with her gun, this time in the back. She nudged me down the road, unaware that I had no house to return to.

The beggars were huddled in clumps on the road, whispering and crying. Some of them held jars of emotions, either stolen or swiped from the commotion.

They all looked at me when I passed by, scanning my hands for any jars. I noticed a knife, clenched in the hands of one of them. He started to laugh, a bone-chilling laugh, causing the others to join in.

Anyone who had survived the wreckage lay crying. Some people hid in their houses, locked their doors, and shut their windows, but most just sat in the street. The survivor's guilt crashed over me in waves, yet again.

It only got louder, as more people began to wake up and search for their loved ones. I heard the wail of a mother and instinctively navigated towards the noise.

"Please! My son!" she cried. "You need to help me! He ran... he ran down there. I know he's down there if you would just help me look."

"You need to back up." the Empath ordered. "Back away from me. Right now."

"Please!" the woman wailed. "Do your job! You have a family too, don't you? Wouldn't you want to save them? I need you to help me! He's all alone, and he's scared, and-"

"No one down there is now alive." the Empath yelled back, elbowing the woman away from him. He didn't even seem shaken to deliver the news, but otherwise happy. One less child to look out for. One less rebel. One less mouth to feed.

In a blind rage, the mother began to swing at the Empath, clawing, spitting, and punching whatever body part she could get her hands on.

A bullet was soon through her heart.

The very heart that broke for her lost son.

My heart broke too but only a little bit.

For every death I witnessed it broke a little bit, but I couldn't think about it too long or I would have no heart left.

The crowd of people who had formed let out a collective gasp as the woman crumpled to the ground. She twitched only once before laying still, which was somewhat relieving because that meant that she died a quick death.

Everyone quickly dispersed after that, trying to find somewhere safe to go. A man bumped into me, sprinting towards his house with his sobbing daughter in his arms.

A little boy struggled to carry his baby brother down the road, limping from a cut on his leg. The baby was wailing, kicking its tiny feet, and swinging its tiny fists.

An old man slammed his door shut, ignoring the pounds of helpless people trying to get into any house they could.

People were getting shot left and right. For capturing a stray emotion that they illegally stole from the Empathorium.

For asking too many questions about the bomb. Or the basement. Or the bodies. Or the beasts.

For fighting, over who got the sorrow drifting down the street, or which family could go inside which house.

I saw a little boy, sitting on the road, crying. Plumes of fear emerged from his eyes, along with his tears, and created a cloud around him.

Greedy beggars began to circle him, readying their jars and drifting their dirty fingers through the fog.

I ran to the little boy and picked him up, trying to calm him down and escape the beggars that pursued us, upset that I had ruined their chance to get richer.

"Mommy! Mommy!" he blubbered, screeching at the top of his lungs. I doubted his mother would hear him, with all the commotion around the streets anyway.

The emotions had made it to the city now, and the Empaths were trying their best to control both them and the people clamoring for them.

They shot anyone who ran towards the mess, not lethally yet still enough to show that they were willing to shoot. They couldn't stop a hoard of curious emotions, however. They drifted down streets and squeezed into houses, flew around citizens, and drifted up into the sky.

The little boy I was carrying sniffed as he reached for a happiness core. His fingers went straight through it, as they would through fog or mist, but he still laughed.

The happiness didn't last long, a gunshot rang through the air and the little boy burst into tears once more. I needed to find a place to put him, while we waited out the chaos, but there was nowhere in sight.

All of the houses were locked up, whether you lived there or not. People hid behind the houses but there was nowhere to hide since roads and pathways were everywhere.

Then it hit me, one of the only places with no lock since it wasn't a house at all.

I began to sprint towards the blacksmith, while the little boy sobbed in my arms and screamed for his mother. I had nearly reached the door when someone grabbed my arm and yanked me backward, sending me falling to the ground.

"Mommy!" the little boy wailed.

"Kidnapper!" the woman screamed. "Get the hell away from my son! Get away from him!" She snatched her son by his arm and held him close, tears streaming down her cheeks as she screeched every horrible thought imaginable at me.

"You don't understand!" I screamed. "I was trying to help him, you don't understand!"

"Don't hurt us!" the mother wailed, backing away from me. Once she was a safe distance away she began to sprint, down the road and out of my sight.

I saw another child, crying beside a house a couple of roads away, but I couldn't help. Her mother could be dead but her mother could also be roaming the streets with a gun, searching for her daughter and willing to kill anyone near her.

I shoved the blacksmith door open and ran inside, ducking behind some of the heavier equipment. I took a hammer from the tool shelf as protection, even though it could do little to nothing against a gun or a bomb.

I flinched when the door opened again, but was relieved to see it was only a mother, rushing her kid inside before slamming the door behind her.

The mother screamed when she saw me, hunched over and clenching a hammer, which caused her child to scream as well. I dropped the hammer and stood up, trying to be the one to remain calm for all three of us.

"Just protection, just protection," I reassured them, taking a step backward. "I- I'm Seraphai."

"I'm sorry." the mother sighed. "I just... and with today... and all those emotions... and they *shoot*." She placed her hands on her daughter's shoulders protectively. "This is Vera. I'm Crynn."

We all turned our heads towards the door once we heard William's voice. It was booming through speakers, calm and collected. A little *too* collected. A little *too* calm.

"Citizens. Please refrain from capturing the emotions in front of you. Everyone must return to their homes, immediately. Anyone caught outside *will* be shot."

"There are people in our house," Vera said, looking up at her mother with worry.

"I know," Crynn said, looking around as if William would appear behind her any second. She turned towards me. "Beggars," she said. "They had knives. We had our gun inside the house, but we couldn't reach it. They broke in."

"Oh. Yes. Same for me. They broke through our window. I don't know if they are beggars but they um... they looked like them."

I couldn't just say that my house got bombed. I was the one who started this mess. I would get turned on by Crynn and Vera faster than I could argue and explain. They wouldn't listen. No one would.

I would end up on that balcony, just like Mom.

I would end up with a rope around my neck, with tears streaming down my cheeks. Just like Mom.

One push.

One long fall.

Crack.

Swing

Swing

Swing

Vera snapped me out of dwelling on the past. She pointed at her mother's leg and gasped.

"Mommy, you're hurt!"

I took a couple of steps towards Crynn to observe her leg. A giant gash lay, going down her thigh, dripping blood onto the blacksmith floor.

"Oh, Mommy's okay," Crynn said.

"Beggars? The knife?" I asked.

"Oh. Yes. I was trying to grab the gun." Crynn said, sitting herself down on the floor. Vera ran over to her and plopped in her lap, visibly worried.

"I'll get you a towel," I said. "I think we have one around here somewhere."

"Yes, thank you." Crynn sighed. "It should heal, I think. But if anything were to happen... please just make sure she gets somewhere safe. I would ask you to take her with you, but the burden is too heavy... please... just don't let the Empathorium take her and shove her in one of those orphanages."

"Where is her father?" I asked.

"He was a bad person," Vera said.

"He was obsessed with power," Crynn said, moving Vera so that I could wrap the towel around her leg. "He chose his job over us. The thrill and the high of all the control he got was too much for him. I tried to stop him, and he nearly killed me. Just because he could with no repercussions."

"He's an Empath." I breathed. There was no other job that fit such a description. Of course, he fell into the trap of killing. Most Empaths did.

I mean, most *regular* people did. And they didn't even have access to multiple weapons and a free pass to kill anyone who even looked at them wrong.

Crynn thanked me for the towel and Vera plopped right back on her lap. Both of them flinched at the sound of heavy boots, running right past the door.

The door began to creak open.

Crynn placed her arms around Vera, cradling her.

I backed against the wall, staring at my boots, trying to hide my face from whoever was outside.

"You guys shouldn't be in here."

The voice didn't echo off the walls and attack my ears like an Empath's voice usually did. I looked up to see that it was an Empath, but he looked just as scared as I did.

"You need to, um, return to your homes. Now."

He placed a hand on his gun but removed it quickly.

"Why are you helping him?" I asked. The words flew out of my mouth before I could think about the consequences of saying them.

The Empath scanned my face. He tilted his head slightly. I knew I had messed up, as he mentally took note of my features and the clothes I was wearing.

"Hey... wait... what's your name?" he asked, tapping some buttons into his watch and glancing at his gun around his chest.

"Rayah," I said.

"Nuh-uh! You said it's Seraphai!" Vera laughed, looking at the Empath with glee.

Shit.

Amid the commotion, I had forgotten to make up a fake name for Vera and Crynn. Vera was happily playing with her hair while Crynn looked at me with confusion. The Empath furiously tapped more buttons on his watch, glancing up at me occasionally.

"You need to come with me," he said. "Now."

"You don't understand," I whispered.

"You are under arrest and on trial of death for breaking into the Empathorium-"

"They killed my mom," I said, louder this time. I backed up towards where I had left my hammer.

"As well as for the death of an Empath-"

"She shot my friend. He... he died. I tried to keep him alive and I needed to get out because of William. I never would have... if it wasn't for-"

"And finally for breaking inside the Empathorium's vault and releasing the emotions inside, causing this mess. You, Seraphai Vane, are responsible for the deaths of dozens."

I reached down and picked up my hammer. The Empath was still tapping on his watch, probably sending out signals and letting everyone know that I had cut my hair.

"You don't want to do this. You don't have to. I'll stay quiet. They'll stay quiet too, right?"

I pleaded with Crynn and Vera not with my words but with my gaze. Vera looked back up at me, confused. Crynn stared at me for a while, before grabbing Vera by the shoulders and backing away from me.

"Take her away," she told the Empath. "Please. She is a threat to this city. I will not stay quiet and let anyone else die because of her."

The Empath approached me, trying to grab my arm.

"Please, don't make this hard. I-"

I didn't mean to swing the hammer, but my instincts took over. Fight won over flight, leaving the Empath on the floor, his skull bashed in and blood trickling from his wound.

I dropped the hammer, mortified at my actions. Another death added to the tally of everyone I had killed.

Vera started to wail.

Crynn started to shriek, grabbing a sheet of metal off the wall and pointing it toward me as if it were a weapon.

"Help! Help us! In here! Seraphai is here! She... she killed someone! Somebody help us!"

I could barely make out her words over Vera's wails and sobs, which was ironically good for me since if I couldn't hear the pleas for help neither could the remaining Empaths.

I pushed the door open and ran out into the street, despite the warning that William had given. Outside was better than inside, since I doubted I could calm Crynn and Vera down. I looked up and down the street and was relieved to find no Empaths, but I didn't know how long that sweet relief would last.

I knocked on every door, but every one was shut and locked. That meant there were people inside, but they would rather ignore my cry for help than risk their lives.

I was outraged at the utter selfishness of the cowardly adults hiding behind closed doors before I remembered that if I was them I would do the same thing.

To them, I was a murderer. A convict. Someone who had to be dealt with immediately.

Mom used to tell me that my name was sweet like honey. That it was unique and special and I should treasure it, just like we treasured sweet desserts since they were so scarce.

I used to love sugar when we could get it because Mom would always let me have a spoonful and say that no matter how sweet the sugar tasted, my name and my personality were sweeter.

I would laugh and dip my spoon in for another mound of the grainy goodness, and Mom would laugh as well, telling me that we had to save the sugar for cooking and not for eating.

I can imagine how sour my name tasted now, to the people hearing it. Their brains flooded with the fake media of how I was a murderer and I needed to be killed immediately.

If a citizen recognized me in the street, they could very well pull out a gun and shoot me themselves. But the Empaths wanted me alive. So that *they* could kill me.

So that they could make it hurt.

So that they could chant their stupid nonsense, watching as I cried and begged.

I ducked behind a house, trying to hide but no matter where I went there would be a road on both sides of me. Unless I made it to the edge of the city, where there was the gate, but I could never make it that far.

I assumed the Empaths were all down in the dropoff, cleaning up the bodies and sweeping up the debris, and William had only made that announcement to scare everyone into hiding. That meant fewer deaths.

He couldn't be the leader if there weren't any more peasants to lead. He couldn't have a voice if there was no one to boss around. His threats and tactics couldn't work if everyone was peacefully laid to rest.

However, everyone *wasn't* laid to rest. His threats and tactics still worked, there wasn't a soul in sight. Even the beggars had found a door to shut and lock.

Some stray emotions still drifted around lazily. Others either got recaptured or floated away into the sky. Maybe to reunite with the dead souls. Maybe Amin's terror was up there, showing them the way to heaven.

The terror wouldn't need to return to Amin anyway. I hoped he would never feel fear again.

I hoped that he was somewhere with a beach. He could make sandcastles in the soft sand while his parents watched from afar. He could swim in the endless ocean, as far as he wanted, without worry.

What killed me the most was how painful his death was. I kept thinking and rethinking about if there was anything I could have done differently. Or anything I could have said differently.

In my mind he was still next to the cliff, rotting. But in my heart, he was at the beach. And he was waiting for me.

Mom was there too.

She was also waiting for me.

And I hated to admit how many times I thought about turning myself in because I was waiting to see her just as much.

Maybe they'd make it quick after all. Just a quick gunshot and all the pain and all the suffering would be over. It would just be the fear that held me back.

I heard the sound of boots getting closer.

I heard empty chatter between two Empaths.

I didn't even bother to run. There was nowhere to run anyway. Either they found me or they didn't and I would rather be found sitting in the dirt than shot while trying to scale the fence or something.

I hated giving up, I did.

But I had no one left to fight for other than myself and I didn't think she was worthy of all the fighting anymore.

Chapter 13

I could tell that William was relieved to see me. Once he killed me, his city could go back to normal. Everyone would be so much happier if I was dead.

I understood.

I would be happier too.

William sat me in a chair, facing him, with two Empaths behind me standing guard.

"So you didn't try to fight?" he asked. "Or run?"

I stayed quiet.

"But you screamed, however. I almost heard you from here, quite a set of pipes you have."

"They were rough with me," I responded. "But they didn't crucify me right away, like I thought. Why am I here? What do you possibly want with me? I set the emotions free and you caught me. Game over. Just shoot me or banish me and I'll die and we can move on."

"Shooting you would be too easy," William said. He rummaged around in his desk drawer and pulled out a piece of paper. There were multiple names scrawled in gold ink. Mom's and Amin's were what made me realize what the list was.

William had made the list to show me the people 'I' had killed. It was to make me realize how many people were affected by 'my' actions.

"I get it," I said.

William smiled. "Glad. We haven't tallied up the rest of the innocent citizens murdered by the bomb yet but-"

"And who sent that bomb?" I asked.

"Excuse me?" William asked.

"And who provided the gun that shot Amin? And who pushed my mother off the balcony? And Amin's mother? I suppose she fell off the balcony with that rope around her neck?"

William placed the paper down and folded his hands. He smiled at me, but the anger in his eyes was too noticeable to be hidden by his sneer.

"I was hoping you could understand some things, Miss Vane," Willam said. "It seems that you can't. I was hoping we could kill you more peacefully. That is what we had decided after all, but it seems we will go with the latter."

William looked up at the Empaths.

"Please, ready the materials for hebdomad torture."

I was horrified at what that could even mean, but I didn't show it. I needed to stay strong. I couldn't give William the satisfaction of my suffering any longer.

The Empaths yanked me up and led me down the hall. I turned around best I could to see William beaming, right before his office doors were shut in my face.

"What is hebdomad torture?" I asked the Empaths.

They didn't respond. They didn't even look at me. They just continued to march me down the hall, going at a pace that was just fast enough to be uncomfortable.

"If he's going to torture me shouldn't I know how?" I hissed through my teeth. "I'm going to die anyway."

I tried to jerk free from the grasp of the guards. If I could just break loose and start running, they would most likely just shoot me in the head, and I wouldn't have to go through with the pain that was surely headed my way.

My plan to make my death less painless didn't work, since they had an iron grip. They still didn't say a word as I thrashed and swung in their arms. One placed his hand on his gun though, which was a small step in the right direction.

They ended up throwing me into a small room and quickly locking the door behind them. The room had no decorative furniture or giant statues littering the walls and the floor.

It was completely empty.

I was the only thing in the room besides an overhead light above that was way too high up for me to reach.

"This is it?" I screamed. "I starve to death? Or- or die from dehydration? Why can't you just execute me like every other prisoner? Go to hell William! You can be obsessed with me from there!"

My tangent left me with no reply and the room filled with muggy clouds of fury.

I slumped down against the wall and tried to wave it away, glancing up at the ceiling. If my fear remained it would be clouding up the room as well.

I couldn't stop thinking about it. Slowly going insane in the empty room. Starving and dehydrated. I couldn't find a quicker way to die with nothing in the room to help me.

"This can't be it," I whispered. "There are no cameras. He would want to watch you die. He would broadcast it. This isn't it. It'll be quicker than this."

I stared up at the light as long as I could to see if there was somehow a hidden camera in it. I couldn't see anything, but the light was too bright for me to notice anyhow.

I laid down on the cool floor and closed my eyes, dreaming of how wonderful existing would be once I was dead.

Guards woke me up, dragging me to my feet and walking me out the door at that same uncomfortably fast pace.

I kept quiet but was screaming inside. It was relieving to know that they were at least letting me see something other than those four unbearably blank walls.

They led me through stairs and down hallways. I took in all the enrichment I could get. Gawked at unique shapes and colors other than white and gold. I knew that I would end up in that room again. Left to mentally rot. There were no patterns in there, no colors, nothing to interact with.

It was... torture.

Was that what William meant?

Did hebdomad torture mean nothing to see or do? I would rot and mentally decline until I was nothing but putty to Wiliam's greedy fingers. I would probably find a way to kill myself, and William would watch and he would beam at how impossibly clever he was to deprive me like this.

The Empaths pushed open a large door and shoved me inside. Once again the door was shut in my face.

I turned around to see a long table, filled with food and drink. William sat at the end of it, smiling gaily.

I looked to each end of the room, taking a mental note of the Empaths clenching their guns. Perfect. If I could do something bad enough they would shoot me and-

"Don't get any ideas," William said.

I ran my fingertips along the table as I pretended to observe the food, acting as if I didn't have any ideas at all. I had dozens of ways that the Empaths could shoot me and this horrible nightmare would be over with, but William didn't need to know that.

"Those aren't bullets in the guns." He said. "Just darts. They'll make you fall asleep. I told you that you couldn't give up this easily."

His words cut through my soul and left wisps of anger darting around the room. William sneered when he noticed them, straightening his posture proudly.

I took more steps around the table, looking at all the expensive food I had never seen let alone tasted.

It was just what Amin and I had described.

Plates of turkey and steak. Ham and oysters galore, toppling towers of them. Piles of truffles and bottles of wine.

Amin's voice played over and over in my head.

"I guess mice are too poor for William. Bullshit."

I got to the plate of truffles. Dark and light chocolate. Some had more chocolate drizzled on top. They were so perfect. I wished Amin was here to try them. His voice didn't leave my mind, not once.

"They just sound rich."

A big plate of ham lay just before William. It was drizzled in some sort of caramel glaze, sliced in thin, meaty, ovals.

"Ham and oysters. The finest pigs. Freshly caught seafood."

I tried not to show how hungry I was. I figured if I lunged at the food I could get a few bites in before I got shot with one of the darts. Or I could clench it in my arms? Hide some in my shirt?

When I woke up I could check if it was there. Maybe they wouldn't notice. Or they would feel bad.

No, that was stupid. Eating as much as I could would be a better plan. It just might work if-

"Are you going to just stare or are you going to sit?"

I looked up at William.

I said not one word.

"The food is going to get cold," he said. "I suggest you sit so that we can start eating."

"We?"

"Yes. I need to discuss something with you."

He took his plate and began taking his helping of food. I retrieved my plate but didn't touch any food that he didn't get. It was too dangerous.

Once we sat down, he took a bite of his ham. I waited until he chewed and swallowed to take a bite of mine.

Next were the oysters. I waited until he had swallowed them as well.

He didn't touch the truffle on his plate with the lighter chocolate, so neither did I. It was all too dangerous. Too suspicious. He had access to too much poison and too many murderous drugs. Drugs that wouldn't only kill me but would send unbearable waves of pain through every muscle in my body.

"Now Miss Vane. I understand you are confused. I understand that you are upset with me. I am upset with you as well. Why did you murder all those Empaths? All those people?"

"They were going to kill me," I responded. "Self-defense. That's all it was."

"You don't understand what I mean when I say the term 'hebdomad torture', do you?" he asked.

I shook my head, noticing that he had completely chewed and swallowed his potatoes. So I scooped a forkful into my mouth.

"Hebdomad. It's a group of seven. Commonly used to describe a week. Now you see... besides the dozens that were murdered by the bomb... seven murders have happened because of you."

I slammed my fork against the table. A tendril of fog began to circle it. William took a bite of a darker chocolate truffle. I held mine in my hand, waiting for him to swallow.

"There was your mother. And that sweet boy Amin."

The tendril grew into dozens of tendrils.

"Then *his* mother, of course. You smashed a hammer into one of my youngest Empaths, Jerid..."

The tendrils developed into a sheet of anger.

"You shot one, Eruth, and stole her thumb to open and close the gate as you please."

He swallowed his truffle. I angrily popped mine into my mouth. The sheet grew into a cloud. My eyes began to water. The air became thick and hot.

"Oh and then Joel and Culley. Very tricky what you did there... with the flour? Now that talleys up to seven. I assume you can add those simple numbers... not by the looks of you. No schooling, I assume?"

"You set that system up. There are hardly any schools. And you are happy to just sit and watch your people fade into nothing. Why don't you have the vaccine William? Why?"

I started to scream, standing up and growing my cloud of anger by the second. The core circled around the room but no one would take it. Again, too quick of a death.

The guards took a lunge towards me and aimed their guns for my head, forcing me to sit back down and bite my tongue until I tasted blood.

"Besides the point," William said. "Seven murders. One day of torture for each murder. The seventh day will be your final day. I do hope you enjoyed your food. I assume you will not be very hungry for long, pain does weird things to a person. Ask your dear friend Amin, who you murdered. He must have been in a lot of pain, hm?"

"I didn't murder him."

"And I wish he could be here to testify for you."

"I didn't murder him."

"Perhaps your dear mother could bail you out. Or your father? Any would be acceptable."

I stood up and headed for the door, flipping the plate of oysters nearest me on the way out. The two Empaths who had escorted me were waiting. They grabbed my arms and began the long walk down the hall.

I left streams of anger as I walked, marking my trail.

The once-extravagant flavors of the meal now tasted nothing but bitter on my tongue.

To punish my behavior, they placed me back in the barren room. To punish them back I showed no emotion. I counted seconds in my head, trying to time them perfectly.

I thought about Mom.

I tried to think about Mom, at least. I was on the verge of tears after only a couple of minutes and I was too deep into the plan of showing no emotion to cave now.

They took me out once, and led me to a bathroom. It was below them, to let such a prisoner piss on their pristine tiles.

I took in everything that I could. The feeling of the cold water from the sink. The taste of it as well. The smell of the soap. The different atmosphere.

I rubbed some of the soap on the back of my hand to smell later, so that I didn't go completely insane. I stuffed balls of wet toilet paper into my clothes so that I could get some sort of stimulation in the room.

When I walked out the guards were waiting. They gave me a pat down and removed most of the toilet paper but couldn't remove the soap. I was disappointed but remained calm, any emotions shown would be a gain in the egos of William and every Empath that worked here.

They sent me back to the room immediately after. I tried to fight them, so that they would just shoot me, but they resisted. I landed on the unforgiving floor with a bang, grunting due to the pain that shot through my ankle.

I tore out the rest of the toilet paper from my clothes and laid it out in front of me. I shuffled it around with my fingers, trying to think of something to do. The frustration came over me in a wave so I ended up balling it up and chucking it against the door. It did nothing, hardly even made a sound.

I made sounds though.

I cried and screamed and cursed William until I fell to the floor, my voice hoarse and my head throbbing. Waves of anger throbbed with me, emerging from my head and clouding up the already claustrophobic room.

I placed my hands over my head and wallowed, trying to close my eyes and sleep the week away. The Empaths woke me up, barging into my room. In their hands they held a loaf of bread and a pill.

"We aren't leaving until this is swallowed." one said. "One way or another."

They approached me, sliding latex gloves onto their evil hands, and pried my mouth open. I tried to scream and resist, letting them do as little as they could to me, but they forced me to swallow the pill.

In return for my 'compliance' they gave me only half the loaf of bread, chucking it behind them on their way out.

I hated that I pounced on the thing.

I hated that I nearly swallowed it whole.

And I really hated that I was behaving exactly how William wanted me to.

I woke up the next morning with a throbbing pain in my neck. I groaned and touched it before pulling away. Touching it only made the throbbing worse.

The Empaths barged through the door and pulled me to my feet. They began to drag me down the hall. I recognized the pattern of the hallways, they were taking me back to where I had a feast with William.

I tried to defy.

I tried to get shot.

I screamed and wailed all the way down the hallway, cursing William, cursing the Empathorium, and cursing any people who could hear me. I caught a glimpse of a window and could make out that it was around noon. I tried to remember as much as I could about the outside world, it stopped me from going crazy. Slowly and slightly, but still certain.

My neck was killing me but no Empath answered the questions I was throwing at them in between my screams.

They pushed me through the same doors and sure enough, a feast with William.

There were some of the same foods, ham and truffles and wine, but there were new foods, little cookies and a giant turkey and pitchers of lemonade. I ran my finger against the tablecloth once again, wanting to run and strangle William but the Empaths were still in the corners, armed with the darts.

"If you sit, I will answer your questions," William said.

I glared at him as I sat, grabbing a turkey leg and taking a massive bite. I couldn't care less about the poison anymore, if the pills kept increasing my pain I would rather go out some easy way. Poison wouldn't be too bad.

"The names of those guards? What are they?" William asked. I stayed silent, causing him to answer his own question. "Empaths. And this building, Empathorium? It's all about empathy here, Seraphai."

I scoffed, reaching for a bottle of wine.

"I wish you could understand how badly I care about this city running smoothly. It's life or death to me. Hence, I make it my biggest effort to control the emotions through the virtue of everlasting empathy. And it's what's causing the pain in your neck."

When he mentioned it, the pain got worse.

"Me *feeling bad* doesn't cause this," I responded, my tone drenched with disgust and annoyance. "It's that pill."

"Well of course. But we would never torture you so randomly. William continued. "Everyone you killed, they all, for the most part, died differently, pained in a different location. Today, we started with your mother. Oh, how horrible. A rope to the-"

"Neck," I said, gasping in utter realization, cutting him off. I didn't want to understand him but I did.

William raised his eyebrows.

I touched my neck, my fingers slightly shaking as they brushed against the irritated skin. The wave of frustration returned, stronger now than ever.

I grabbed the nearest fork and slammed it into the table. It stuck standing upright. Streams of rage blew across the table towards William.

"For seven days?" I screeched. "A different... how they... just to torture..."

I was so angry and horrified that no words came out but instead only sounds. I didn't storm out again though, and I took note of the Empaths clenching their guns tighter.

I was too hungry and thirsty and sensory deprived to willingly storm back into that room, no matter how angry William made me.

I sat myself back down and tried to ignore my neck the best that I could, shoving more and more food into my mouth.

William smirked at me, pleased with how vulnerable I was acting. He reached for the ham.

I scanned the table. There were no knives, all the food was pre-cut and pre-portioned. I couldn't do any harm with the serving forks, and I couldn't break the glasses quick enough to do any harm before I got shot with a tranquilizer.

I thought about what William had said while I forced myself to eat and drink as much as I could.

Amin's mother and Mom got hung. Two days with my neck like this. Amin was shot in his stomach. I hit the Empath on the head with the hammer. Oh shit, Culley and Joel... their whole body was in flames...

But they wouldn't.

They couldn't.

My whole body feeling like this?

No.

I reached upward to touch the ache in my neck but stopped myself when I noticed William's smirk widening. He had no business enjoying the pain he put me in. Instead, I busied myself by drinking another cup of wine, hoping that forcing myself to become drunk would help take the pain away.

William ate and drank his fill too, trying to break the silence with scattered attempts at conversing with me. I stayed silent, ripping another leg off of the turkey or unwrapping another truffle.

Finally, he said something that piqued my curiosity and interest. But not in a good way. The torture never ceased.

"Ironic. The death of your parents."

I froze. A strand of anger circled my fingers. My neck continued to throb, causing me to become even more agitated. It was a struggle to calm down and ask William what he meant in a civilized fashion.

"How so?" I managed through gritted teeth.

"Your death too. An entire bloodline lost to protect the hidden emotions." he sighed. "And it was all for nothing anyway. They got out. The people know. Lives were lost. And that's part of the reason we had to make you endure this."

He had to bring it up, he always had to. Every time he did I remembered the pain and it began to bother me again. It was a battle not to show my agony.

"So, have you learned your lesson yet?" William asked, smiling as he topped off his glass of wine.

"I gain nothing from saying yes," I responded. "It only makes your ego swell. The people have done quite enough of that, haven't they?"

"That's not the question. Have you learned that you aren't as powerful as you think?"

"Only if you have."

The room fell silent. One Empath took a daunting step towards me.

I ended the conversation at that, leaving the table with my fork still in my hand. I burst through the doors and allowed the Empaths to lead me back to my room, trying to resist when they ripped the fork from my fingers.

"Visitation hour is soon." one told me, before shutting the door. I didn't know why. If they wanted to deprive me of information and entertainment, telling me something to look forward to couldn't be their best effort. On the other hand, they were only people.

I was only a person.

Maybe just one Empath held true to their name and cared for someone other than William.

It was a stupid thing to hope for but it was something to hope for and that was golden.

It felt like an eternity, sitting in that room, throwing my old toilet paper balls and wishing that the pain would just go away.

I tried hard to sleep and not to cry but a couple of tears unwillingly slipped out. I hid my face from the camera, if it was even there, and silently wept, letting out just a bit of my agony but not enough.

The guards ended my pity party by bursting through my door. They grabbed my arms and lifted me up, starting my long walk to what I assumed was the visitation hour. I had no free arms to wipe my face, leaving anyone who wanted to visit me able to see my puffy eyes and tear-stained cheeks.

I had no living family or friends. It was a pointless hour. At least I got some enrichment.

If only visitation hour was what I thought it was.

I assumed I would be sat in a room, hopefully with a comfortable chair, and anyone who wanted to see me in my final days could.

Oh, but that wasn't torturous enough.

I wasn't in enough agony.

I wasn't embarrassed or humiliated enough.

They led me out the Empathorium doors and hustled me down the stairs. I blinked rapidly in the blinding sunlight, inhaling massive amounts of fresh wind. It was tainted with the remains of lost emotions, but clear nonetheless.

Once my eyes adjusted, I noticed the box.

It was big enough for me to move around in, made of pure glass, with a grid of holes lining the ceiling.

Crowds of any remaining citizens waited a couple of feet from it. They screamed and cursed when they saw me, stopping themselves from rushing to beat me up only because of the Empaths.

I eyed the crowd, wondering how such great minds could be tainted by William's words. I was their enemy. *I* was the one who killed their family, not the leaders who dropped the bomb.

The Empaths opened a hidden door in the glass and shoved me inside. I hit the floor with a thump, turning around to the glass getting slammed in my face. The Empaths keeping the people tame started to move out of the way, breaking the floodgates.

The crowds lined every inch of my box, screaming barely comprehensible insults at me.

It was unbearably overwhelming, too many lights and noises and words after being locked in that room for so long.

I covered my ears and tried to curl up in a corner, getting startled out of it when people started to kick my box, sending violent vibrations through the glass. I only hoped it was strong enough.

My neck continued to throb, adding to my discomfort. There was nothing I could do but cover my ears and ball up in the middle of the box. I tried to block out the insults, but multiple slipped past my fingers, no matter how hard they tried to cover it all up.

"You killed my brother! You useless piece of-"

"My wife was down there! We could have lived in peace but you were greedy and you were-"

"You had to kill every Empath you saw? You shot my daughter you disgusting, wretched, diabolical-"

"You weren't happy with the government because they hung your useless excuse for a mother? I swear if you weren't hiding in that damn box I would-"

Wave after wave of insults. People poured vile smelling substances and shoved garbage down the air holes on top, but were stopped by the Empaths when they tried to block them. Suffocating would have been a nicer death than torture, but I was still happy the Empaths stopped them.

When one person got tired of yelling another took their spot and picked up the slack.

Kids wailed and sobbed about their parents, pressing their snot-stained noses against the glass.

Teenagers experimented with curse words and tried to kick and punch my box best they could.

Adults shattered my self confidence, hurling the most creative yet hurtful insults at me with astounding speed. Even though there were what felt like a million voices at once, I could still somehow hear just about every insult clear as day.

Some were unserious.

Lots were overused.

Some broke my self confidence down so low that I made it my best attempt to smush my fingers into my ears even tighter, in order to block out any more hurtful words.

My neck was what made the whole thing so horrible. I could handle insults, especially after hundreds of them, but when I was so vulnerable and weak it was harder to stay strong.

There were one or two kind souls, who somehow understood me and saw past what William had probably lied about to make all the people hate me so much.

Those people screamed not insults, but kind words at me. They told me that it was alright, that I was just a kid and didn't deserve this. They tried to tell the other people in the crowd too, but quickly got shoved aside and replaced by another insane heckler.

My ears and palms were sweaty within minutes. At least the headache I developed numbed the pain my neck was in. The more comfortable I got, hands over my ears, curled into a ball on the glass floor, the more insane the crowd got.

They even tried to pry open the glass door to get to me, but it was sealed shut. Only the Empaths could open it, I assumed with fingerprints.

When they couldn't open my door, they settled with rocking my box back and forth until my weak body was slammed against every wall. The Empaths made them stop, however, when they almost tipped the whole thing over.

Clouds of fury and sadness fogged up the outside, which only increased the yelling as people tried to search for any cores they could snatch up.

It was the longest hour of my life, and I was beyond relieved when the Empaths shoved everyone aside and opened the door. I sat upward and stared at their cold expressions, feeling the weight of the world being lifted off my shoulders.

I had to use every bit of my self control to prevent myself from leaping into their arms and skipping back to my quiet little room with glee.

Instead, I stayed quiet and let them drag me upward, stumbling out of the little box and into the hot air.

The crowd reached out and tried to grab me, but got shoved backwards. They continued to yell however, wishing me the worst of death threats and spitting in my direction.

It was a struggle to walk up the stairs, especially after being hunched in a ball for an hour. It was even more of a struggle with the mob that followed, marching up the stairs with a sense of false importance.

The Empaths yelled at or shoved anyone who got too close but said nothing about the endless screams and outbursts of profanity.

The crowd continued to yell and pound on the door even after I was back inside the Empathorium. My mind still swam, although it was grateful for the silence. I got led to the bathroom, where I refreshed myself best I could, given the circumstances.

I splashed water on my face. It was freezing but it helped my mind clear.

I rubbed more soap on the back of my hand, and I stuffed more toilet paper down my clothes. I wet my hair, just so that I could feel it drying. Funny enough I was excited about it, my mind was slowly disintegrating and just water in general was enough to keep it entertained for hours.

I kept myself busy until the Empaths pounded menacingly on the door and threatened to tear it down if I wasn't out soon. I got a chill that told me they weren't joking.

"I'm sorry... that room..." I whispered. Only I could hear my plea but that was how I wanted it. No signs of weakness. I couldn't let it happen. I had to face that room until tonight, when I would get my pill and then sleep.

It was bright outside, during visitation hour at least, which was disappointing because that meant it was a while until I was tired enough to fall asleep.

When the door slammed, I took out any toilet paper they didn't find and inhaled a whiff of the soap on my hand.

"They killed Mom. You didn't kill her." I muttered. "They killed her. They killed Amin, it wasn't you. They are confused."

I froze in fear when I heard the marching of what I assumed were Empaths in the distance. My neck hurt horribly, and I couldn't bear it if they decided one form of torture wasn't enough. If they marched in and decided to beat me or let citizens beat me.

But the coast was clear after a while, the boots stomped right past my door and on into the next hallway. I continued to convince myself that I was innocent, forcing the insults and curses out of my mind best I could.

"I didn't, did I? No, it was Drew. He... he kept you in that room and he chased you down into the emotions and you had to kill to escape."

The voice in my head, the one that I wanted to be anywhere else at the moment, argued with me.

You didn't have to shoot anyone lethally. Or kill by hammer. Amin's mother did nothing wrong, you did. Oh... and poor Amin died because you were waiting for him to.

"No. No. That's not right." I whispered.

Culley and Joel, they were trapped already. Did you have to drop that match? You could have run and they would be fine. You would have gotten away anyway.

"Oh God..."

And Mom. Did she stumble across those stray emotions? Or did she just get hung for it. And did you beg and plead with William and give yourself up to spare her? Or did you watch from the crowd as she fell?

I hid my face from the camera while I wept. Begging the voice to stop. It couldn't stop because it was me and I was right.

I could only pray that the week would be over soon. That *I* would be over soon.

I did fall asleep, eventually, but it was a struggle. I felt that as soon as my eyes and mind closed for good, I was being shaken awake by Empaths. They said nothing but handed me another pill.

I was almost grateful to take it, something other than my neck would hurt. Unless of course Amin's mother was next, in which case my neck would hurt the exact same.

"What happens if I don't take it?" I asked. "You kill me? You torture me?" my voice was raw, from all the sobbing and screaming. It hurt to speak but I managed to choke out those words.

"We hold you down and inject you," one of the Empaths answered. "With the same medicine."

"We figured we'd give you a *choice*." the other sneered. His smile caused a wisp of anger to flee from my hand and disapparate into him. My expression of emotion only made him smile wider, knowing he made me horribly infuriated.

"How *empathetic*," I muttered, swallowing the pill and lying back down on the floor. I felt four evil eyes staring into my back before the thump of boots let me know that they had left.

I had cried horribly from agony and fear, but I nearly cried tears of happiness when the pain in my neck began to subside. I fell asleep before the new pain kicked in, somewhat content to the naked eye, but, based on my past experiences, exceedingly comfortable all the same.

I woke up before the Empaths led me to my meal with William. I winced when I sat up, clutching my head.

"The hammer," I whispered, touching the wound and then pulling away. I didn't know if having the pain in my head was better or worse than in my neck. On one hand, it was a more condensed spot, but I already got migraines during visitation hour and I didn't know how much pain my head could take before I went crazy.

I entertained myself and tried to forget about my pain, by trying to make myself believe that I was innocent. I needed a reason to fight or I would die a lamb, clenched in the bloody jowls of the lion that was the Empathorium.

"They killed Mom. William pushed her off that ledge. They killed Dad with the poison. He just wanted firewood..."

I flicked a ball of toilet paper across the room.

"You survived. You are going to die but you survived. They are trying to make you crazy, do *not* give in. You are not crazy."

I flicked another ball.

"The Empaths you killed... it was self-defense. They would have shot you... one shot Amin... Amin was afraid to die.

He was afraid." I started to yell. "And you stood there and let him, why couldn't you have died instead!"

I hurled the last ball at the wall, but it didn't shatter into a thousand pieces or make a satisfying thud like I needed. It barely sailed across the room before fluttering to the ground.

My head started to throb as streams of anger poured from my fingers. I placed a ginger hand on top of where it hurt, but the pain wasn't a pain that could be solved by pressure or bandages. It was something within, something horrible that ached and twisted my brain into knots.

I inhaled the sweet smell of soap on the back of my hand in an attempt to calm myself down. The waxy waft of fresh fruit calmed me down a bit but did not ease nearly as much pain as I needed it to.

My eyes flickered to the door as the Empaths walked in, grabbing my arms and leading me away.

"Why do I have to see him?" I groaned. "Please don't make me see him, I can't listen... he's..."

I didn't expect them to respond and they didn't. The only thing they would respond to is if I had a heart attack and dropped dead, even then, they would probably just be grateful and burn me.

They shoved me through the doors, nearly pushing me right into my chair. I sat myself down with a sigh, fighting not to touch my head or show any signs of pain.

"The *youngest Empath ever*," William said, grinning. "And you put a hammer against his fragile skull. Shame isn't it."

I eyed the table. There were platters of seafood more than anything else, most of the fish I had never seen before and definitely never learned about.

There were the same old things, a honey glazed ham, wine, truffles, that were gold this time, and different pitchers full of colored liquid. I couldn't tell if it was juice or more alcohol, but I hoped the latter so that I could become drunk and my pain would subside.

"Why do you make me do this?" I asked.

"We've gone over this," William said. "You need to pay for your actions to bring back *some* of the peace that you wrongfully destroyed."

"Not the torture." I continued. "Why do you bring me here and sit me down at this table and place all these rich foods in front of me and let me gorge myself? What do you gain? Are you fattening me up to burn at the stake? So that everyone in the city can try a bite of the famous criminal?"

William reached for a pitcher of gold liquid. It looked shiny, too shiny, just as fake as everything that was rich.

"I want to know why you murdered the innocent," he said. "What did *you* gain from it?"

Why *I* murdered the innocent?

I murdered the innocent?

I murdered the innocent.

I racked my brain for an answer. I knew it was self defense, that was what I had been repeating to keep myself sane, but I had let the accusations and harsh words cut me to the core.

"I don't know," I whispered.

I could hear my heartbeat in my head, sending horrible vibrations through my skull.

"You're the monster," William told me.

"I'm the monster," I repeated.

"So you agree that this is a fair punishment? It's only right after all. Don't you wish you could have taken Amin's place? He could be alive and thriving, with his wonderful mother by his side."

It was hard to think, all I could repeat in my head was how much pain I was in. I hoped that I could get the strength to do something other than shovel food into my mouth, something that would get me shot with that dart. I would slip into my dreams, my pain disintegrated.

"Yes. It's all my fault." I murmured.

I hated the feasts with William. He ripped any shreds of empathy from my soul and used them to torture me, both literally and figuratively. He twisted my words and rearranged my thoughts, leaving me to believe I deserved the torture. A tiny part of me knew I didn't but was too afraid that he would torment me more to speak up.

It was only fair after all.

It was only fair?

Was it only fair?

The tiny fire that kept me reaching towards freedom and equality ignited once more, not as severe as before but enough to push me the step forward that I needed.

"So you'll die at the end of the week too?" I asked. "And the pills... you must be taking those."

"Excuse me?" William asked, eying his guards.

"Well I caused seven deaths," I responded. "But a lot more than seven people have died inside these very walls... haven't they?"

William fell silent.

"Haven't they?"

"I didn't murder them. Not like you did. I didn't pull the trigger, or swing the hammer, or go snooping inside other people's basements." he sneered. "They died of their injuries. Or starvation."

"And who limited their food? Anyone who eats like this can spare enough to save the starving. Anyone with this many rooms can afford to spare some for the homeless."

I stared right into his two evil eyes, unafraid.

"And who pulled the trigger on Mortia? Who made her hide with the beggars because of the rumor *you* made up?"

With no warning, Empaths burst through the door and took me away. William smiled while I kicked and fought in their arms. I don't know how they heard me, or how William could have alerted them, but the whole Empathorium ran like a hive and I had just upset the king bee.

Chapter 14

Before I knew it I was in that box, surrounded by the same people, who had everything and nothing to say all at once.

That was the thing with people. And noise. It could fill an empty room but it was mostly meaningless. The insults that were thrown at me only proved my point. Meaningless gossip. Chatter. Yelling. Loud.

I don't know how they managed to come up with new insults for an hour straight but they did, and the ache in my head only increased.

It went from a dull throb to a searing flash in a matter of minutes. I clenched my sweaty hands around my ears and dug my fingernails into my skull but nothing helped. I couldn't tell whether the liquid dripping down my face was my sweat or my tears. It could have been blood too, I wouldn't have noticed the difference or cared enough to check.

"You deserve every ounce of pain you are in! Every sharp pain, every dull twinge, every-"

"I hope your death is as slow as you made my son's! You disgusting, wretched, selfish-"

"My daddy! You killed my daddy!"

Each one hurt but the children sobbing for their dead parents hurt the worst. Any remaining figures in their life brought them there on purpose, I could tell. With the one intent to torture me further.

When the people concluded that words didn't hurt me enough, they resorted to shaking the box again. The Empaths had to stop them once more, before they tipped me over or sent me tumbling.

"I'm sorry!" I wailed, hoping someone could hear me. "I'm in pain, I'm in so much pain! I'm so sorry!"

The noise got quieter but never subsided. Some people began to stand up for me, probably after hearing my cries, pushing the mob back and yelling at them.

An angry father punched a man who pushed him aside. Two teenagers yelled over who was right and who was wrong about me. A mother and father tussled for their child, one adamant on leaving and one adamant on teaching the child that criminals deserve punishment.

A handful of small bickers turned into dozens of full out fights. The Empaths had to pull me out once a body slammed against the glass I was in, streaking blood from their nose onto it.

They elbowed and shouldered anyone trying to get to me out of the way, pushing me forward and up the stairs. I stumbled up them, wanting to cradle my head but my arms were pinned.

A couple of stragglers followed me and yelled but most were still either fighting or caught in the mess. All I could think about was getting through the bathroom and then finally returning to my little corner of my little room to sleep.

I rubbed some more soap on my hand, even though I was usually too busy sleeping and writhing in pain to smell it. I took the time to wet my hair just to feel something other than my head throbbing, and willingly let the Empaths throw me through my door. I hit the ground hard, staying down.

However, instead of shutting the door, one Empath began to walk down the hall while another stayed to look at me.

I curled into a ball and clenched my head, still feeling two eyes on my shoulders but too fed up to care. Of course I wondered what the Empaths were doing, and the feeling of being left in the dark gnawed at me but I had to stay strong.

I finally gave in to curiosity, after about five minutes of sitting quietly in pain, and demanded to know what was going on. I knew they probably wouldn't tell me, but hope kept me asking anyway.

"Here to make sure I don't feel an ounce of comfort?" I asked the Empath. He stayed silent for a while, barely moving a muscle, before answering me.

"William has decided it's too humane to let you sleep the pain away," he responded. "You are to feel what others felt and you are not to cheat the system of this hebdomad torture."

"No one besides Amin spent over three seconds in pain." I snapped back. "You can try to justify this and recite William's lying decrees to me but you know that this is wrong, no matter how hard you try to believe your king."

The other Empath returned, carrying a projector and rolling a small gold and white table behind him. He set up the table in my room, and placed the projector on top of it, perfectly centered. The gold began to hurt my eyes, after staring at it for too long.

The spotless setup certainly didn't belong in my room, which had begun to smell horribly and became musty from the amount of fury lost in it.

"Yay, movie night," I said, rolling my eyes.

The Empaths ignored me and turned out the single light in my room. I adjusted my eyes to the darkness and immediately became exhausted. I knew they would never let me sleep, and was horrified at what the screen could possibly show, but thought that maybe they would forget to turn the light back on when they left.

The Empaths pressed some buttons on the projector and a crisp image appeared. It was of a sobbing woman, who seemed to be in another room of the Empathorium, based on the array of white and gold items behind her.

"This is an innocent woman." one of the Empaths said. "On a live feed, broadcasting from this very Empathorium."

"What are you doing to her?" I whispered, my eyes stuck on the woman who was screaming and crying for her life.

Another Empath held out a pill towards me. I eyed it but didn't dare take it. I wouldn't unless they forced it into me.

"She is going to die in five minutes. A horrible death. Her worst fear actually, decapitation. And she knows this."

"How is this about me?" I screamed. "William is going to execute this woman and it'll get blamed on me?"

I stood up and reached for the projector to turn it off but the Empath holding the pill sent his boot into my back and I fell to the floor once again.

They both grabbed an arm and pinned me down, angling my face so that I was forced to watch the wretched screen. The woman was begging me, pleading with me to spare her life.

"Yes!" I screamed. "Yes, I spare her! What the hell is this? Why are you doing this?"

I squirmed and fought in the arms of the Empaths, kicking and yanking but they were too strong for me.

"If you ingest this pill," one said, his voice drenched with struggle due to the fight to pin me down. "Your pain will double and the innocent woman will be spared. You have five minutes to decide."

"What?" I cried, struggling even more now. "Please stop this! This isn't my fault if she dies! How is this my fault?"

"Four minutes."

"Please!" The lady begged, taking a break from sobbing to plead. Even though she couldn't see me, she still found a way to stare directly into my eyes. The hand from one of the Empaths, I couldn't tell which, clenched my jaw, forcing me to stare into her eyes as well.

"Please stop. Please." I whispered.

I couldn't double the pain, I just couldn't. It would kill me, I was already mentally drained just from feeling the sting in my head for half of the day now.

"Stop this!" I screeched. "Stop! This isn't my fault! This is William's fault! God, someone please believe me! Oh God, please don't kill her! William, please don't kill her! You don't understand!" Tears began to stream down my cheeks, fast and hard due to the built up pain and frustration I had locked away for most of the day.

The woman began to struggle in her chair. She looked left and right, around the room, searching for anyone to help her besides relying on me. If only she heard my cries as much as I heard hers. If only she understood how badly I wanted to help her, how horribly I felt.

In her mind I was letting her die on purpose, no doubt. She either thought I was too selfish and too weak to double the pain or she had no idea about the pill and thought I simply wanted her dead because I was a ruthless killer.

I bet on the latter. There was no doubt in my mind that William was broadcasting me to the city right now, showing the people what a coldhearted killer I was. How selfish I was.

It's easy to judge someone for being selfish when you aren't the warm body at stake. When you aren't in pain.

"Three minutes."

"Are you understanding me?" I screamed murderously. "There's got to be some other way, you've got to understand! Don't make me the murderer for this! Don't make me watch this! Please!"

The Empaths held fast, gripping my face with sheer power and strength. I tried to plead and scream and let the people, who were no doubt watching me since I assumed I was being broadcasted, know that I had no intentions to harm the sobbing lady in front of me.

No one listened. No one cared. Nothing stopped or changed. No one came to save me and fight on my side.

"Two minutes."

My head screamed with pain, worse than it had ever been today, letting me know that I simply couldn't handle taking that pill and doubling my agony.

"Please save me! Please save me! Somebody please help me!" the woman screeched, her voice ringing in my ears. Her fear turned to anger, which was expressed in waves of smoke.

The camera obtained a red hue, which only further expressed the pure anger of the woman on her deathbed.

I blinked away my tears, trying to fight the growing feeling that told me I was being selfish and pushed me to just take that pill. The feeling was diminished by the searing hot pain throbbing through my skull, letting me know I simply could not take double.

"Wouldn't you want someone to help you? Please, oh, I have a family at home. I have a little girl. I have a husband. I've done no wrong, nothing wrong!"

"That makes two of us," I whispered, trying to look anywhere other than at the screen. Even if I closed my eyes, the torturous screams would still be heard and re-lived in my nightmares.

"One minute."

The pleading got louder and my headache grew stronger but I didn't give in. I gave up trying to explain my situation with anyone watching. I would always be the villain in their eyes and they had good reason to believe I was a ruthless killer, with the picture being painted of me by the propaganda William shoved down their gullible throats.

I squeezed my eyes as tight as I could and tried to block out the horrible sound of screaming and pleading once a minute was up. All too quick I heard the swish of a blade, a disturbing squelching sound, and then... finally... silence.

But it wasn't the sweet silence I hoped for. It wasn't silence that mended my headache and left my ears feeling still and sweet.

It was the deafening silence that constantly drilled a reminder through my aching brain. That an innocent person's head was on the floor because of me. Because I was a coward.

The selfishness continued when all I could hope for wasn't peace for her family or justice for her soul but that I wouldn't get another day added onto my torture for this.

The Empaths finally left me alone, scoffing at my weak little body as they left. I curled up into a ball, hands clenched over my ears, as if that could make up for the screams I had just heard.

They would pound on the door occasionally, a loud and sharp boom that would shake me out of whatever sleep I had finally slipped into. They never did it regularly either, every five minutes or so. *Sometimes* it would be minutes in between the thumps, and other times mere seconds.

All I knew is that it kept me awake and kept the pain thriving. I also knew that there was something so horribly wrong about anyone who became an Empath. There was nothing you could pay me to torture and watch the tortured like this. I had to do it enough just surviving in the city, let alone for fun.

I tried distracting myself from the pounding on the door and the pain by rolling the spheres of toilet paper around but most had been crushed by a boot or kicked across the room.

I couldn't even get myself up to get them, I could only switch between cradling my ears and cradling my head.

"That wasn't your fault," I whispered.

Someone pounded the door.

Thump.

"William captured her. And put her in that chair. And killed her. That was not your fault."

It sure felt like my fault. I couldn't do anything about the endless murders but it was torture within itself to sit and watch them happen.

Thump.

There had to be someone out there that thought like me. And understood that William was behind this, not me. But they were doing what I would probably be doing too. Hiding in their homes, locking the doors, sheltering what little crap they had left and stockpiling food for whatever apocalypse was sure to come from this.

I couldn't even think of any apocalypse that was worse than living inside the city. A tsunami would bring water at least. Same with a hurricane. A tornado would tear the Empathorium down. A nuclear war would kill us all, and quickly.

The only apocalyptic murderer was sitting on his gold and white throne, hiding away resources so that he could pretend like he was gracious giving the people what he did.

Thump.

And it angered me how much his plans worked.

I fell asleep at some point, somehow. The Empaths either stopped pounding on my door or I had found a way to block it out. Either way they shook me awake and handed me another pill, reaching out their hand as if I had a choice.

I took it, only because I didn't want them to pry my mouth open and nearly rip my jaw off again. I scoffed as I got a better look at the pill. Of course it was white and gold, I couldn't escape the two colors I hated most.

They were too clean.

Too rich.

Too bright.

I reluctantly took the pill, too drowsy and weak to even wonder what came next. I knew that I still had Culley and Joel left, which was going to kill me since they burned to death.

I also had Amin's mother, and Amin. And the guard that I shot although I couldn't remember where. I thought it was the head but I had seen too many deaths to remember who got shot where or who died when.

I laid my head back down and breathed a deep sigh of content when the horrible, hot pain in my head began to fade. Much like before, I fell asleep too quickly to feel any other discomfort settle in.

The Empaths woke me up, but not to have my meal with William. I was afraid they would roll that projector in and make me choose again but they only woke me up so that I couldn't sleep the pain away.

My stomach hurt horribly, a deep, fleshy pain. It was centered around the abdomen, but more or less hurt everywhere. I blinked back tears as I felt poor Amin's suffering. He had dealt with it for days, barely complaining but rather just surviving.

"Oh Amin, I'm so sorry," I whispered, struggling to stand up. I could argue that Amin had it worse because he didn't only have to deal with the pain but the endless blood and ichor pouring from the wound as well.

I took a couple of painful steps around the room, trying to remain calm and breathe deep. The Empaths and William wouldn't let me skip out on a day of walking just because I was in pain. If anything, they'd make me run a marathon or take laps around the Empathorium.

And it wouldn't matter how much agony I was in or how much I apologized. It would never be enough and I would always be the enemy.

I was everything and nothing to the people all at once, everything to torture but nothing to help. Everything to blame but nothing to understand. Everything to worry about but nothing to worry for.

The Empaths smiled when they saw me struggling. That was the only reason they hadn't slammed the door yet, to watch me stumble around the room and find any position that was comfortable enough to relax.

I tried to remember best what positions Amin had laid in so that he looked slightly comfortable. All I could remember upon hearing his name was his death. Slow, and full of torture, and devastating. But he had no family to cry for him and place flowers by his grave. He didn't even have a grave. His body was still out in the unforgiving sand, the sand that he hated, cold and alone.

I pressed my back against the wall and slid down to the floor, saying no words and showing no emotion, until the Empaths grabbed my arms and took me to have my meal.

I walked with importance, keeping my pace. I knew William would blame me for the innocent woman's death as soon as I walked in but only Amin's death was on my mind.

The Empaths shoved me through the door and lingered, probably not trusting that I could last a full five seconds without needing to be removed again.

"Well well well," William said.

I bit my tongue and sat down, resting my hand on my stomach in an attempt to lessen the pain.

"Now we know where your priorities lie," he continued.

"How is it my fault again?" I asked, in a strained yet calm voice. "Who kidnapped her, William? Who held the blade that sliced her neck? You can't pin *your* murders on me once I'm gone you know."

"Good reason to keep you around then."

I began to stuff my face with food and drink, not even bothering to place it on my plate first. I ate to avoid thinking about how great it would feel to murder William in the most painful way humanly possible. Preferably in front of a large crowd. Preferably now.

"Now, why didn't you take the pill?" William asked, pouring himself a glass of gold wine.

"Because I'm a bloodthirsty villain," I replied coldly, reaching for a vanilla cake with gold frosting. It had a serving fork but I just grabbed a chunk from the top, letting the frosting slide down my fingers.

"Hm." William reviled. "And that's what we have been hoping you would accept. *You* are the problem. *You* are the soul responsible for this mess. And you need to suffer to make up for the pain you caused dozens of families."

"Well it was easy to become like this," I said, playing along. William grinned, happy that he had finally broken me, happy that I had finally caved into the torture and believed his lies and rumors. "I mean, watching you all these years. It was only second nature."

I licked the frosting off of my fingers, glancing up to get a good look at William's face. He was angry but was fighting not to show it.

"We can increase the pain at any time," William told me. "Keep that in mind while you think about where your smart little mouth has gotten you."

The guards burst through the door and grabbed my arms, dragging me away before I could argue.

"Oh, I can't *wait* to avenge Culley and Joel." William laughed, forcing the last thing I saw before the door closed to be his cackling face.

I'm dead.

That was all I could think of. Over and over.

I'm dead. I'm dead. I'm so dead.

I could hardly stand the pain I was in now, not to mention if it was over my entire body.

What was he going to do to me?

How could he somehow twist everything I said and did to make me the villain? And have people believe him?

Why did everything he say have to fill my body with unimaginable fear that closed up my chest and sent me spiraling?

The only thing I could do to prevent a full-blown panic attack was to shove the feelings down deep and only worry about the pain that was in the present.

And it was there all right.

The Empaths pinned my arms so tight that I couldn't rest them on my stomach no matter how hard I fought. They only gripped me tighter and tighter, as they stormed through the halls just quick enough to leave me stumbling.

I had vague knowledge of how to get from place to place. It was the same routine every day.

My room, to the meal with William, to the bathroom, to visitation hour, and back to the room. I used my time in the bathroom wisely, with access to only one trip a day.

They had changed it to only one trip a day. I guess two trips were too kind. Too much water wasted on a living corpse.

The Empaths had shortened my time though, they started to pound on the door after around five minutes, yelling for me to get out if I didn't want them to break the door.

I barely had time to wet my hair and rub soap on my wrists before they opened the door and yanked me away from my stimulation. They left the water running too, money meant nothing to them.

Or perhaps it was a little rebellion towards William, letting the pristine water from the shiny gold tap run. He was the one who limited the water anyway and raised the bills for it.

I knew it was only the pain talking. An Empath rebelling was unheard of. They were too proud to have been chosen. Too spoiled with riches and guns.

Being an Empath was the safest job for your body but the most dangerous job for your mental health. If you were humane, but most weren't.

They threw me back inside the room, and I breathed a tiny sigh of relief when they didn't return with the projector.

I was also relieved because I didn't have to walk much anymore.

Walking hurt terribly, which only made me feel worse about how much I pressured Amin to walk to and climb the cliffs. It brought me back to our big argument, where I found it such a hassle and such a struggle to apologize to him.

I turned my head towards the ceiling, overwhelmed with guilt but too proud to burst into tears in front of William. I still suspected that the light had a camera in it, and any emotion I showed was surely being broadcasted to everyone in the city.

"I'm so sorry," I whispered, hoping that Amin could hear me. Hoping that he would forgive me, even if I was days too late. I told myself that he could, to calm myself down enough to get some sleep.

I had just closed my eyes for a couple of seconds, finally finding a comfortable enough position on the hard floor to doze off for a couple of hours. It felt pretty nice too, my wet hair providing a crisp chill to the back of my neck.

But it was too good to be true because the Empaths made it their liberty to pound on the door like there was no tomorrow.

I ended up drifting in and out of consciousness, which created a mind bending false reality. I didn't know if I was hallucinating or dreaming but whatever it was left me sweaty and confused once I woke up.

I rubbed my eyes and groaned, placing pressure on my aching stomach. It didn't help, but it tricked my mind into thinking it helped.

The guards came in a few minutes after I had woken up. They burst through the door and hustled me to my feet. I stumbled down the hallway with them, trying to match their pace, but I was in too much pain and too groggy to keep up.

They ended up halfway dragging me, clenching my wrists so tight that it almost distracted me from the pain my stomach was in.

The screaming started as soon as the people saw my face. They were more angry than ever now, after watching what 'I' had done to the innocent woman.

Their brains were replenished with waves of brand new insults, and they didn't hold back. They began pounding on my box with rage as soon as I was thrown in. I took only a second to look at my surroundings before huddling in a ball with my hands over my ears.

I had never seen so many emotions. Billows of rage and despair clouded up the glass and left stragglers wheezing. No matter where I turned there were faces, all of them angry.

Children lined the bottom half of the box, screaming and crying, trying to be angry because their parents were but ultimately unaware of my crimes.

I locked eyes with a scared little girl, who looked at the mob around her with fear. She tilted her head just slightly when she got a good look at me, which only proved my point regarding the innocence of the children brought to make me feel bad.

A sharp pound next to my ear caused me to flinch and break eye contact. After one pound came another, and another.

The Empaths didn't stop them. They weren't trying to flip me over or suffocate me and those were the only two things that required a break up to happen.

The horrible echo of the kicks and punches sent me to the ground, sheltering my ears and my stomach best I could with only two hands.

The noise didn't end. It filled my ears, diminishing whatever sanity and serenity was left in my brain.

"Murderer! Filthy murderer!"

"Justice! She was innocent!"

"Which one of us is next? Who will you decide to kill next? What's another tortured body to you?"

Any sensible person would stop and think. They would realize that William was the enemy and that it wasn't my fault.

None of this was.

Right?

I begged the Empaths to let me go back to my room once my stomach felt like it was being ripped apart and sewn back together again but they couldn't hear me. And they wouldn't let me. No matter how many tears I shed and how much pain was visibly shown on my face.

I could decide which was worth my hands, my stomach or my ears. I chose my ears because although shielding my stomach made the pain *seem* better, I knew it did nothing to help.

I rolled over to my left side, which is what Mom always told me to do when my stomach was in pain. It didn't fix anything and only reminded me of her death, leaving me both tortured *and* depressed.

"Get up and face us!"

"You deserve it! You can't make us feel bad for you, you disgusting scum of the earth!"

"Mommy? Daddy? I wanna go home!"

Me too, kid.

Me too.

If only there was a home for me to hide in.

As soon as I returned from visitation hour, the Empaths left the door open again. One waited while one disappeared.

"No. Please no. I can't do it." I begged.

But they didn't roll the projector in. Instead the Empath returned with just the pill.

"I don't even get a choice anymore?" I asked. "I just automatically have to endure it?"

"This pill will take away all of your pain. For a full twenty four hours you will be pain free. We will see you up not in this room but in one of our finest guest bedrooms."

"Very funny." I scoffed. "Either you're lying or there's a catch. I... I'm *not* killing anybody."

"They're already asleep. You just need to pull the trigger. No pain."

"I'm *not* killing anybody."

"William won't be happy if you-"

"If I don't comply? If I don't listen? I tried to listen to his rules my entire life and look where it left me. Tortured until I die."

The Empath twirled the pill in his fingers before leaving and shutting the door behind him. I looked up at the light, where I was sure the camera was now, and ignored the burn in my eyes.

"You see that?" I cried. "I didn't kill. But you're still going to yell at me tomorrow!" I stood up, yelling my heart out to the camera I had made up my mind about. Waves of anger poured from my head and circled my waist. "I'm still the villain aren't I? You're still mad at me aren't you! Not William, who spilt the blood and gave us that damn vaccine! Of course it's *all my fault!*"

I fell to the floor in a ball, clutching my aching stomach. Screaming and standing didn't help the pain, but it helped with the built up frustration.

Again, I thought only of Amin, and how he must have felt after our big argument where he both yelled and stormed off. And he was completely right. I should have ran to him and told him that, but my pride got in the way.

No matter how bored I was, or how eager I was to stand up and walk around so that my legs could stretch, I stayed on the floor. I wasn't going to give William something to watch and broadcast.

He was everyone else's king bee but mine. To me he was nothing more than an annoying pest.

But bees really are useless if you don't let their stingers affect you. One little sting takes away their power completely, meaning you just have to endure the pain and they'll drop dead.

So I endured, hoping William would drop dead as well.

Chapter 15

William looked happy to see me when I walked in for our meal, which was surprising since I hadn't killed anyone.

That meant he couldn't make me the enemy, at least for today. At least for a couple of hours before he conjured up some other insane rumor.

I rubbed my aching neck as I sat down. The pain was somehow worse than it was the first day my neck hurt, which only left me more frightened on behalf of what was going to happen to me for Joel and Culley.

"You didn't take the offer?" he inquired. "We thought you would for sure. I had the bed all made for you."

"A *bed* isn't worth a *life.*" I snapped. "At least to people with morals. You can name this mansion and your guards after empathy but that doesn't give you any."

William ignored me.

"How were we to make you the enemy when you wouldn't take the bait? Good thing I had the livestream shut off before you had your tangent. The people would have seen some good in you."

"Oh I have good in me? Maybe I could give you some lessons." I said, filling up my plate. "Besides, I thought I was a power-hungry terrorist killer with no remorse for her victims."

"That's the picture we've painted," William said. "And you can't change your mind about a painting after the brush has hit the canvas."

"So no one noticed that you just *decided* not to show me choosing between a painless night and murder? No one cared or questioned that you broadcasted nothing last night?"

"Oh we broadcasted something. Would you like to take a look?"

I said nothing, taking a bite of ham. The lights dimmed and another projector was rolled in. The Empaths aimed it at the wall, pressing the buttons to start the video.

I reluctantly turned my head, trying to act uninterested but the curiosity was killing me. What could William have done now to make the public hate me more? I had said nor done anything murderous, I had only called out William for his actions and laid on the floor until the Empaths gave me my pill.

The video started. I immediately noticed that I was in it, clear as day. There was a man in a chair, screaming and crying for me to stop and help him.

"How did... this didn't..." I gasped.

In the video I held a gun, smiling menacingly at the man. He screamed and cried and thrashed in his chair, begging and pleading before I pulled the trigger. Blood splattered all around the room, droplets even landing on my face.

William looked pleased, proudly watching his lie. I turned to face him in shock, trembling a little but fighting not to show it.

"I didn't kill that man," I told William as if he already didn't know. "Why can't you just let me die in peace? How are you going to fake my murderous intent once I'm gone? Turn me into a ghost that kills so I can be hated in the afterlife?"

"Don't act high and mighty now." William snarled. "You can play it nice now that a camera is in your face but let's not forget the deaths you caused when your life was a secret."

I resisted the urge to stab my fork into the table. I was too hungry and thirsty to get taken away. Instead, I stayed silent and refilled my cup with ice cold water.

William nodded at the Empaths who took the projector away. The next few minutes were filled with the sound of plates and silverware clinking, which was oddly soothing, before he spoke again.

"Do me a favor today. Choose the pill. It's a lot of work having to edit you murdering someone, although the reward comes when the city is enraged."

"You wouldn't know work if it hit you in the face," I replied. "I'll take the pill if I want to take the pill, which will happen over my dead body."

"I guess we just need to increase the pain then," William said, smiling. "If there's no motivation to stop it."

He nodded at the Empaths, who exited the room. One stayed behind though, so that he could tranquilize me if need be. I continued to eat, hoping that William couldn't smell my fear.

Increase the pain?

I couldn't kill anyone else, I couldn't. I didn't care about how people saw me or what people whispered behind my back. I couldn't take someone else's life just because I wasn't strong enough to endure the pain given to me.

William wanted to see me suffer and he wanted to see me cave. He wanted me to become like him through the torment and the agony, giving anything for sweet relief.

But if that's what William *wanted* I was going to do everything I could to ensure that he was disappointed with the results of his sick little experiment.

Visision hour hit me like a brick. Insult after insult, mostly talking about how disgustingly happy I looked to have killed someone else.

I gave up on covering my ears and rubbed my neck instead. The Empaths had given me another pill which spread the pain down to my chest, nearly down to my stomach.

I didn't even bother to curl up into a ball to avoid the insults, I just sat and endured. I rubbed my neck to try and ease the pain but it only made it worse. I looked at the dozens of angry faces surrounding me and wondered how I could have caused so much pain in so little time.

I could have tried to tell them that William faked the video, but they wouldn't hear me and wouldn't believe me if they did.

They were train cars, fueled by anger, blindly following the engine that was William, leading them to the sweet end of the tracks that was my death.

I tried to ignore the pain and the screams and instead focus on the beautiful afterlife in front of me.

I wanted to look death in the face, standing tall and brave, but I couldn't resist the beckon of anxious thoughts.

There was no way that William was going to kill me quickly after spending so much time making sure I was in pain.

He probably had some sick plan in mind already, and withholding the information was just another way to torture me.

The Empaths grabbed my arms and led me out the door after what was one of the quicker visitation hours, ignoring the pained look on my face.

Some people followed but most didn't. Each day there were less and less people visiting me. They had either run out of insults or didn't care enough anymore. I even heard some people stick up for me. It was unbelievable and believable all at once.

I had never doubted that everyone in this town cared for each other but the doubt settled in once I was made a public enemy. A disgusting traitor. A murderer.

"Please slow down," I murmured, as the Empaths all but ran up the stairs. My neck and my chest were on fire, screaming at me to stop moving and sleep the pain away.

One Empath slowed down, only a little, before changing his mind and quickening his pace again.

Ironic. The Empaths who cared only for William had some morals in them after all. They certainly didn't care about morals when they force fed me pills to watch me suffer, but anything that proved the *whole* Empathorium wasn't evil was enough for me.

If only it weren't so hard for me to believe myself.

I patiently, yet anxiously, awaited which horrible decision would come to me later in the day.

William's words echoed in my mind, and he certainly reminded me of his power by increasing my pain.

But if he could make me feel worse with ease than why make me choose? To continue making me the enemy? Wasn't I already seen bad enough in the eyes of people who were once my peers?

My coworkers?

The people who would trade me fresh fruit for some eggs or resew my clothes in exchange for a bottle of sadness. The people who would pass my house when they walked the streets, carrying their children and laughing with their spouse.

The very people who made this hellhole of a city feel like a home were also the very people who now couldn't even say my name without spitting, scoffing, or swearing.

"Seraphai," I whispered.

Was it really that bad?

"Seraphai Vane. My name is Seraphai Vane. And I did nothing wrong. I don't deserve this."

"Sure you don't." a voice replied. I whipped around to see an Empath, standing in the doorway. He held a gold pill in his hands.

"Please don't make me," I whispered. "Don't make me choose. William doesn't have to know just help me-"

"If you take this pill." The Empath said, harshly. "Your pain will diminish immediately. The pot is sweetened with this offer: you will not die on the final day of your torture, but instead be released back into the city."

I froze. It was a tempting offer, sure, but what was the catch? What could the other end of the deal possibly be?

"He wouldn't let me off that easily." I breathed.

"However." The Empath continued. "Ten random people will be chosen from the city and they will suffer the same fate as you. Hebdomad torture followed by death."

"Absolutely not." I sputtered, crawling backwards. I touched my neck lightly, with my fingertips.

The pain I had felt... to ten innocent people... just for me to get off scotch free?

"I have no one left to live for," I said. "Nothing and no one is waiting for me back there. I will not take the pill."

"I must tell you again. Your pain will-"

"I will not take the pill," I demanded, pressing my back against the wall, distancing myself from the pill as far as I could so that temptation couldn't drive me to take it.

The Empath looked angry as he left, throwing the pill into his pocket and walking out the door.

"I'm excited to see your little video come tomorrow," I called, getting in one good laugh before the door slammed in my face. No pain got taken away from me but knowing how angry my defiance made an Empath, and probably William, was enough reward for me.

I woke up the next morning groggy and confused. The Empaths had announced their payback by endlessly pounding on my door and bursting through it to shake me awake.

Needless to say I got about an hour of sleep and it didn't help that my head was throbbing harder than my heart.

Which day was this?

I had already gone through the day of the Empath I killed with the hammer, and it couldn't have been Joel or Culley's either.

My mind raced to remember, trying to search in the depths of my mind. Too much had happened over the past couple of days for me to remember every trigger pulled and every body on the ground.

And then, suddenly, it came to me.

The Empath who had shot Amin. The one death that I was not at all ashamed or regretful about. She deserved to die... she smiled when she shot Amin. She *smiled*.

I pressed a couple of fingers to my head, pulling away once the pain increased. She deserved to feel this but did I? Her death was quick, she probably didn't even feel the bullet.

Who would have guessed that one impulsive trigger pull, one frightened drop of the match, one desperate swing of the hammer, would lead to all of this.

I didn't *want* to die. No one did, really. I knew it was a much better alternative but that didn't stop me from having nightmares about what William could possibly do to me. It didn't stop me from feeling a twisted pain in my gut every time I thought about how stupid I was to drop that match on Culley and Joel.

"Stupid," I whispered. "Stupid, stupid, stupid."

I ran my fingers through my hair, debating whether or not I should pull it all out in a blind rage.

Wisps of anger emerged from my fingertips and swirled around my feet with fury.

"Why did you have to kill them? Why did you have to kill so many innocent people? Why did William have to find out? God, I want this to end!"

My whispers of defeat turned into blind screams of pure rage in a matter of seconds. I knew William was watching and recording and editing videos of me but I didn't care anymore.

My emotions could be bottled up on the outside, and sold for a couple of vegetables or a box of clothes, but they couldn't be bottled up on the inside too.

Once I had finished screaming every horrible thing I possibly could to the Empaths and the Empathorium, I lay on the cold floor, resting my burning head against it.

My fury filled the room, and my lungs, adding another layer to the musty heat and thick, hot air. The core circled my tortured head before finally returning to me. The rest of the fog took ages to disappear, lingering in a cloud around my head.

I imagined William having a field day, taking the footage and creating some deliciously wicked video that would knock me down *another* peg.

Just another reason for people to hate me.

Just another disaster I had caused.

Just another reason for Seraphai Vane to die.

The mixture of sweat and tears under my cheek made an unsatisfying ripping sound when the Empaths dragged me away for my meal.

I tried to play it nonchalant but I really was curious about what William could have made up about me. There wasn't much he could work with, because I hadn't been in any other rooms.

But I was also wary about what he would do to me for not complying. Last time he spread my pain down to my chest but I had an unsettling feeling he would do something horrible like double it this time.

My head already felt like it was on fire, so painful that I could hardly think about how much pain I was in. Somehow, even though my legs weren't burning, it still hurt to walk.

I wanted to do nothing but lay on the ground and mope. But that wouldn't be torturous enough for William. That wouldn't be a big enough punishment for my *despicable* actions.

I slumped in my chair, reaching for a glass of wine.

"Before you eat," William said. "Why don't you take a look at the screen?"

I turned to my right, noticing that the projector had already been set up. It was eerie, how the Empaths stood around it, still as statues, ready to watch my reaction.

The projector started up and a fuzzy image began to appear. It cleared up as the video went on but still had a weird glitch to it.

It all fell into place. William made the video look as if it was unknowingly captured by a security camera. It took away the scripted and planned vibe of the first video, which of course no one but me noticed.

The video only showed two people, familiar people.

It was me, in a room with William. William was tied up, pleading for me to let him go. He shook and shivered, quaking in the chair with rope around his limbs.

"The Empaths will be here soon! I'll let you go if you just don't hurt me!" he cried. "Please, don't do this!"

"Long live the *Empathorium*," I said, smiling smugly.

I pulled a gun from my pocket and aimed it at William. He cried and begged and pleaded for his life, but my finger still pursued the trigger with importance.

An Empath came from behind and grabbed me, right as I pulled the trigger. The bullet shot William right in his arm, causing him to scream a bloodcurdling blare of torment.

The camera glitched and cut to William, in a white bed with gold sheets. An Empath tended to his bloody shoulder beside him.

"She's out of control." William gasped. "We can't... we can't contain her. Not to worry... we have her detained. I- I promise we will kill her soon. After she has served her time."

The video ended and cut to a black screen.

I turned to William, my face blank.

"Impressive," I muttered sarcastically, reaching for the wine again.

"Now to talk about avenging Culley and Joel..." William said, smirking. "Tomorrow is auction day. The very reason I've had to... villainize you... if you will."

"You're going to sell me?" I gasped, my heart dropping to the soles of my shoes.

"Tomorrow you will feel no pain. Culley and Joel's revenge will be combined into your final day." William told me. "I was going to let you feel their pain until your execution on the final day, but my scientists informed me that the suffering over your entire body would more or less kill you."

His wicked grin grew the more that my horror grew. He didn't stop once to let the information soak in but instead continued to bombard me with details of my death.

"Whoever pays the most at the auction will be brought here, and will obtain the liberty of deciding how you will be executed."

I froze, nearly dropping the bottle of wine I clenched in my hands. Everyone in the city hated me, and with how much they had disparaged and berated me, I assumed they wouldn't choose a quick death.

With how creative their insults were, I figured that they could conjure up some harrowing ways to kill me.

"This is why you've kept me alive," I whispered. "To make sure their hate for me grew. As much as it could. To make sure it reached the limit before they grew bored and realized you are the real villain."

William nodded his head, only once, before filling his plate. He ignored both the elephant in the room and the bomb he had just dropped.

I gave up pouring the wine in my cup and began to drink straight from the bottle. The pain in my head was replaced by fuzz and static, the more intoxicated I got. It still lingered though, in an annoyingly repetitive way.

I tried to eat too, but my stomach was too terrified to willingly accept the food I offered.

I had already, surprisingly, survived a death sentence by immolation. I figured that whoever bought me at the auction would choose something even more painful, although I couldn't imagine something worse than burning alive.

No matter how much wine I drank, the pain still cut through my brain like a knife. I managed to dull it, but not stop it. The only way to stop the pain was by sleeping, but the Empaths would pound on the door to prevent me from sleeping if I returned to my room.

Unless...

I eyed the Empaths in the corner. The ones with the guns. The guns that contained some very helpful tranquilizer darts. The very darts that would send me into a beautifully deep slumber.

Every time I had yelled, I had only gotten dragged away, which meant I had to take more drastic measures. There were no knives that I could threaten William with, which set me back. Everything was sliced and cut already, with nothing but tongs to serve and a small fork to eat with.

I could charge at William with the fork, but I doubted that would be drastic enough and I would end up being dragged away instead of shot.

The wine glasses were made of glass, that could be a daunting weapon but I didn't know if I could smash one and grab a chunk fast enough without getting dragged away.

That left me with one option, playing it safe and then charging.

I began to walk to William's table, slowly. He had a bottle of wine right in front of him, that I didn't take my eyes off of while I made my way down the table.

I made it halfway without getting dragged out the door, which I considered a win. The Empaths were fast, and they were stronger than me, so if at any moment they barged through the doors my plan would be ruined.

"Sit down," William ordered. "The food is the same."

"Yours looks better." I retorted, acting as if I was reaching for a slice of ham.

In an instant I grabbed the wine bottle and smashed it over William's skull. His instincts kicked in first, so he had time to place his hands over his head before the bottle made contact.

The last thing I saw was a mixture of blood and wine running down William's infuriated face, before a tiny prick in my side made the world spin.

My eyes opened sharply, exposing me to too much light too quickly. I was bombarded by light, even in my secluded room, hidden away from the rest of the white and gold.

"I did it," I whispered, being whipped side to side by two Empaths. They had one goal, to wake me up, and it worked.

I had fallen into the beautiful black pit of unconciousness, which had spared me a couple hours of pain.

The Empaths continued shaking me violently, which didn't help with the anguish..

"Get up." one ordered. "What were you thinking?"

"I was thinking about getting some sleep." I snapped, sitting up to avoid getting whiplash. "I was *thinking* about being pain free, even if it was only for a couple of hours. Or a couple of minutes. Or even a couple of seconds."

The Empaths stayed silent, and the satisfaction of knowing that I had outsmarted them settled in. The crude realization that I was still in pain, and it hurt like the devil, crashed down upon me only moments later.

They brought me to the bathroom, and only gave me two minutes to freshen up before bursting through the door and bringing me to visitation hour.

I went from a high of knowing I was wiser than the Empathorium to feeling like dirt under everyone's boots when I remembered that some 'lucky' citizen would choose my death.

And none of them looked particularly pleased to see me. Especially after William's new video in which I shot him. Some looked disgusted, some looked horrified, and some looked enraged. There were less people then there were the day before, which I knew made William upset because people were losing interest in me.

I studied their faces as I entered my box, thinking about what would possibly happen to me if anyone watching me was chosen. My mind raced with ideas, none of which brought me any relief or comfort.

Mom always told me that my creative ways of thinking were my greatest strengths, but right now they were my biggest weaknesses, filling my mind with terrifying ideas.

She would also praise me for thinking outside the box, but that didn't come in handy right now, as I sat inside a *literal* box with no way to think outside of it.

I doubted that I could properly think anywhere, with the pain in my head growing stronger by the minute.

The voices didn't help.

They never did.

They never would.

I stared at my shoes in silence, ignoring the words and the pounds on the glass. The anger of the shouting citizens only increased when I ignored them, which didn't help my case with the whole auction ordeal.

Everything felt fuzzy. It felt like a nightmare that I couldn't wait to wake up from.

Maybe the pain had gotten to me and my brain was shutting down, or perhaps I had truly given up. No matter what I did, William would turn it worse. Even if I slept my final days away, there would still be videos of me on a killing rampage until my death.

I would always be the enemy.

There would always be someone spitting on my grave and scorning the ground I walked on.

There was no good reason for me to fight so desperately for peace in a world fueled with unexplainable and inexcusable violence.

So it baffled me why I continued to.

Chapter 16

"Seraphai Vane."

It was auction day. I was back in the glass box, but instead of being bombarded by barbs, I was being sold. What looked like the whole city lined the streets in front of me, clutching bottles of emotions. Some couldn't even carry them all and brought heaps of them in bags or sacks.

"Criminal. Murderer. Thief. We opened our arms to her, and look at where that left us."

William had a bandage wrapped around his shoulder, and he continuously winced or pointed to it, reminding the crowd about what I had 'done'.

My box was no longer down near the streets but instead on top of the stairs, close to where William was standing. The rest of the crowd lined the streets below, standing oddly neat for how angry and unorganized their faces and gestures looked.

I suppose the Empaths with their giant guns helped with some of the peace and order. They lined the streets, pacing back and forth, eying anyone who moved too fast or too far.

William cleared his throat, glancing at me.

I sat defeated, my back against the cool glass, determined not to give William the satisfaction of hearing my screams or pleas. Not to mention the crowd below, hungry to hear my suffering. Thirsty for my tears.

"We will start the bidding low," William announced. "Five bottles of terror."

I held back a laugh. Five bottles of terror meant so much for people like Mom and I but nothing to William. He scanned the crowd, as did I.

Around half of the crowd raised their hands, all willing to give up five bottles of fear or more to watch me suffer.

Others watched, just curious about the whole ordeal.

"Ten bottles of fear!" a voice called.

"Six bottles of anger!" another yelled.

Empaths pinpointed the highest bidders and yanked them from the crowd, settling them in a line on the bottom of the staircase.

"Five bottles of happiness!"

"I'll do six!"

"Three bottles of fear and four bottles of rage!"

The Empaths continued to pick and choose the highest bidders, checking their bags to make sure they weren't lying about the amount they were willing to give up.

When someone didn't get chosen they would scream louder, bringing up insane amounts.

Once a dozen or so top bidders lined the bottom of the stairs, William spoke again.

"We will go higher. Ten bottles of happiness. To those on the stairs, advance if you are prepared to pay said amount."

Out of the handful of people, only three advanced. They were all men, which increased my fear. They were all looking directly at me, menacingly.

Every step they took was another step towards me. Towards ending me.

"Ten bottles of happiness, one bottle of sorrow." one spoke, still staring me down.

"I'll throw in two anger." another yelled.

They both took a step forward. The man who had advanced with them stayed behind.

The closer they got, the clearer their faces became. They both looked to be mid-forties, clutching bags of emotions no doubt stolen from my little show of freeing them.

How could they show up to an auction, set on buying me, with emotions from nowhere else than the vault I had broken into?

"Ten bottles of joy. One bottle of sorrow. Two bottles of fury..." William said, contemplating. "I'll be raising the price to fifteen bottles of joy, fifteen anyone?"

Both men hesitated. I saw them glance at their bags, and then back at me.

"Flattered to be worth so much," I muttered.

The man on the left, who looked slightly older but not kinder, finally took a step.

William smiled, his lips curved in an evil sneer.

He gestured for the man to join him on the top of the stairs, next to me. The man got a good look at me, his eyes filling with evil intentions as I backed as far away from him as I could.

"Your name?" William asked.

"Slate." the man said, not taking his eyes off of me. "Slate Ploith."

"Congratulations on the win, Mr. Ploith," William said. He nodded at the Empaths who began to clear the crowd.

"An honor," Slate said, handing William the appropriate jars of the emotions he had bid. William held out a hand to stop him.

"Come inside. We will deal with your payment later. For now, it is time to discuss how to kill Miss Vane."

One Empath grabbed the bag of emotions from Slate's arms, while another helped me out of the box. He bound my arms behind my back while we walked, Slate taking in every fake piece of crap like it was a museum.

William made menacing small talk the whole way there, not forgetting to clench his shoulder in pain.

I blocked out the sound of his voice, breathing small breaths of relief because, for the first time in weeks, there was no pain.

My head felt fine.

My stomach.

My neck.

Of course, it was my last day on earth, so I was terrified out of my mind, but with what I had been through I took what I could get. I could finally keep up with the uncomfortable pace of everyone in the Empathorium without having to grit my teeth in pain or lag behind.

William led Slate into a room at the end of a long hallway. In the center lay a sprawling gold table, with a clear glass box taking up most of the center.

I assumed that the box wasn't to put precious artifacts in but instead a criminal on death row.

William took one end of the table, gesturing for Slate to take the other. They matched each other's energy, sitting smug and with power.

They smiled as the Empaths hoisted me inside the box.

They straightened their positions once I was sealed in.

I was cramped, hardly being able to sit up without my head brushing the ceiling and blocking my limited air holes.

I knew it was inconvenient for William too. I was blocking him and Slate from seeing each other without having to look around or through me.

Like many other things, putting me in a box served no purpose but to humiliate me. There were only a couple of people in the room, yet it was still William's sole purpose to make sure I was as uncomfortable and embarrassed as I could be.

"Now, you understand the gist of things, don't you Mr. Ploith?" William asked.

"I understand," Slate said. "The punishment I choose must relate to fire to correctly ensure equality with the anguish felt by her final victims."

"What are your first ideas?" William asked. "We have access to virtually anything you may need to fulfill what execution you deem fit."

"Many things come to mind," Slate said. "Burnt at a stake seems equal to what they felt, but old fashioned. People could easily stop it if they wanted to, with just a bit of water."

"Understandable. Has there been talk of an uprising?" William asked. He seemed nervous to hear the answer. But why? With the power he held, he couldn't handle a couple of people thinking what he did was wrong?

"Not much, but some. People who don't understand that criminals shall be punished according to their crimes." Slate answered.

"I see," William said, glancing at the Empaths scattered around the room. "Any other ideas?"

"Of course, an explosion comes to mind," Slate said. "But it could injure anyone that got too close. And the fire itself..."

William looked at me, thinking about what kind of explosions he could conjure up.

"Those boxes..." Slate said with much curiosity. "Are they... could they be made fireproof? Explosion-proof?"

William grinned.

"What do you propose?"

"Nothing too serious. Put her in a box, like the one she has outside. A bomb is attached to the wall, one that couldn't be stopped or thrown out. Air holes so she could breathe, but not big enough to slip the bomb through."

William stood up and walked around to the side of the table. He eyed the box, his brows raised.

Slate stood up as well, walking around the table to stand by William. He stared into my eyes, which made me feel even more vulnerable.

"A regular bomb wouldn't be enough. The audience would get bored too quickly. I suggest a twenty-four-hour timer."

"Twenty-four hours?" William contradicted. "Mr. Ploith need I remind you the goal is to kill her, not to give her one final day to celebrate her life."

"I understand," Slate explained. "However, the audience could lessen the time on the bomb by giving up various emotions. A couple of seconds for terror, a couple of minutes for rage, maybe a half hour for joy. The audience would participate."

William gained a horrifying twinkle in his eye.

"Yes. Yes..."

A bomb was better than burning alive. It was quick and it wasn't too painful because I would be gone in an instant. But of course, it had to be dragged out for an entire day, just me alone in that box. The people who I once viewed as neighbors and coworkers giving up their hard-earned emotions just to kill me faster.

Maybe it was hate.

Maybe it was pity.

But none of it was right.

"I admire your thinking," William said, after a while of silently finalizing the plan. "I believe I have a bomb in stock that could do the job. I'll get the Empaths to create a fireproof box right away."

"Excellent sir. Happy I could help." Slate agreed.

He followed William around like a lost dog, around the entire room, and out the door.

A couple of Empaths left, to tend to William's demands no doubt, but one stayed to lead me down the hallway. They kept my hands behind my back, which just made me even more aggravated.

Plumes of anger began to trail behind me, leaving my mark. It was unwanted but at least it proved I was alive.

That I was in the moment.

That no matter how I was treated I *wasn't* just an object to be crucified. Some doll to be tortured. I was alive and I was angry and sometimes I was glad it showed.

William would glance behind him sometimes, to check if I was still there. As if I had escaped. I was confused at first, he had a tight grip and at least four eyes on me at all times, so why was he so concerned about my potential escape?

My eyes fell on Slate and I remembered. To every citizen, I was a criminal mastermind who had shot William and was capable of escaping any clutches.

Every time William turned Slate did too. Both of their faces would be filled with disgust. I stared back, nothing but disgust in my face as well. The only difference is that I was better at hiding it.

William turned into a room and beckoned for Slate to enter first. He waited until the Empath had led me to the door frame before placing a hand on my shoulder.

"One word... one word about the videos being fake... and I'll kill him. *And* I'll kill *you*. And I won't ensure it's as painless as the bomb." he whispered.

I kept a calm composure but on the inside, I was boiling with rage. Leave it to 'King' William to treat someone like a true friend only to kill them if things didn't go according to plan.

And of course, just like things had been the past couple of weeks, the death would end up being my fault.

It wasn't even a surprise anymore.

A couple of Empaths lined the walls of the room. It was eerie how they were always exactly where William needed them, even without proper instruction.

The room contained a metal box, identical to the ones I had been put in for the past couple of days. It even contained scattered holes across the top of it. On top of the box was a small rectangle which I assumed, after reluctantly hearing the previous conversation, was a bomb.

Slate ran his finger along the box.

"Only a prototype," William said. "We use it to test the bombs. Hers will be made with proper air holes, of course, we wouldn't want her to suffocate before the big bang."

Slate glanced at me. The Empath kept my hands behind my back which made my arms cramp. I figured complaining would only make my situation worse so I kept my mouth shut.

"Why have holes if not for air?" Slate asked, inspecting the box even further.

"For the fire to escape," William responded. "Otherwise, with bigger explosions, the box would be at risk of cracking. Or of course, explode itself."

Slate took a step back.

"Shall we test it?" he asked.

William nodded at the Empaths who placed the bomb inside of the box, pressing a couple of buttons on it first. I tried my best to back away from everything, but I was held steady.

Slate backed away even further, joining William near the door. I kept my eyes locked on the box, not knowing if it would be better for the explosion to be big or small.

Either way, I died.

I tried not to think about it but the thought of death was persistent in my mind.

It was almost as if-

The explosion ripped through the room, sending a ring through my ears. Jets of fire poured from the holes, sending turrets of flames nearly reaching the ceiling.

My stomach and any courage I had left turned to mush. The searing heat continued for what felt like ages before it finally died down. I could see the heat waves, headed my way, ready to intensify and kill me.

Slate began to clap.

"Wonderful. Simply wonderful. You've outdone yourself fulfilling my request, sir."

"The fireproof box is being manufactured as we speak," William said. He looked right into my eyes. "Made just for you. For your special day."

"Can't wait," I responded, dejectedly.

It was getting clearer now that I was going to die. All those weeks I had spent wishing I was dead were worth something after all. My wish was coming true.

It was a shame that I had changed my mind.

William led Slate on a tour around the Empathorium. I was forced to follow behind them. It was mildly interesting at first but quickly became boring. How could one person squeeze so many useless rooms inside of one palace?

Maybe if William cared about his people, he would rent out some of the rooms for them to live in. At least if a storm passed through.

The kitchen had hundreds of food choices. Fruit and vegetables and meat and drinks littered the cabinets and the fridges.

But of course scarce pickings of rice and beans, maybe some meat, were sold in the markets.

Slate seemed to notice it too. His gaze hardened with each room we walked into, every one adorned with extravagant objects and furniture.

William didn't notice a thing, he was happy as could be. His plan had worked after all. I was the villain and I was going to be mercilessly executed in his hands.

It was too bad Slate hadn't picked the guillotine to kill me, I'm sure William would have loved my head on his wall. A friendly reminder of who he could blame other than himself.

After what I assumed was an hour of walking around the Empathorium, listening to William painstakingly describe each room's importance, Slate spoke up.

"Simply wonderful sir," he said timidly. "However, it is getting late. And I... we... have a big day tomorrow. Shall I return home or are there accommodations here for me?"

William's demeanor became more aggressive. I knew what he was thinking: *How dare he speak to me in such a way? In such a tone?*

I halfway expected Slate's body to hit the floor, bullet to the head, but instead William smiled.

"Yes, of course. I will set you up in our finest bedroom," he said his words through gritted teeth and a fake smile but at least another person wasn't dead.

"Shall I return to help with the execution?" Slate asked.

"Help?" William scoffed. "Oh, Mr. Ploith. You've helped enough. We will be watching the execution as kings, not setting it up as commoners."

"I'd be honored," Slate said.

William turned around and faced me. It took everything in me not to warn Slate to run while he still could. There had to be some way I could warn him about William's true intentions without getting both him and I executed before dawn.

"Take her to her room," William ordered the Empath handling me. "As for you Mr. Ploith... follow me... I have just the room for you."

"Mr. Ploith!" I called, struggling to face him while the Empath yanked me down the hall.

Slate turned around with caution and stared me down.

"Don't listen to her," William ordered. "She's crazy."

Slate nodded his head slightly but continued to face me. He was waiting. He had a shred of humanity and dignity left in him. Not all hope was lost.

"Never..." I uttered. "Never meet your heroes."

William placed a menacing hand on Slate's shoulder, turning him forcefully in the right direction.

"She's behaving irrationally on purpose." I heard him say. "Don't pay any attention to her or what she lies about. This whole ordeal will be gone *very* soon."

I was only allowed to get a couple of hours of sleep. Ironically, it was the best sleep I had gotten, with no pain to keep me awake. Empaths woke me up at the crack of dawn, letting me know it was time to die.

I had my final meal with William, joined by Slate.

"Let's make this quick," William said. "Everything is ready for you, Miss Vane, and I'd like to not waste any more time keeping you alive."

"Finally, something we agree on," I responded coldly.

"She wants to die?" Slate asked.

"Of course not," William told him. "She plans to convince herself she's ready. No one wants to die, Mr. Ploith. But some people deserve to."

"I agree," I told Slate, staring right into the cold, dead, eyes of William himself. "Some people don't deserve to live. Of course, they get to anyway. The higher your rank, the higher your lifespan."

I noticed a small scar above William's eyebrow. It was where I had hit him with the wine bottle, but why not broadcast that? I had actually injured him that time.

Did it make him seem weak? Not to others but to himself? It was easy to fake an injury and keep the power and strength to yourself, knowing it was all a ruse. But to actually get injured by someone so tortured?

By someone locked up and guarded at all times?

That must have been a jab at William's ego.

It was probably also the reason why there were no wine bottles in sight. I wished there were, it would be a lot easier to die if I was drunk.

Slate kept his eye on me for most of the meal, but it wasn't a cold stare that sent shivers down my spine.

Instead, it was a stare of confusion.

Did my words affect him?

Was he realizing how cruel William was, hoarding all the riches and food to himself and watching his people starve?

Was he realizing that behind the scenes, I wasn't a bloodthirsty murderer with a taste for killing but instead just a tortured girl with no family?

I stared at him for most of the meal as well, hoping he could read the suffering in my eyes. Hoping he would understand.

William must have noticed too. Noticed that Slate wasn't talking horribly about me or glaring at me.

"She's on her best behavior today," he said, taking a sip of his drink. "Don't let it fool you Mr. Ploith. She killed her entire family with no remorse."

"Yes... yes... I remember." Slate said, in a soft tone. He slid some food around on his plate.

William cleared his throat.

"I think we are done here," he ordered. "Get her ready and wake the commoners."

Two hands grabbed my shoulders and forced me out of my chair. I resisted best I could but they were stronger than me. They were always and would always be stronger than me.

Slate stood up too, glancing at my body being dragged out of the room. His eyes were filled with pity but he didn't act irrationally.

William stayed seated, smiling at my demise.

"It's time."

Much like before, crowds of people lined the streets, except they didn't yell or scream when they saw me. Their anger was quiet but noticeable.

My heart dropped when I noticed how many emotions everyone carried. If they were willing to give all of them up, I would be dead in minutes.

William and Slate stayed at the top of the stairs, while two Empaths led me down the stairs to the end of my life. I kept my eyes on the ground. I didn't have enough courage to look at the bomb that would murder me.

My limbs felt weak. I found it hard to move. I had heard the phrase paralyzed with fear but I hadn't felt it until now. Adrenaline kept me going when fighting for my life but there was nothing and no one to fight except William and he had successfully turned everyone against me.

I couldn't win a fight against someone who pulled all the strings. Who more or less controlled my actions.

I heard a few scattered whispers and shuffles as I got led into the box, but no protests. No shouts of disagreement. I saw no revolutions or rebellions.

Nothing that would save my life.

William smiled when the box was sealed. Slate smiled too but he didn't look as happy as his face suggested.

The crowd cheered when the box locked and the Empaths stepped away. They raised their fists and clapped their hands, growing louder when the countdown started.

I positioned myself against the glass, as far away from the bomb as possible, as if that would get me anywhere in the long run. It was hopeless. I was a lost cause.

William began to inform the crowd about the prices, but I drowned him out. All I could hear was the sound of my heart, rapidly beating. It echoed in my ears, another annoying sound that I couldn't get rid of.

I heard snippets of what was announced.

Fear took a minute off of the timer.

Sorrow took five.

Rage took ten.

Happiness took thirty.

The prices weren't outrageous. They could have made it so that happiness was an hour. Or two. Or three. It was obvious that William was unhappy with Slate's decision.

A quick bomb wouldn't be painless enough. He had to drag out the whole ordeal for me to feel as much pain as I could. Of course.

I buried my head in my knees.

I couldn't bring myself to look at all the people giving away emotions. I couldn't bring myself to hear the ticking of the bomb, each second closer to my death.

God, I couldn't bring myself to die.

I wasn't ready.

It was too slow.

It was too fast.

It was everything except for what I wanted it to be. Everyone was dead and I was going to join them, the fantasy of every good dream for the past couple of days, yet the moment didn't feel as whimsical.

"I'm not ready," I whispered. "I'm not ready."

"That's one jar of sadness!" William announced. "Five minutes off of the timer!"

Upon hearing the announcement, I dragged my head up. Hiding was worthless if William was dead set on announcing every emotion given up.

I saw a man hand in three bottles of happiness, glaring at me after he did so.

A teary woman gave up a multitude of jars, also giving me an eerie death stare.

A teenage boy handed in two jars of anger. He walked up to my box after doing so, holding eye contact.

"My parents were down there," he told me, pointing to where the bomb dropped. "One jar for each parent."

"I didn't drop that bomb," I responded.

"No," he said. "But you made them believe that they could save their family from poverty. Because you couldn't leave well enough alone, could you?"

His words cut me like a knife.

The whole time I had thought it was just a horrible misunderstanding, and that they were blaming me for William's actions, but the boy's words had opened my mind.

"I made them think that?" I breathed, staring back at my shoes. The boy walked away.

"I was just trying to do the right thing," I whispered, but he was too far away to hear me. I knew that even if he did hear me he wouldn't believe me.

Death was a powerful motivator that silenced every other idea, no matter how moral or just.

I knew from personal experience. It was death itself that motivated me to set the emotions free in the first place.

Deaths that William caused but who was counting?

Who cared?

Who was listening?

Certainly not anyone who approached me, each voice filled with hatred and misunderstanding. Certainly not anyone who gave up an emotion, each jar filled with horrid intentions.

My gaze softened when I saw a young girl, no older than eight, giving up a jar of rage. She walked over to me and stared into my eyes.

"Why are they doing this to you?" she asked.

"You don't know? Why give up an emotion then?"

The girl pointed behind her, at a woman who was glaring at me. She took a protective step forward as if I could reach through the glass and hurt her daughter.

"My mommy said I should. To get rid of you faster."

I sighed.

"But why are they getting rid of you?"

I paused before answering.

"I hurt a lot of people. I didn't mean to. I thought I was doing the right thing."

"Maybe you did do the right thing," she told me, placing a hand on the glass. "Sometimes I try to do the right thing but I get yelled at anyway. Maybe we are alike."

A tear slid down my cheek, even though I fought my hardest to hold it back.

"Yeah," I said, letting out a small laugh. "Yeah, maybe we are the same."

The girl's mother stormed over and grabbed her arm.

"Cora you begged me to see the girl and now you've spent too much time talking to her. What did she say to you? What did she do to you? Forget everything, we are going home right now, come on."

Cora took her hand off of the glass, giving me one last look and one last innocent smile.

"I was trying to do the right thing," she told her mother. "Just like her."

I smiled back, watching as the innocent little girl got dragged away to her home, and scolded for talking to a murderer for too long. She tried to look back at me multiple times, only to be whipped around and scolded some more.

"Just like me," I whispered.

The hours blended together.

It was even harder to tell what time it was since the amount of time on the bomb kept dropping lower. It wasn't by much, since hardly anyone wanted to give up their happiness, but it was enough to keep me worrying.

After the first couple of hours, most people began to leave. They got bored of standing around and I didn't blame them, it wasn't an exciting execution yet.

I figured they would come back to watch me die and then continue with their lives. Unaware that I was innocent. Not caring about the people I lost or the feelings I felt.

William ordered some Empaths to bring chairs for him and Slate. Followed by drinks. Followed by dozens of bowls of appetizers, which Slate looked at woefully.

I looked closely and saw a tiny wisp of sorrow escape from Slate's fingertips. He waved it away before William noticed but that was all I needed to see. Slate felt bad for me. He knew what he was doing was wrong and yet he didn't speak up. William was frightening and had horrible intentions but I still wished that Slate would speak up.

He had been gifted with the finest treatment that William could give. A giant bed, no doubt. Decadent food and drink, and elegant architecture to explore. But I knew that Slate saw beyond the expensive gifts.

He saw the mother on the street, frantically picking vegetables from her neighbor's garden so that her child could eat.

He saw the beggars, huddled together, ecstatic over a stale piece of bread dropped from a basket.

He ate the cheese cubes and the soft pretzels. He enjoyed the sparkling wine and the juice of every color. But that only opened his eyes to the family on the side of the road, trying to plead with Atlas to lower his prices.

Ever since I had set the emotions free, the prices rose like crazy. I heard commoners yelling about it. They yelled at *me* about it. It was my fault. I should be punished for it. The same old insults that still hurt my heart.

A wicked smile seldom left William's face. He would call out every emotion given up, eyes flickering to my face to watch my reaction.

The timer dropped. Lower. Lower. And lower still.

Two bottles of sorrow.

Three of rage.

Six of terror.

The bomb would tick. And tick. And tick. It drove me mad but there was nowhere else to go. My brain had nothing else to do except drive me deeper into the abyss of confusion, anxiety, horrific thoughts, and rage.

Some plumes of rage did come out, but I quickly waved them away. I couldn't give them the satisfaction. That was below me. I wasn't perfect and I was below a lot of things but giving the people what they wanted was too weak.

I wasn't weak.

I had to stay strong for only a couple more hours. It was a hard battle, keeping a calm and composed face, but I managed.

I thought of Mom. I thought of Dad. I thought of how complete our family would be when I was finally up there with them. As far away from William as one could be.

"Four bottles of happiness!" William called. "Two hours off of the timer!"

"Shit," I whispered.

The end was near. Most everyone had disappeared into their houses, bored of the drama. A couple of people lingered, making small talk with each other and walking around out of pure boredom. A few emotions were given up. Some bottles of terror or sadness but a lot of people hoarded their joy and their rage. It was too expensive for me.

Perfect.

Screw this whole show of killing me. William couldn't entertain the people forever and he certainly couldn't portray the character of the villain on me if I was stuck in a box.

I didn't know what everyone was doing besides watching me die, but I didn't blame them for hiding. Sheltering their kids from the gruesome sight. Protecting their hearts from seeing an innocent girl burn alive.

William noticed it too. And he was angry. He stood up and made menacing announcements, ordering everyone around just like he was best at.

"All citizens must report to the execution. One hour remains. No more donations will be accepted so as not to run down the timer too quickly. Any citizen caught hiding, running, rebelling, or otherwise disobeying will be dealt with." he said, speaking into a small microphone clutched in his right hand. The announcement boomed around the city, projecting from what I only imagined were hidden loudspeakers.

"One hour?" I muttered.

Oh no.

It was real.

This was real.

I couldn't breathe. The only breaths I could manage were choppy and shallow. Any words of protest I tried to muster up got caught in my throat.

My eyes flickered around the box I was in, landing on various unhappy faces of commoners forced out of their safe little homes.

I grabbed at my chest, twisting my shirt in my hands.

Calm down. Calm down. Please calm down. It's going to be quick. Oh, God. I can't breathe.

My heart wanted to leap out of my chest. I could feel it everywhere. It echoed through my ears and just about echoed through my gaping mouth.

I gasped for air, squeezing my hands into little fists to prevent them from trembling. The bomb kept counting the worthless little seconds until my death.

Tick. Tick. Tick.

Calm down. You need to calm down or it will be the longest hour of your life. It's almost over. It's okay, it's almost all over.

I didn't want it to be over.

But nothing was my choice, was it?

I began to breathe slower, tapping my hand against the glass repeatedly. Tap. Tap. Tap. Tick. Tick. Tick.

I focused on the colors. The soft breeze barely blew through the array of air holes on the top of my box. The sound of my breathing, and tapping. Anything but the ticking.

Oh, God, please, anything but the ticking.

I ran my free hand through my hair, noticing that it was trembling but too occupied trying not to hyperventilate to do anything about it.

There were so many voices.

Some yelled in agreement. Some yelled in protest. Some just yelled incoherent words that I couldn't make out even if I wanted to.

Tick. Tick. Tick.

Tap. Tap. Tap.

"Set her free! She did nothing wrong!"

"Let us donate! We want her to burn!"

"Kill her! Kill her faster!"

"She's innocent!"

My hands grasped at my hair, desperate for something to hold on to. It created a false sense of stability, knowing I was clutching onto something balanced.

William continued yelling through the microphone, his voice frantic. His desperate attempts to calm everyone down were shattered when the first brave soul began to rush up the stairs. They held a gun and shot wildly at William.

The Empaths killed him in a matter of seconds, his body resting on the steps. Blood pooled from his head and ran down the stairs. A waterfall of cold, hard truth.

A few people screamed out of horror. Others screamed out of anger. Waves of terror and anger began to fill the air, masking the crowd. They yelled at William and each other. Fistfights broke out, leaving more bodies on the stairs. People clamored and ran to get away from the scene, only to get shot.

"No," I yelled. "Please, stop! Please!"

Tick. Tick. Tick.

Slate lay lifeless on the ground next to William. A bullet had made its way into his heart. A discarded tray of cheese cubes lay beside him, splattered in blood. The Empaths shot the people and the people retaliated by shooting the Empaths.

A wall of guards stood in front of William, protecting him while he shouted into his microphone. He was desperate to calm everyone, but no one listened.

A woman reached my box, a hammer in her hand. She began to swing furiously, sending vibrations through my body but not leaving a crack.

I saw an Empath aiming his gun at her. She was too busy trying to free me... helping me... to notice.

"Watch out!" I shouted, but I could hardly get the words out before she collapsed to the ground. Her dress became an unforgiving red. A deep red that was the all too familiar color of shed blood.

One man tackled an Empath, which sent both of them tumbling down the stairs. I heard multiple gunshots go off from down below, but the clouds of sorrow, fear, and rage were too thick to see far in.

"Everyone remain calm!" William announced, his voice stained with horror. "Go inside of your houses and we will remedy the situation! Please!" he glanced nervously at the sky, as if looking at the clouds would save him.

Tick. Tick. Tick.

I heard the wails of multiple children, crying for their mothers or fathers to come pick them up and save them. Dozens of little feet ran home, too scared to realize that their parents had died.

The Empaths were screaming too, shouting orders at the citizens. Everyone was too enraged to hear or listen.

"Should we drop another bomb, sir?" I heard one yell.

"Not yet!" William yelled.

"Sir, we need to!"

"If we drop a bomb we kill every damn person in the city!" William responded. He continued to scream into the microphone and look up at the sky with no results.

A splatter of blood hit the side of my box, causing me to flinch and scurry to the other corner. It meant I was near the bomb but I didn't care anymore. I didn't know what was going on but I knew that the time was still ticking and it was soon going to burn me alive.

Two men were fighting beside me. Neither of them had guns, which only made the entire ordeal more brutal. One ran to my box and tried to pry it apart, banging at the material to try and free me.

Tick. Tick. Tick.

The other came up behind him and pushed him to the floor. They continued to tussle, backing away, and disappearing into the unforgiving clouds of emotions.

Endless cores filled the sky, swirling around the yelling citizens and each other. Greedy hands reached up to the clouds, again valuing money over their own lives. Multiple palms were stained with blood. Multiple hands were filled with cuts and bloody knuckles, but they continued to stuff as many cores as possible inside whatever jars they had.

I looked towards William who had given up screaming orders into the microphone. He seemed genuinely terrified, but of what? That people had finally seen his true self? That they were finally rebelling?

An Empath's body landed right beside me, adding another splatter of blood onto the wall. I could hardly see what was going on, with the amount of blood and emotions that blocked the commotion. Even if I could see past the ichor, a foggy abyss of rage and sorrow clouded up the clear skies.

Tick. Tick. Tick.

"Shit! Shit!" I heard William scream. He was still staring at the sky, but only for a second. He began to sprint back inside the Empathorium, leaving the Empaths confused.

One took a step forward to follow him, but William was long gone. The microphone he once held so importantly lay discarded on the ground.

"What's going on sir?" I heard an Empath yell.

I turned my face upwards, searching the sky for what William was so afraid of.

Three planes flew overhead, adding a mysteriously low rumbling sound to the multitude of noises flooding my ears.

Some people noticed them too, stopping and staring at the sky. Their eyes were either filled with awe or confusion. Parents were shocked and frightened, while their oblivious kids pointed up at the sky with glee.

We had never had planes fly over us before. Most people hardly knew what they looked like or what they were. I had always wanted something new and exciting to happen but the planes seemed frightening.

Unpredictable.

A hatch began to open under all three of them, dropping mysterious metal ovoids. A high whistling sound accompanied them. Everything was hazy and confusing, but then it clicked.

They were bombs.

There was hardly enough time for anyone to scream or move before the colossal explosives made contact with the bloodstained sand.

Tick.

Tick.

Tick.

Boom.

Chapter 17

Either the smoke or the deafening silence woke me up.

My face was pressed against the glass, sore and hot when I finally ripped it off. Smoke was everywhere. It entered my box through the air holes, choking me, engulfing me.

"Help." I choked out, wiping my eyes to see the scene in front of me.

Everything was gone. The Empathorium lay crumbled, a giant pile of gold and white. Broken pieces of wood and clay, drenched in blood, lay askew on every open surface.

A couple of stray fires lay across the scene. There were three giant craters, laid out across the city. My box had been blown far away. I could tell, even though there was virtually nothing but debris to tell me where in the city I was.

A faint ticking sound snapped me back to reality.

I was in a box. With a bomb.

"Help! Help me!" I cried frantically. I hoped, and *prayed,* that someone else was alive but I was met with disappointing silence. The bomb had only one minute left. One minute until I would join the hundreds of souls scattered across the wasteland.

I turned around. The box had been tipped over, to where the top was now directly to my left. I let out a breath of disbelief when I saw it.

The explosion had cracked the small spaces in between the various air holes. It wasn't too damaged, but it was damaged enough to give me a chance to live.

I lay on my back and began to kick the side of the box, wildly. A flash of pain shot through my feet with each kick, but I didn't dare give up.

Tick. Tick. Tick.

"God, please!" I screeched.

I began to kick even faster, slamming my feet into the cracks and the gaps, my brain screaming at me to hurry up.

I glanced over at the bomb.

Ten seconds remained.

My feet slammed through the material and most of the space between the scattered air holes gave way. I launched myself through the gap, just big enough for me to squeeze through, and burst into the smoky air.

I had just enough time to sprint a couple of steps before the explosive detonated, sending a wave of fire to scorch the earth. The force caused me to stumble and left me on top of a large slab of concrete.

I breathed in the smoky smell of the air.

The fire behind me crackled softly.

The concrete I sprawled out on was cool and fresh on my warm, throbbing head.

I began to sob, crying to anyone that could hear me. I was overjoyed to be alive, but at what cost? Everyone around me was dead. Everything was dead.

It took an eternity for me to pick myself up and take a proper look at the disaster around me. I walked around the rubble, trying my best to take in everything, calling out for anyone who survived.

I got no reply. No footsteps. No shouts.

I searched the remains of the Empathorium for William. He knew about the bombs. He kept checking the sky because he knew they were coming. But why didn't he escape sooner? Why didn't he stop whoever sent them?

"Hello?" I called, my voice hoarse and raspy. "Please, is anyone alive?"

A shred of an Empath's uniform lay stuck under a pile of white bricks. The vases that lined the halls were everywhere, pounds upon pounds of shattered glass.

I wasn't scared to find William. He had nothing he could use against me. No weapons. No soldiers. No citizens to believe his every word.

I saw nothing that told me he was alive. Only piles upon piles of rubble. Useless trash piled up. Expensive crap.

I was hysterical. Filled with paradoxical laughter and adrenaline. I picked up a shard of a vase, discarded next to a small fire. It warmed my shaky hands.

"It's useless now, isn't it William?" I screamed, laughing diabolically. I was in utter shock and disbelief, hardly able to put one foot in front of the other. "It was so important then, but it means *nothing* now!"

I flung the shard to my side, watching as it shattered over a block of concrete. It felt relieving. Uplifting. Exciting.

I was doing the wrong thing and I wasn't going to get punished for it. I wasn't going to die for it.

I picked up another shard of glass. This one looked as if it came from a dinner plate, cracked everywhere it could be.

I threw it over my shoulder maniacally.

There were sheets of paper everywhere. I didn't know what they were but I also didn't care. I lit just about every last one on fire, watching as it crumbled into ashes in my hand.

I dropped the flaming paper only when I couldn't stand the heat anymore. They fluttered to the ground, turning into a neat pile of cinders.

There was so much blood.

It dripped into divots in the ground, creating pools.

It bubbled next to roaring fires.

It dried on merciless concrete, once belonging to an innocent person. It wasn't fair. William was the only person who deserved to die, and I was glad he was gone, but of course, he couldn't go down without taking everyone else down with him.

Besides the obvious fact of being proud I was alive, I was filled with more pride since the one thing William wanted to happen didn't happen.

I was alive and walking over the rubble of his palace. I crushed shards of glass under my feet. I burned his papers, and any important documents became lost to the flames he created. I kicked rocks and stray pieces I found. Broken pieces of furniture, cups, silverware. I threw and bent and kicked and broke everything in sight until I was pleased with myself.

I was smart enough to know it did virtually nothing, the entire city was destroyed. But I was too filled with adrenaline and shock to care.

Every limb of mine trembled.

Some softly and some violently.

It took a while for me to stop punishing a deceased king and stop mourning the loss of people who, just a couple of hours ago, wanted me dead.

I gathered my senses, as best I could, and headed for the cliff. Any cliff. Any ticket out of the city that only brought me bad memories.

The bluffs were steep but not unconquerable. I was fueled with the indomitable human spirit, the one that had kept me alive for the past couple of days.

The whole climb felt swift and easy, even though if I fell I would be faced with the consequence of multiple broken bones.

"Come on." I huffed, grabbing the top of the bluff with one arm and hoisting myself up. I brushed myself off before looking upward at the scenery ahead of me.

"Holy shit."

The cliffs were beyond what any natural cliffs could form. They lay in straight lines, positioned in grids, forming too many squares to count. In each square lay a small, yet bustling, city, much like mine is.

Was.

I dropped to my stomach so I would not be seen because something felt unnatural to me. Why was my city one of many to be set in the manmade cliffs? Why hadn't William told us? We could have traded supplies.

The climates were insanely different. One right in front of me had multiple trees, each one thick with leaves and foliage. I glanced around to see multiple people, each one walking or trading at booths.

The booths were positioned in front of a white and gold building, a mansion to say the least. The houses were poor, most fashioned out of wood. Just like mine is.

Was.

Oh God.

Oh my God.

What was this? Why were there so many? All of them had a main white and gold building and a busy city taking up the rest of the space. They all had gates surrounding the city and barren bluffs surrounding *them*. I observed the one below me, trying to get more information.

A lady stood screaming at a guard. She waved her hands and yelled wildly, tears streaming down her cheeks. A man stood behind her, frantically trying to console her. No emotion came out. From either of them.

Okay. Maybe she lost her sorrow and anger a while ago.

A baby laughed happily in the arms of a man a couple of feet away. The child waved his arms with glee while the man holding him rocked him up and down.

No happiness emerged from the child.

How cruel of them to take their child's emotions so young.

But the longer I looked, the longer I realized that there was no fog or mist.

No smoke, tinting the sky.

No emotions emerged from screaming children or worried parents.

No cores darted around the city, hands waving wildly to capture them.

No animals getting primped and preened in a last attempt to score a bottle of happiness.

"What...?" I murmured, crawling closer to the edge of the cliff to see better. I was wary not to crawl too far. If I somehow managed to slide down the cliff I would either die or get taken in by this new city.

And for some reason, death seemed to be the safer option. The quicker option.

I squinted my eyes to see if any of the trading booths had buckets of emotions under them, or even any stray jars that had been traded that day.

I was a good bit away, and my vision wasn't perfect, but I still didn't see anything.

There were no jars in sight. Citizens walked around clutching their children in their arms instead.

The guards still held guns though, clenched in their hands. Why would there be a need for guns in such a seemingly perfect town? In a city where emotions could be shown? Where you didn't have to be wary of laughter or scared of sobbing?

I stopped myself from thinking irrationally and crawling down the bluff to join what seemed perfect to the naked eye. Something felt off.

The city was so identical to ours.

Too identical to ours.

And that meant evil lurked in the center of it all.

So many towns. All like ours. All eerily oblivious of each other. All different yet all the same. They ran like clockwork, every one filled with the same rows of houses, the same white and gold buildings, the same trading centers, the same people.

Something was not right with the whole ordeal. I needed to get far away before someone noticed me and I got dragged down into another wicked town led by another wicked leader.

I gathered my composure, making sure I was able to think straight, before standing up and sprinting for my life.

I ran with my city to my left and a new city to my right. One thriving and one rubble. One filled with little people to poke and prod and lead, another filled with wandering souls.

I wanted to get information. I wanted to cry. I wanted to go back down into my city and mourn the loss of everyone I had ever known. But I needed to escape. I needed to get far away from whatever was going on around me.

My legs burned, having been contained in a small box for the past couple of hours, but I knew that stopping was too risky. I wouldn't and I couldn't stop until I was somewhere safe. Far away from the horrifying grids of cliffs. The towns all running and looking the same. The leaders, no doubt cruel and murderous, just like William.

My mind twisted into circles while I ran, frantically trying to piece together the random bits of information shoved at me. It disappointed me that I couldn't figure anything out.

I couldn't gather enough information.

I couldn't stop my eyes from wandering to the debris and bloody rubble beside me.

I forced myself to think about the sweet relief of escape. I forced myself to look forward, where I could see the end of the cliffs. I could see the end of the grid.

I could see where I was finally going to escape.

You need to keep running. Keep running and don't stop until you are far, far away. Get the hell out of here.

My hands hadn't stopped trembling ever since I had gotten into the box hours ago.

My legs trembled too, slightly. I was lucky they didn't buckle every time I took a step. One step away from whatever sick test was behind me.

I was still in a wasteland, filled with nothing but sand, dust, and a couple of scarce trees, but I was free.

The air smelled... *clean.* It wasn't filled with muggy emotions or the tainted screams of the tortured.

It was something new. Something exciting.

For Amin's sake, I hoped that there was a beach close by. He wouldn't be able to see it but I would have seen it for him. And if I had to choose between his dream of the beach and my dream of the jungle I would pick the beach every day.

"Stop," I muttered to myself. "Stop thinking about people you can't save."

I had to think about the one person I could save and that was myself. Amin was gone and Mom was gone and everyone that had raised me or interacted with me my entire life was gone.

I had nothing more to do but push forward.

For them.

I walked for a while, trying my best to ignore the pain in my legs. The sun went down and the stars appeared, which was nice because it meant the blazing heat was gone and the cool breeze was back.

I stared at my shoes, concentrating on putting one foot in front of the other. I looked around for any source of water, or maybe food, but I knew I would find nothing.

Any resources for a long while would go to the cities behind me. Whatever was going on took a lot to power and if there were no resources in front of me that meant I was still in their backyard.

The daunting realization hit me that nothing else would be out there. That civilization was behind me and I was digging my own grave by straying from it. The planes had come from somewhere but it could be miles and miles away.

My heart began to race again. My chest tightened which forced me to take those awful shallow breaths. I clenched my hands into fists, trying to regain my composure.

"Something is out there," I whispered. "Something has to be out there. This can't be it."

My throat burned. It begged me for water, it forced my eyes to flicker around the dusty nothingness, searching for a little oasis I could call mine.

My stomach was angry with me. It attacked my insides, pleading with me to fill it up with something. My eyes flickered to the skimpy trees, hoping to find a squirrel, a mouse, a bird, anything edible.

I had nothing to give to my dehydration and starvation other than dust and dead tree limbs.

Maybe if I was desperate. But not now.

I squinted my eyes, searching in the darkness for anything of use. Virtually anything that could either aid me in survival or explain everything about my life that I had missed.

And that's when I saw it.

A giant building, a good bit away from me. I shook my head and squinted my eyes again, to make sure I hadn't hallucinated my oasis.

Sure enough, it was there, towering over the wasteland with pride. It made the Empathorium look small, with the sheer size it was.

It wasn't adorned with gold or white, however. It looked quite average in materials. It had hardly any windows, from what I could see, and a flat roof, uncommon for vast mansions.

I began to sprint towards the building, as fast as I could without falling over or getting sick. I didn't take my eyes off of it, afraid that if I did it would disappear.

The closer I got, the more frightening it got. It didn't scream welcoming. There were barely any lights illuminating the front of it. Nothing homey like porch swings, flower pots, gardens, or even a fence.

It was simply there, a giant rectangle of confusion.

I was filled with a mix of adrenaline and terror, a combination that lifted my hand to the giant metal door to knock without me even thinking about it.

I figured it would take a while for someone to answer, due to the grand scale of the giant building, but the door swung open fairly fast.

It wasn't comforting how quickly I was greeted at the door, but instead added to my wariness.

I cleared my throat, already pleading with my eyes.

"Please," I begged, my voice hoarse. "Help me."

Chapter 18

"Are you a refugee?" the person at the door asked. He looked to be in his thirties, wearing white pants with a white formal shirt. His belt was gold, as were his cuffs.

"What? I- yes." I said. "Please do you have any water?"

The man beckoned for me to come inside, and I didn't think twice. I let out a small gasp of disbelief when I walked through the door.

The inside of the colossal building looked nothing like the outside. It was so decadent. So fancy. Comfortable furniture, exquisite lighting structures, and eye-catching centerpieces.

They had it all.

"What is your name?" the man asked.

"Seraphai," I said. "Seraphai Vane."

He began to walk to another room so I followed him, relief flooding my brain when he handed me a cup of water.

"That sounds so familiar." the man told me. "Have you... where did you come from?"

"I don't know," I told him. "I don't know... everyone is gone... it's just me."

"What happened?"

I froze. It all came rushing back to me. The bomb. The collective screams of horror. All the blood. Pools and puddles of bubbling blood. The Empathorium, crushed to smithereens.

"I don't want to talk about it," I whispered.

Once I had finished my water, the man led me upstairs to a different room. This one wasn't as fancy. It looked suspicious to me instead. Beakers and instruments and beeping computers.

Other people were in there, all wearing the same white and gold formal shirts with white pants. They all started to look at me when I walked in.

"She's a refugee." the man said.

"Shall we prepare her for trial forty-eight?" a lady asked.

"What's trial forty-eight?" I said. Everyone looked at me but no one answered me.

"Ask Gorgon. She may need the pods for a few years."

"Yes, for her memory."

I opened my mouth to speak up but there were too many people talking. They talked about me right to my face, as if I wasn't there.

"We have to clean up from trial forty-four before we even begin to *build* trial forty-eight."

"Someone tell me what is going on, right now!" I yelled. My voice projected through the room, causing everyone else to fall silent. A wisp of anger emerged from my shoulder.

A couple of people let out small gasps when they saw it. Others stared at me, eyes wide, mouths agape.

Did they not understand what it was?

Was this weird place filled with weird people finally somewhere safe? They had an obsession with experiments but maybe they could craft a cure from my emotions.

I opened my mouth to try to explain, to say that I wasn't magical or cursed, that it was from my horrible past city.

The man who brought me in placed a hand on my shoulder, gripping me tight and startling me away from my thoughts.

"You need to come with me."

"I promise it's not contagious or anything. Please, listen to me. I know you are confused but I can explain. Just *slow down,* please."

The man walked me down the hall at the same brisk pace the Empaths always did. The deeper into the giant building we got, the less gold and white I saw. Everything turned into computers, blinding white lights, test tubes, and monitors.

The man burst through a door and brought me inside with him. He was flustered.

"Gorgon."

There was a man at a white desk, wearing the same uniform as everyone else, except the colors were reversed. He was writing some things down and didn't even look up at first.

"This better be important," Gorgon said.

"She escaped." the man said. "From trial forty-four."

Gorgon looked up, his eyes flickering all over my body. I was too stunned to speak. Everything began to click into place, but it wasn't as satisfying as I had hoped.

"Trial forty-four?" I whispered.

Gorgon and the man began to talk but none of the words made it through my brain. My vision began to blur, from anger or fear I couldn't tell.

Strings of rage began to emerge from my fingertips and float around the room. The man pointed them out to Gorgon, who nodded slightly.

The grids.

All the cities, divided from each other.

All just like mine.

The damn white and gold found both here and there.

Everyone here wearing the same uniform, messing with bubbling beakers and beeping machines.

Scientists.

"We're all experiments?" I muttered.

I got no answer. Gorgon and the scientist continued to talk frantically, words flying out of them. The anger boiled inside of me, turning from a shocked annoyance to full-blown rage.

"I'm an experiment?" I snapped, shaking free from the scientist's grasp. Clouds of rage began to pour out of me, fogging up the room. "My entire life? An experiment?"

I stormed to Gorgon's desk, slamming my fist down onto the wood. He wasn't frightened or taken aback, but instead intrigued.

"You are going to tell me what the hell is going on. Right. Now." I demanded, shaking from the absolute ire and fury that filled my body and fueled my actions.

Gorgon nodded at the chair behind me. It took every ounce of dignity inside of me not to pick it up and smash it to bits on the ground. Still quaking, I sat, digging my fingernails into my skin.

"Open the door, Arsure," Gorgon ordered. "Clear the room of this... beautiful anger."

My fingernails penetrated my skin, causing me to wince slightly. I pulled my hands away, hastily.

"Where to begin..." Gorgon said.

"Anywhere. Just answer me." I fumed.

"I assume you saw beyond the cliffs of trial forty-four," Gorgon told me.

"Yes." I seethed.

"Those *are* all experiments. Each one is different. Yours was, as you *unnecessarily* demonstrated, various emotions being capturable and used as currency."

I dug my fingernails into my legs again, to stop myself from digging them into his neck.

"So you raise us there? You raise generations of people just as a sick little experiment?"

"Miss Vane... you weren't raised there."

I sat back in my chair, breathing heavily. "But..."

"Your experiment," Gorgon told me. "Trial forty-four. It was only running for a year."

"I..." the words couldn't come out. They just didn't. A year? I had remembered living in the city my entire life. The memories were hazy, sure, but wasn't that what all memories were like? False reminders of the past, altered by what one's brain perceives as reality?

I could only muster one word.

"Why?"

"The world is broken, Miss Vane. The world needs a leader. Someone to provide stability and order in the chaos. And that person is me."

I rocked in my chair, horrified.

"But the world will not be governed easily. They will not listen. They will not obey. The trials... are to see which circumstances will lead to citizens depending on their leader the most. They are to see what conditions will result in easy governing. Your experiment was on the right track, before the short-lived rebellion."

"Why didn't you save William first?"

"Mr. Rowen? I didn't need to."

"And why is that?"

"My son understood the risks," Gorgon said. "All of my children do."

"What the hell is wrong with you?" I whispered. "You continue to have children just to... just to force them into a false leadership position? Until you find an experiment successful enough for you to lead?"

I was disgusted that I was even in the presence of such a person. That I was in the same room, breathing the same air. He did this to me. He killed everyone. Everyone who ever died in the city, even if it was due to old age, he killed them.

"We almost had to call off your experiment sooner." Gorgon continued, staring right at me. "Someone nearly escaped. But she turned around when her friend died."

I stared back, unafraid. I was too angry and stuffed to the brim with too much horrible information to care about anything else that could happen to me.

I glanced around the room for anything that could kill Gorgon. A knife, a club, a sword, anything.

But one question was left unanswered, and it gnawed at my brain until I finally asked it.

"Where do you find everyone?" I whispered.

Gorgon smiled. "Bring her to the pods, Arsure."

Arsure pinned my hands behind my back and walked me out of the room. Gorgon followed, with difficulty. I noticed a small metal chip in the back of his neck. I connected the dots and assumed that chip was the reason he stayed alive. The reason he was able to wait for a successful experiment. The reason he had so many children to govern them for him.

I made a mental note to rip it out and drown him in his own blood as soon as possible.

Arsure walked slower this time, keeping pace with Gorgon. I squirmed in his grasp, trying frantically to escape so that I could kill everyone in this wretched building.

We reached the door fairly quickly. Arsure turned around to seek approval. Gorgon nodded.

Arsure let go of me with one of his hands to open the door but still held me tight. I was too curious as to what horrors were beyond the door to try and escape.

I took a wary step inside, letting out a gasp of disbelief.

Hundreds, maybe even thousands, of sleeping pods. Inside, men and women of all ages, floated their days away until they were deemed worthy of Gorgon's attention.

"The world is a wasteland," Gorgon repeated. "There is nothing out there. Resources were limited. People fought over the smallest logs. The stalest slices of bread. It led to the nearly unlivable conditions you see outside. We offer a helping hand. A place to stay."

I was too furious to form proper words. My mind screamed at me to kill him. But Arsure kept me restrained, obviously reading my mind. My fingers began to twitch, itching to do something.

I turned away from the inhumane sight, unfortunately facing the man who caused all of this.

"Please tell all units that prep for trial forty-eight should start immediately," Gorgon told Arsure. "Have the appropriate number of subjects live the false memories from their 'years' in the city."

He turned and began to walk away.

"Sir," Arsure called.

Gorgon turned back around.

"Should I wipe her memories as well? Place her inside of a pod? Have her live the fake memories of trial forty-eight and place her inside when the time is right?"

My mouth fell open.

Live it all again? Oh, God, please no.

My mind screamed at me to protest. To run and hide—anything to avoid going back.

Gorgon smiled at me. Instead of filling me with comfort, his smile filled me with terror. "No. Don't wipe her memories."

I was confused, but I knew that whatever Gorgon meant couldn't be a good thing. Everything was bad, nothing was good, and my life would never be stable again.

"I think we've found the ruler of trial forty-eight."